HARD EVIDENCE

A chance meeting with the attractive young Julie
Dawson should have been no more than a pleasant interlude for DS Lambert of Cannonbridge
CID. However, two months later she is reported
missing by elderly relatives and Lambert is
sufficiently intrigued to look into the matter. A
crotchety DCI Kelsey, low because of lingering illness, orders him to drop the inquiry – there is no
reason to suspect foul play – but Lambert takes
advantage of his chief's enforced absence from
work to carry on with his investigation.

Tracking the woman proves complicated but
Lambert becomes increasingly convinced that she
could be at risk. A childhood contact yields the
information that Dawson, who has always been
obsessed with detective novels, may be conducting
her own private investigation into a possible
blackmailer. Armed with only the sketchiest of
information, Lambert must follow in her footsteps
– but will the trail, which has already turned up
suspicious deaths from the past, lead to a present-
day murder?

A tense new crime novel from the ever-popular
Emma Page which will keep the reader guessing
until the very last page.

HARD EVIDENCE

Emma Page

HarperCollins*Publishers*

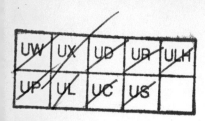
Collins Crime
An imprint of HarperCollins*Publishers*
77–85 Fulham Palace Road, London W6 8JB

First published by HarperCollins*Publishers*
in 1996 by Collins Crime

1 3 5 7 9 10 8 6 4 2

Copyright © Emma Page 1996

The Author asserts the moral right to
be identified as the author of this work

A catalogue record for this book is
available from the British Library

ISBN 0 00 232604 3

Set in Meridien and Bodoni by
Rowland Phototypesetting Ltd
Bury St Edmunds, Suffolk

Printed and bound in Great Britain by
Caledonian International Book Manufacturing Ltd,
Glasgow

For M. H.
in unceasing admiration

CHAPTER 1

The thriving, bustling town of Millbourne looked its best on this sunny Tuesday afternoon in the third week of April. In his first-floor office overlooking the main street, Donald Fielding closed the file on which he had been working. He stood up from his desk and returned the file to its cabinet. He was a tall, lean man, thirty-seven years old, with thick, dark hair and sharp grey eyes. He was the proprietor of the *Millbourne Advertiser*, a highly successful freesheet, one of a number of such newspapers he owned in this part of the county.

He glanced at the phone, looked at his watch, expelled an impatient breath and crossed to the window. The top sash stood open to the soft air, laced with traffic fumes and the scents of spring.

After a few moments he turned from the window and went back to his desk; he began to work again. All his movements were quick and decisive. He glanced frequently at his watch. Whenever the phone rang he snatched up the receiver on the instant.

It was almost four when the call he had been waiting for, the call from George Gresham, head of Gresham Enterprises, at last came through.

Fielding sat leaning forward, rigid, listening, then his expression began to lighten, his shoulders relaxed. By the end of the call he was smiling broadly.

His tone was now briskly cheerful. 'Right, then. Ten o'clock tomorrow morning. I'll be there.'

He drew a deep breath of relief. He felt exuberant, charged with energy. He had the look of a man long resigned to old hindrances and restrictions, who sees all at once exciting challenges opening out before him.

Then his expression altered. Before those new opportunities could be grasped an existing association must be ended. He was foolish to have let it continue so long when it was plain weeks ago that the time had come to cut loose.

He rested an elbow on the desk, cupped his chin in his hand. He remained for some time frowning, pondering, calculating.

Wednesday dawned chilly and overcast but by lunch time the sun had broken through.

In the walled garden of Honeysuckle Cottage, in a secluded spot three miles from Millbourne, Audrey Tysoe spent the afternoon as she had spent many other afternoons since her retirement a few months ago at the age of fifty-five: working in her garden.

The cottage stood on its own at the end of a lane, some distance from the nearest village but within easy walking distance of a bus route into town. The garden was a fair size but she managed it herself.

Today she was busy clearing a tangled corner; the wheelbarrow beside her was now full. She wheeled it across the garden and emptied it onto the compost heap.

She was a dumpy woman, strongly built, with a slight, habitual limp. A shrewd, weathered face that no one had ever thought pretty; hair taken back without artifice into a scanty bun. Neat and tidy, even in her old gardening clothes; the air of a woman who has never bothered overmuch about her appearance and certainly doesn't intend to start bothering about it at this stage of her life.

As she turned from the compost heap she heard the sound of a car in the lane. She glanced at her watch: just after 5.30. She gave a little nod. It would be Donald Fielding; he had phoned to say he intended coming. She had worked for Fielding until her retirement.

She heard the vehicle turn in through the gateway. By the time she had walked round to the front of the house Fielding was getting out of his car in the parking bay at the side of the drive.

He raised a hand and called out a greeting. He came up to her and put an arm round her shoulders, kissed her affectionately on the cheek. They sat down close together on a garden seat and were soon deep in earnest conversation. They had just about reached a satisfactory conclusion when there came the sound of another car approaching.

Julie Dawson came along the lane in her white Mini. As she

turned into the driveway she saw Fielding's car parked in the bay.

She drew a trembling breath, hesitated, then drove slowly round to the garage at the rear of the cottage, flicking a glance as she went by at the pair sitting side by side on the garden seat. They both looked across at her but neither waved, neither smiled. She felt a nervous tremor run through her.

She sat for a moment in the car, steadying herself, then she picked up her holdall and shoulder bag. Before she came into view again she squared her shoulders and assumed a confident smile. She was slightly built, twenty years old, with a pretty, heart-shaped face, sharp little features, a satiny skin. Hazel eyes, very bright, flecked with gold. A wealth of curling brown hair, full of russet lights.

She walked jauntily towards the other two, chattering cheerfully as she approached. 'It wasn't so terrible, after all. Just one filling, no injection. I could hardly feel it.' She worked at the *Advertiser* and had been allowed to leave early to keep a dental appointment. 'I went shopping afterwards, I felt I deserved a treat. I bought myself a jacket.'

She halted, reached into her holdall and drew the jacket from its wrappings. 'It was marked down quite a bit. It seems a terrific bargain to me. I can't see anything wrong with it.'

She held it up against her. An expensive-looking garment, fashionably cut; fine, smooth cloth in a muted grey-green check. 'Do you like it?' she asked. 'Do you think it suits me? It goes with all my things.'

Neither of the other two responded to any of this with so much as a smile or a glance at the jacket. Fielding got to his feet and Julie's stream of chatter fell away.

'We need to talk,' Fielding told her brusquely. 'We'll go inside.' Without another word or look he went into the house.

Julie stood irresolute. She turned her head as if about to make a run for it, then she gave her shoulders a little shake and followed him with an air of compliant meekness.

But the look in her eyes as she stepped across the threshold was far from compliant.

Audrey sat gazing after them with an expressionless face, then she stood up and went limping over to a bed of daffodils. Here and there she nipped off a faded bloom, to be cast down later onto the compost heap.

CHAPTER 2

Rain began to fall early on Friday morning, dying away by eleven. It was almost noon as Detective Sergeant Lambert drove back to Cannonbridge. His inquiries had taken him to a couple of outlying villages where he had spent a fruitless morning chasing shadows. He felt tired and irritable, hungry and thirsty.

The sun shone down from a clearing sky. His route took him along minor roads little more than lanes, between flowering hedgerows, grassy banks starred with primroses, past orchards of pear trees snowy with blossom. His sour mood began to evaporate.

When he was still some half-dozen miles from Cannonbridge he rounded a bend and saw on the grass verge, a short distance ahead, a white Mini, standing sideways on to him, its back wheels sunk in the ditch. As he came up it became clear that the rear bumper had got itself hooked under a boulder, one of several strewn along the verge, which had fallen from the crumbling stone wall backing the ditch.

A girl crouched beside the vehicle, trying to free the bumper. She got to her feet as Lambert pulled up close by. He ran an appreciative eye over her. A pretty girl with strikingly beautiful brown hair glinting in the sunlight. She was trimly dressed in a dark green skirt, a smartly cut jacket in a muted grey-green check.

She was delighted at his offer of help. 'I overshot the turning,' she explained. 'I was reversing and I skidded back into the ditch.' She gestured over to the right. 'I'm going to Calcott House.' She saw the name meant nothing to him. 'It's a hotel,' she added. 'Quite near here.'

He got her to move aside the stone as he eased up the rear of the car. The end of the bumper was twisted and dented. 'It's no great damage,' he assured her. 'It won't cost a fortune to put right.' She thanked him profusely for his assistance.

'This hotel you're going to,' he said. 'Do they serve lunch to nonresidents?' The notion of a decent meal in civilized surroundings appeared distinctly cheering. Particularly with the chance of a pretty girl to share his table.

'I think they do,' she told him. 'I haven't stayed there before. I used to live round here, in Calcott village, but I left three years ago. This is the first time I've been back – I've no family here any more. Calcott House used to be just a residential hotel but there were changes a few years ago; they did a lot to the place. I think maybe it changed hands at that time but I can't quite remember. Anyway, they started doing bed and breakfast, catering for holiday-makers. I'm pretty certain they began doing meals for nonresidents at the same time.' She gave him a friendly smile. 'I'm sure they'll give you lunch.'

He followed her Mini till they came in sight of tall wrought-iron gates standing open to a long drive flanked by flowering shrubs, running up to a large Victorian house framed by mature trees. A board by the gate assured him the hotel did indeed serve lunch and dinner to nonresidents.

In the car park the girl suggested it was time they exchanged names; hers was Julie Dawson. She wore an air of pleased expectancy as they walked across to the pillared entrance. 'I always longed to come here when I was a child,' she confided. 'It seemed a mysterious, romantic place. But I never even set foot in the grounds. I used to make up stories about it. I used to tell myself: "One day, when I'm grown up, I'll go and stay there." I imagined that would be about as far as anyone could get in the high life.'

She gave him a grin, like an excited child. 'Now here I am, walking in through the doors. I decided to come this weekend on the spur of the moment. I rang up and found they could take me. I was delighted.'

He waited for her in the lounge bar while she checked in. When she rejoined him he asked what she would like to drink.

She looked at his glass. 'What's that you've got?'

Nonalcoholic lager, he told her. She shot him a surprised, amused glance. 'I still have to drive,' he pointed out. 'Unlike you.' After a moment's hesitation he added, 'I'm a policeman. I'm on my way back to the station in Cannonbridge.' He waited for the friendly expression to vanish from her face, for a look of cool wariness to succeed it.

11

But she leaned forward with an air of eager interest. She ran her eye over his dark suit, his white shirt. 'Are you by any chance a detective?' she asked. He admitted that he was. 'I'm a detective sergeant, to be precise.'

She clapped her hands and gave him a gleeful smile. 'How marvellous! I've never met a real-life detective before – I've never met any kind of policeman on a social level. I've always loved reading detective novels.'

'I'm afraid it's not always like it is in the books.' He changed the subject without subtlety; he had no intention of spending the next hour talking about his job.

When she had finished her drink she suggested an inspection of the garden; there was plenty of time before lunch. They went out into the bright sunshine. The grounds were of considerable size and had clearly been laid out with much care at the time the house was built. They strolled past lawns, shrubberies, rockeries in full springtime splendour of pink and mauve, yellow and white. A dolphin fountain jetted cascades of diamond drops into the sparkling air; purple irises bloomed beside a pool. They followed a woodland walk through dappled green shade under an arching canopy of branches. The ground was carpeted with bluebells, forget-me-nots, violets, anemones. A relaxing air of peace and tranquillity brooded over the whole.

They wandered back towards the house and came upon a series of small individual gardens enclosed by formal hedges of clipped evergreens, each garden designed round a different theme. One had been entirely devoted to aromatic foliage plants in shades of silvery grey. Julie asked Lambert if he knew what the plants were. He had to admit he didn't.

On a stone bench a few feet away a woman sat leaning back with her eyes closed. Beside her on the seat lay a folded newspaper and a spectacles case. At the sound of their voices she opened her eyes and sat up. She looked across at them and after a moment got to her feet and came over. A stocky woman, mid-fifties, with a vigorous appearance. Blunt features; short, iron-grey hair taken to one side and secured with a plain brown slide. No make-up; a scrubbed, clinically clean look. She wore a dark grey, chalk-striped suit tailored on lines of uncompromising severity.

With the briefest preamble of an apology for breaking in on them she began to identify the various plants for Julie, who listened with appreciative interest. A lonely woman, Lambert judged, snatching at any chance of conversation. As she gestured at the plants he saw that her stubby hands were bare of rings.

The stream of information flowed on unabated, and Julie began to exhibit signs of restlessness. She flicked a speaking glance at Lambert and started to walk away from the woman – still unflaggingly voluble – towards an archway cut through the hedge. Lambert fell in behind her. Undeterred, the woman went with them, continuing to hold forth about the garden and the grounds in general.

The three of them reached an open stretch of sward set at intervals with fine specimen trees in full flaunt of blossom. Some yards away a man, young and powerfully built, knelt with his back to them, working on a border. 'That's Luke Marchant,' the woman said. 'He does all the gardening here.' She saw that Lambert didn't recognize the name. 'The hotel belongs to the Marchants,' she explained. 'Evan Marchant and his wife, they own and run it. Luke Marchant is Evan's brother, he's a lot younger than Evan. He's done a wonderful job since he came here. It's all he thinks about, the garden. He works all the hours God sends.'

Julie looked intrigued. She moved away from the other two, over to where Luke knelt, absorbed in his work. Lambert saw that she was attempting to engage him in conversation about what he was doing, her manner easy and affable.

'She won't get much change out of Luke,' the woman beside Lambert observed in a sardonic tone. And from this distance it certainly appeared that Luke's response was confined to a nod or shake of the head.

'You really must take a look at the water garden,' the woman advised Lambert. ' "Water canal", I gather, is the correct term for it.' She indicated where it was. 'It's well worth seeing. Luke cleaned it out himself. He dredged it, repaired the stone and brickwork, a real labour of love. I'd come with you myself but it's damp underfoot down there and I'm wearing a new pair of shoes.' She gave a little laugh, glancing down at her shoes with pride, sticking out one foot for Lambert to admire. 'I only bought them this morning. I couldn't resist putting them on right away. I know they're walking shoes but I'd rather not get them wet the first time I wear them.'

'Very nice,' Lambert remarked politely. Her feet were short

and broad, the ankles thick and shapeless. The shoes, a laced pair made of stout leather in a shade of oxblood, looked as if they could withstand any amount of water and hard usage.

She wriggled her foot with satisfaction. 'I never believe in skimping on shoes. If there's one thing I learned early on in my working life, it's to take good care of your feet, then they'll never let you down.'

Julie came back and Lambert took her off to see the water garden. The woman returned to her seat on the stone bench.

Left to himself again, Luke Marchant sat back on his heels, his hands idle. He turned his head and gazed fixedly after the departing figure of the girl, her beautiful brown hair gleaming in the sunshine.

CHAPTER 3

Lambert's watch showed five minutes to one as he and Julie made their way back towards the hotel. Lambert was by now ravenous.

A woman came along a nearby path, progressing gracefully in the same direction with the aid of an elegant walking stick. Not far off seventy, Lambert judged. She was chattering to a small pug-nosed dog, a black-and-tan King Charles spaniel, trotting docilely beside her at the end of a lead. From time to time the dog uttered a little bark by way of reply, tilting its head to look up at her.

The woman smiled in friendly fashion and spoke a word of greeting to Lambert and Julie. An aura of expensive French perfume drifted to Lambert's nostrils as she went by. She was a lady of generous proportions, with the remains of great prettiness. Very well groomed, carefully made up; immaculately dressed hair of a subtle shade of ash blonde. She wore a light, flowery, floaty gown – the word 'dress' seemed too mundane for such an airy creation; it looked as if it had cost a great deal of money.

A long-term resident of the hotel, Lambert guessed; she had a relaxed air, as of someone very much at home in her surroundings. She came into the dining room – without her spaniel – a few minutes after Lambert and Julie had been shown to a table. She made a regal progress across the room, dropping a word here, a nod or smile there, till she reached her small table laid with a single place, not far from Julie and Lambert. Her name, Lambert gathered from exchanges during a stop she had made close by, was Mrs Passmore.

Julie made her choice after briefly scanning the menu but Lambert, in spite of his hunger, took somewhat longer to decide. He eventually settled on salmon but even then found himself torn between salmon mayonnaise and poached salmon with hollandaise sauce. The waitress, a cheerful woman with bleached hair and bright red lipstick – 'Call me Iris, everybody does' – guaranteed both dishes to be delicious. The chef was first class, she assured them, a young Frenchman who had been at the hotel a couple of years.

As Lambert finally opted for the mayonnaise the talkative grey-haired woman in the chalk-striped suit came into the dining room and took her seat alone at a table some distance away. She gave the two of them an acknowledging nod in passing.

'I see you've met our Miss Hammond,' Iris observed.

'A very knowledgeable lady,' Lambert remarked. 'About plants, at any rate.'

Iris smiled. 'That's a recent craze with her. She's bought herself a cottage out at the back of beyond; she's moving there very soon. It's nothing but gardening now all day long. Gardening books from the library, gardening programmes on the television and radio, gardening pages in newspapers and magazines. Six months ago I don't suppose she could tell a daisy from a dandelion. But I'm pleased for her, she needed a new interest. She used to be a nurse – private, not hospital. She's retired now.'

Iris suddenly became aware of the presence of a man and woman who had appeared in the doorway of the dining room and now stood murmuring to each other, their eyes everywhere, raking the tables, the guests, the food, the service, with practised speed. 'The Marchants,' Iris said in a low voice. 'I'd better be off or I'll be in trouble.' She vanished towards the kitchen.

The pair in the doorway stood murmuring together a few moments longer. Evan Marchant was a dapper man in his mid-thirties, impeccably groomed, conventionally dressed. Sleek black hair, slicked back; dark eyes, alert and calculating. He looked poised and self-contained, very much in control; a man never likely to be taken by surprise.

Lambert put Mrs Marchant at a good ten years older than her husband. A little pouter pigeon of a woman with bright, darting eyes, hair elaborately dressed in a lofty style designed to add inches to her height; it was tinted an unflattering shade midway between dead leaves and Oxford marmalade.

Mrs Marchant left the dining room and her husband began

a ritual tour of the tables. He leaned forward slightly as he progressed, gliding rather than walking, his hands lightly clasped before him. Lambert half expected to hear the strains of the 'Skaters' Waltz' burst forth at any moment from an orchestra secreted behind the scenes.

Marchant paused at every table. His face wore an urbane, professional smile. When he reached Lambert's table he inclined his head at Julie. He had already welcomed her to Calcott House when she checked in. 'I hope everything is satisfactory?' He had an unctuous voice. She assured him that it was. He inclined his head at Lambert. 'We shall hope you'll find yourself able to come and stay with us at some future date.'

Iris approached with the food and Marchant took a couple of paces back. He stood watching for a moment as she deftly served it, then he inclined his head again and resumed his circuit of the room.

The food was as delicious as Iris had promised. Julie chatted in an entertaining fashion, scarcely ever, Lambert noticed, saying anything very personal about herself. He managed to gather that she was living on the outskirts of Millbourne, she had a job in the town, and that was about all. He asked about her job but she made a face, implying it was of little interest. 'Is it so dull?' he pursued. But she would only say: 'It's certainly not what anyone could call exciting. I'll be back at work on Monday morning. I'd just as soon forget the job till then.' He asked no more personal questions.

When Iris brought the coffee Julie said to her: 'I wouldn't at all mind coming back here for a longer break, say a week or two, quite soon. Do you think that would be possible?'

'I think you'd be all right,' Iris told her. 'It's still pretty early in the season. It would be a different story if it was July or August. And two of the residents are leaving soon. Miss Hammond's off to her cottage in the next week or two and Mrs Passmore's going to join an old friend who's been widowed – they're going to try sharing her house together, to see if it works out. I should think it would, Mrs Passmore's easy to get along with.'

She caught Lambert's quick glance at the nearby table where Mrs Passmore sat over her coffee and liqueur, selecting a chocolate from an expensive-looking box in front of her. 'You needn't worry,' Iris assured him. 'She won't hear us talking about her. She's pretty deaf, though she'd never admit it. You have to face her straight on and talk quite loudly if you want her to hear. She'll have to come round to wearing a hearing aid sooner or later but she's putting it off as long as possible.' She grinned. 'You'd think folk would have got beyond vanity at her age but it seems they don't. Take that hair of hers. Looks well, doesn't it? That's a wig. Funnily enough, she doesn't make any secret of that. Wigs are quite a hobby of hers, she has half a dozen in different styles and colours, they cost a fortune.' She turned to go. 'Yes, I'm sure you'll be all right,' she added to Julie. 'Give them a ring as soon as you've settled on a date. I'm sure they'll be able to fit you in.'

As they were finishing their coffee Lambert saw Miss Hammond push back her chair and walk across to Mrs Passmore's table. Mrs Passmore looked up at her, watching her lips; Miss Hammond spoke slowly and clearly. 'I'm going over to the cottage this afternoon; I'm leaving in a few minutes. I wondered if you'd like to come with me and take a look round, see what you think of it. I'm sure you'd find it interesting and you may have some ideas about improvements.' Her voice took on a cajoling tone. 'It's a beautiful afternoon. I'll be sure to bring you back here in time for tea.'

'It's very kind of you, Olive.' Mrs Passmore's voice already held a refusal and Miss Hammond's face drooped. 'But I'm playing bridge this afternoon, I'm being collected at half past two.' She didn't offer Miss Hammond a chocolate. 'Some other time, perhaps,' she added in a tone that didn't promise much. She picked up her coffee cup and drank from it in a manner that spoke unmistakably of dismissal.

Miss Hammond gave a resigned nod. She wore a faintly dejected look as she left the dining room. 'Poor dear,' Julie said lightly. 'She didn't even get to show Mrs Passmore her new shoes.'

Lambert looked at his watch. 'Time I was moving.' As they came out into the hall he said, 'I enjoyed our lunch. I hope you have a pleasant weekend.'

Julie smiled. 'It was very kind of you to help me with the car.' She slid him a beseeching little look, open, unguarded. 'Will I be seeing you again?'

For a moment he was tempted; for a moment he felt himself a green lad again, her own age. But common sense at once brushed aside the thought. Whatever he was currently in the market for, it very definitely wasn't for naive, immature young girls, however winning their ways, however pretty their clouds of hair.

By way of reply he made a noncommittal sound. He consulted his watch again with deliberate openness and gave her an impersonal smile that very distinctly said goodbye.

Her beseeching look fell away. She smiled brightly back at him, raised a hand in a departing wave and turned to go upstairs to her room.

She had got the message.

Lambert came down the hotel steps and set off for the car park. A short distance in front of him he saw the stocky, chalk-striped figure of Miss Olive Hammond, walking briskly in the same direction.

Miss Hammond's car, a Volkswagen Beetle, was parked a few yards from his. 'A glorious afternoon,' she called across as he halted to fish in his pockets for his keys. She looked pleased to see him. 'I'm making the most of this weather; I'm going to do some gardening at the cottage I've bought.'

She suddenly walked swiftly over to Lambert's car and positioned herself strategically in front of the driver's door. 'I'm moving into the cottage very soon,' she continued in a rush. 'I've been going over there, making a start on the garden. It's quite a wilderness, the place has been empty for years.'

Lambert had by now found his keys. He went up to his car but Miss Hammond showed no sign of budging. She went rattling on. 'It's an old cottage, Victorian. It was modernized – after a fashion – back in the year dot. A lot of people would be put off by the state it's in but I know it will be very attractive when I've finished with it. I'm looking forward to it all tremendously. I've never owned a property before.'

'I've never owned one at all,' Lambert said.

'I'm going to see about plans for an extension. Then there'll be all the repairs and improvements, it's going to be very exciting.' She pulled a face. 'You'd be astonished at how much it's all going to cost. I know I was. It's only when you actually get down to it that you realize what prices are these days.'

Lambert mustered his patience as best he could. 'I dare say you can get it added on to your mortgage,' he suggested.

19

She waved a dismissive hand. 'Mortgages are not for me. I wouldn't want to be saddled with one at my time of life. Cash on the nail, that's the only thing at my age. I won't be taking a holiday this year, I'm devoting all my time to the place.' She jerked her head. 'I've started going to salerooms and auctions. I've bought a few odds and ends, just the bare minimum to start with. I've got them in store, ready to move in. I want to get old furniture as far as I can – not real antiques, of course, they cost the earth, but you'd be surprised what nice little cottagey pieces you can still pick up cheap. I've been reading up about old houses, old furniture, the different styles and periods.' She grinned. 'They're getting to know me at the public library.'

Lambert tossed his keys into the air and caught them again. Olive ignored the hint. 'Are you fond of gardening?' she asked.

He tossed the keys again. 'I can take it or leave it.'

'I've had a look round the garden centres and shops but the plants and shrubs cost a small fortune. But I've thought of a way of getting round that.' She made a pleased little face. 'I intend cadging cuttings and plants from Luke Marchant. I can slip him a few bob – much cheaper than buying them.' She raised a cautionary finger. 'Mum's the word, of course. No need for His Nibs to know anything about it.'

Lambert's patience came suddenly to an end. 'I must be getting along,' he told her brusquely.

Still she stood immovable. 'I'm going to be all alone at the cottage after I move in. It'll be quite a change, after living in a hotel for the last four years.' She looked up at him. 'It's going to feel very strange.'

'You should get yourself a pet. A dog. Or a cat. Very good company.'

She shook her head at once. 'They'd take too much looking after.'

'A bird, then.'

'A bird,' she echoed on a note of lively interest.

'Get a budgie,' he suggested. 'Teach it to talk.'

She smiled. 'I might just do that.'

He took a step forward. 'If you wouldn't mind.' He gestured at the car door. 'I really must be off.'

She moved reluctantly aside. As soon as he had got in and closed the door she stooped and rapped on the window. He wound it partway down. She seized hold of the top of the glass and stuck her face in at the opening. 'You'll have to come over and see the cottage. You and your young lady.'

Lambert switched on the engine. 'She's not my young lady. I just happened to come across her today. I won't be seeing her again.'

'Then come by yourself. Any time you're in the neighbourhood, do call in. The cottage isn't on the phone yet but no matter about that, you can just drop in, take me as you find me. I can give you a cup of tea – something stronger, if you like. I can always rustle you up a meal.'

'Very kind of you.' He managed a smile of sorts. 'I'll bear it in mind.'

She began to rattle out hasty directions for finding the cottage. He made to start winding the window up again and she was forced to withdraw. She was still calling after him as he pulled out without further ceremony. He was off and away, down the drive, out through the gates, heading for Cannonbridge.

All at once the day took on a totally different complexion. In no time at all he would find himself giving the chief inspector an account of his wasted morning. Not a prospect he relished.

Before he had put a couple of miles behind him all thought of Olive Hammond and her cottage had gone from his mind.

CHAPTER 4

The cuckoo had barely uttered his first hollow notes when the spring weather turned abruptly fickle, with gusts of rain, showers of sleet and hail, followed by a succession of grey, damp days, giving way all at once to another spell of cloudless skies and warm breezes. Horse chestnuts blossomed white and pink along the avenues, lilac and laburnum bloomed in suburban gardens, hanging baskets of lobelia and trailing geranium sprouted from lampposts; floral clocks appeared in municipal flowerbeds.

Bank holidays, agricultural shows, festivals and carnivals. Children danced round maypoles. Grown men dressed up as Cavaliers and Roundheads and fought pitched battles over stretches of harmless countryside. The cuckoo was in full voice.

In the DIY stores staff worked overtime. Gallons of paint, acres of wallpaper, were loaded into the boots of cars. Householders erected scaffolding and climbed up ladders.

Sergeant Lambert's landlady was afflicted, as every year, by her own variety of spring fever. With her it took the form of prodigious exertions in the garden, a sustained attack upon the contents of cupboards and drawers: sorting, discarding, cramming into cardboard boxes to be piled outside the back door and borne off by the dustmen.

At the end of May a nasty virus made its stealthy appearance, insinuating its way into the country from abroad by means of the aeroplane, cutting a swathe through the population and certainly not minded to spare the main Cannonbridge police station.

Sergeant Lambert endured an attack of average ferocity but Detective Chief Inspector Kelsey was very unwell indeed. He struggled back to work earlier than he should, unable to endure any longer the tedium of an invalid existence alone in his flat – he had lived on his own since his divorce years ago.

He dragged himself up the station steps. A big, solidly built man with craggy features, green eyes normally bright and sharp but heavy now and lacklustre; a head of thick, carroty hair, devoid today of its usual shine and spring.

Outside the windows the season swept joyfully on but the Chief knew none of it, huddled glumly in his office, wheezing, reeking of liniment, sucking lozenges powerfully fragrant with menthol and eucalyptus.

One morning in the middle of June Sergeant Lambert ventured to suggest to the Chief that what he needed was a holiday. The sergeant was still not in top form himself. He had already booked his own holiday for September – he was going to Greece with friends – but he had a couple of weeks in hand. If the Chief decided to take himself off for a break, Lambert wouldn't at all mind fixing himself some leave at the same time, very convenient all round. He could go and stay with his sister and her family in Sussex or with married friends in Wales.

The Chief didn't bother to give him any kind of rational reply, he merely dismissed the notion with a shake of his head. He had so far made no plans for any leave; he was never attracted by the vision of long days of leisure; holidays always served to emphasize his aloneness.

A day or two went by and still the Chief felt no better. What I need is a really good, strong tonic, he decided. Something stronger than he could buy over the counter. He went reluctantly back to the doctor who came up with precisely the same remedy that Sergeant Lambert had proposed: 'What you need is a holiday.'

The Chief shook his head stubbornly. 'All I need is something to make me feel a bit livelier.'

But the doctor could be equally stubborn. 'I am giving you something,' he countered. 'I'm giving you sound advice. Instructions, if that makes it any easier for you to swallow. Take a holiday. Now.'

As he closed the door behind him, Kelsey shook his head slowly and with determination. On his way back to the station he went into a health-food shop and bought himself a large bottle of a fiendishly expensive herbal elixir, brewed in the back yard of some monastery in the Balkans. The moment he got back into his car he took a long swig from the bottle. He immediately felt so hideously unwell that he knew beyond doubt it must be doing him good.

He said nothing of all this to Sergeant Lambert.

On June 21st the Chief awoke in a sourly irritable frame of mind. He felt no better. If he must be honest, he felt worse.

Sergeant Lambert greeted him at the office with a reminder that it was the first day of summer, a remark that did nothing to lift the Chief's spirits. He tackled without enthusiasm the pile of mail awaiting him.

Before long he came upon a letter written in a slow, shaking hand. It was from a Mr Eardlow, with an address in a hamlet a few miles from Cannonbridge.

Eardlow apologized for writing instead of coming over to the police station in person, but his circumstances made a visit difficult. He and his wife were advanced in years and suffered from various health problems. They no longer owned a car and public transport in the area was very limited.

They were worried about a young relative. They had been trying to get in touch with her for some time but hadn't been able to make any contact, nor, indeed, to discover her present whereabouts. They would be most grateful if an officer could call on them; they would supply him with full details.

Kelsey sighed and shook his head. Eardlow hadn't even given the name of the missing relative. No doubt it was another case of an inconsiderate, harebrained youngster taking it into her head to abscond temporarily for the most trifling of reasons, sometimes for no reason at all, never giving a thought to the anxieties of family and friends.

He tossed the letter across to Sergeant Lambert. 'Better get over there and have a word with these folk,' he instructed. 'I doubt if there's anything in it.'

In the afternoon Sergeant Lambert drove over to the hamlet, having first phoned the Eardlows to fix a time. They were nervously awaiting him in the spotlessly clean parlour of their little cottage. The furniture gleamed, the brass shone. A table was set with an elaborate lace cloth and what were undoubtedly their best china cups.

Mrs Eardlow had the kettle already on and she brewed the tea right away. She moved slowly and with difficulty. Her husband walked with the aid of a stick, his hands were swollen and knobbed. In Lambert's estimation neither of them would see eighty again. He felt a pang at the thought of all the painful domestic activity on the part of this frail old couple that must have taken place in the little dwelling after his phone call.

He didn't ask questions to start with, he didn't press them in any way. Over an excellent tea they began to relax. They stopped treating him as if he were minor visiting royalty and began to unload their worries.

The missing relative was a girl of twenty. As soon as they told him her name, Julie Dawson, bells began to ring in Lambert's brain. By the time they added her address, Honeysuckle Cottage, near Millbourne, he was almost certain. He asked if he might see a photograph.

They couldn't produce anything very recent but showed him some snapshots taken during Julie's last visit two years ago. Lambert looked down at the pretty face, the impish smile, the beautiful hair.

'I've met this girl,' he told them. They looked startled. He gave them a brief sketch of his encounter with Julie by the roadside near Calcott House. After a burst of astonishment the Eardlows took up their story again.

It seemed that Julie was an only child, born late in her parents' marriage. Her father – fifteen years older than her mother – had been a first cousin of Mrs Eardlow. Both Julie's parents were now dead and the Eardlows were her only living relatives. Julie worked for the *Millbourne Advertiser* as a telephone sales clerk; she had been there three years.

During her first year in Millbourne she had visited the Eard-lows two or three times. Two years ago she had moved into lodgings at Honeysuckle Cottage. Since then she had written a few lines occasionally and had sent cards at Christmas and on their birthdays, but she had never once visited them.

They had replied without fail to her letters and cards, giving her their bits of news, repeating the invitation to come for a visit, a weekend, or a longer holiday. They had always been fond of Julie, had always been on good terms with her and her parents. As far as they knew, Julie was happy in her job, had settled down well at Honeysuckle Cottage, liked her landlady, a Miss Audrey Tysoe.

The Eardlows had celebrated their golden wedding in the first week of June. Julie had long known about the planned gathering of friends. She had definitely told them she would be there.

Not only would she attend the party but she would stay with them for a night or two. This had been settled months ago and had been referred to on both sides more than once since then.

'We were very disappointed when she didn't come.' Mrs Eardlow looked on the verge of tears. 'Very surprised, too. She didn't even write or phone.' They had thought at first that the date had somehow slipped her mind, but she would remember after a day or two and they would hear from her.

But the days went by and they didn't hear. They began to wonder if she was ill, or had met with some accident. In the end Mrs Eardlow rang Honeysuckle Cottage, not without misgivings. The Eardlows came of a generation who had grown up without telephones. It was only in very recent years, since their health had grown frail, that they had had a phone installed. They regarded it as an instrument to be used in emergencies and with due respect for the cost of calls. Nor had they any wish to appear to be prying into Julie's life.

It was the first time Mrs Eardlow had spoken to Miss Tysoe; she had found her pleasant enough. Miss Tysoe told her Julie wasn't there, she hadn't been there for some time, she was on indefinite leave from her job at the *Advertiser*. She had gone for a holiday to Calcott House in May. Miss Tysoe didn't know her present whereabouts but she wasn't anxious; she was confident Julie would turn up again when it suited her.

The Eardlows were at first reassured by this but after mulling it over for a day or two their uneasiness surfaced again. Why should Julie have decided to go on indefinite leave? Had there been difficulties at work? And what about the money side of it? How was she managing?

So they finally rang the *Millbourne Advertiser* and spoke to the proprietor, Mr Fielding. He told them Julie had not been in touch with the office since going on leave in May. She had given no reasons for wishing to take extended leave and she had not been pressed on the matter. She had always been a good worker and the *Advertiser* was happy to accommodate her in this instance. They were sure she would return when she had resolved whatever it was that had made her ask for leave. Her job would certainly be waiting for her; the Eardlows need have no worries on that score. Fielding had no idea of her present whereabouts.

Again, when the call was over, the Eardlows felt reassured

to some extent, but again, after a day or two, their anxieties sprang up as strongly as ever.

This time they phoned Calcott House and spoke to Mrs Marchant. She told them Miss Dawson had stayed at the hotel from May 10th to May 16th. There had been no trouble or upset of any kind during her stay; she paid her bill on the day she left. The only address the hotel had any note of was her Millbourne address, Honeysuckle Cottage, but Mrs Marchant seemed to remember that Miss Dawson had said something on leaving about going to a caravan. No, Mrs Marchant had no idea where the caravan might be. She couldn't even be certain she was correct in associating that remark with Miss Dawson; it could have been some other guest. No, the hotel had had no communication from Miss Dawson after she left; there had been no mail or phone calls for her since then. Nor had anyone come to the hotel asking to see her.

By now the Eardlows found themselves very far from reassured. They talked it over for another couple of days, arguing back and forth. Probably there was nothing at all amiss – but if it later turned out that there was, they would never forgive themselves if they had just let the matter go.

In the end they decided with a good deal of trepidation to write to the Cannonbridge police and leave it up to them to judge if any inquiries were necessary.

Lambert told them he would report back to his Chief. 'I'll let you know what's decided,' he added as he stood up to leave. 'In the meantime, try not to worry. Young women can be very impulsive. Julie could turn up any day, astonished to hear you've been so anxious about her.'

'I dare say you're right,' Eardlow agreed. 'We're not able to get about much these days, we do tend to sit and chew things over. I suppose we're inclined to get things out of proportion.'

They thanked the sergeant profusely for coming over to see them. They insisted on going with him to the door, shaking his hand on the threshold. Mrs Eardlow looked up into Lambert's face as he took her frail old fingers into his strong, warm clasp.

'I'm still not happy in my mind,' she told him earnestly. 'Whatever kind of sudden notion Julie may have taken into her head, she'd never have forgotten our anniversary.' She shook her head with feeble force. 'Not Julie. Never in a million years.'

27

CHAPTER 5

Chief Inspector Kelsey was about to drag himself off to a conference for a few days and wasn't looking forward to the prospect. He certainly wasn't disposed to feel overmuch concern for Miss Julie Dawson. 'Skittish young females,' he said to Lambert on a note of trenchant censure. Over the years he had come across many of the ilk, light-minded creatures who woke up one bright morning and took it into their heads to skedaddle without a word to relatives or friends – to give those same relatives and friends a good fright, as often as not, or merely to gain attention. Or indulging themselves in a fit of the sulks after a few cross words. Or scarpered with the latest boyfriend. Or simply decided to cut loose for a while. Needless work for the police, needless worry for the family. 'All it takes is a postcard,' he said sourly. 'Or a phone call. Never enters their silly heads.' No doubt Miss Julie Dawson would stroll blithely in where she belonged when she'd had enough of the sulks or the boyfriend.

He was strongly minded to do nothing whatever in the matter. But there were the Eardlows, old, frail, anxious. 'Better look into it,' he told Lambert grudgingly. 'But don't go making a big production number out of it, just fit it in with everything else.' Lambert knew the form well enough, he'd been over this kind of ground often before. He knew precisely how much time to spend, how much to do, just enough to be able to reassure the relatives the police were reasonably certain the girl had come to no harm. And that was what he set about over the next few days. His first step was to discover via a series of phone calls which estate agents in the area handled holiday lettings of caravans. He found three and went off to visit them all. He was in luck. At his first call, an office in the centre of Cannonbridge, the manager produced records which showed that a caravan had indeed been rented by a Miss Julie Dawson, giving the Honeysuckle Cottage address. She had taken the caravan from Tuesday, May 16th, to Saturday, May 27th. She had paid in full, in advance, by cheque, on Monday, May 15th. He could supply no further details himself, he didn't attend to such bookings, but he passed Lambert on to the female clerk who had dealt with Miss Dawson. The woman did recall the matter. Two details in particular stood out in her memory: Miss Dawson's unusually beautiful hair and her insistence on the cheapest possible let. She didn't mind where the caravan was or how basic its amenities but she wanted to move in as soon as possible. The clerk was able to suit Miss Dawson immediately with the cheapest caravan on their books. It was old, isolated, furnished and equipped to a bare minimum, and in consequence difficult to let. It belonged to a fishing enthusiast, a bachelor, who kept it principally for his own use, whenever he could get away from his city job to fish the local streams. It was vacant at the time Miss Dawson made her inquiry; the next booking was for May 27th. Miss Dawson took it for the whole of the interim.

The caravan stood on a small farm a few miles from Calcott village. The clerk gave Miss Dawson directions for finding the farm; the keys were kept at the farmhouse. 'Something else, I remember,' she threw in suddenly. 'Miss Dawson didn't stay quite the full time at the caravan. And she didn't return the keys to the farmhouse. They were dropped in here.' She had found them in the mail on the Friday morning, May 26th; they hadn't been sent by post, they had been delivered by hand. She particularly remembered because there had been no note, no word of any kind with the keys. They had simply been put into an envelope and pushed through the letter box. Every key ring carried a tag giving the name and address of the estate agent, together with a number identifying the property to which the keys belonged.

There had been no further contact of any kind with Miss Dawson. The clerk had no idea where she might have gone after leaving the caravan.

The following afternoon Lambert drove out to the farm, a small, old-fashioned, man-and-wife enterprise that appeared far from thriving. A stream ran between overhanging willows along one boundary. Close by, Lambert saw a sizable stretch of shadowy, gloomy-looking woodland, overgrown and neglected.

He walked across the cobbled yard to the farmhouse. His knock at the door was answered by a harassed-looking woman in late middle age. Her hands were covered in flour, wisps of hair stuck out around her face. She didn't invite Lambert inside but answered his questions on the doorstep, briskly and without embellishment, already half turned back towards the demands of her kitchen. Her husband wasn't in, he was out at a farm sale, she couldn't say when he'd be back.

Yes, she remembered Miss Dawson very well; that is, she couldn't recall the name but she did clearly remember a girl staying in the caravan in the latter part of May. It was the only time she could remember a pretty young girl staying in the caravan on her own, and she too had been struck by the beauty of the girl's hair. Miss Dawson had also been unusual in that she had never called at the farmhouse for milk, eggs or vegetables, had never stopped by for a chat, never asked if it was all right if she took a stroll round the farm. 'In fact, I only ever saw her twice,' the woman added. 'The day she came, when she called in here for the keys, and one other time, a day or two later – I saw her in the distance, walking towards the wood.' The caravan stood at quite some distance from the house and wasn't visible from it.

The woman was paid to clean the caravan after each let. There had been nothing untoward when she had cleaned through after Miss Dawson's stay; she had found nothing left behind.

The caravan was currently occupied by a young couple with a baby. They had gone out for the day and wouldn't be back till it was time to put the baby to bed. They would have taken the caravan keys with them; there was only the one set. She jerked her head. Even if she had a second set she wouldn't have been happy about letting the sergeant take a look inside in the absence of the young couple. But he was welcome to walk over there, to see the location. He must excuse her from going with him, she was up to her eyes just now.

Lambert followed her directions. The caravan was in a secluded spot, well out of sight and earshot of both the farmhouse and the road, provided with an even greater degree of privacy by a thick screen of trees. The caravan curtains had been left closed.

He stood for some moments glancing about. The breeze carried with it the scent of clover fields. From the topmost branches of a nearby tree rang out the clear, bell-like notes of a blackcap.

The situation was certainly pleasant enough. Apart from the glowering presence of the wood.

Next day Sergeant Lambert found himself free in the middle of the morning to run over to Millbourne. The town was somewhat smaller than Cannonbridge, thirty miles away.

As he neared Honeysuckle Cottage the road took him through undulating countryside, past deep gorges running between thickly wooded hills, green copses, bracken-covered slopes, old gravel pits and quarries filled with water, hedgerows decked with wild roses.

Because of the phone call she had recently received from the Eardlows, Audrey Tysoe wasn't surprised at Lambert's visit. She was busy in the garden when he arrived but she broke off readily enough. Lambert noticed her limp. Habitual, he guessed, probably from some old injury; she used no stick, wore no plaster or bandage that might suggest a more recent mishap.

She took him into her charming cottage, sat him down and gave him coffee. No, she wasn't anxious about Julie, she was sure she would turn up again before long. She had left most of her things at the cottage – that must surely mean she intended returning, if only to collect her belongings. She had lodged with Miss Tysoe for two years. Before that she had stayed with three or four other landladies but hadn't been happy with any of them.

Miss Tysoe didn't normally take in lodgers. She had been in charge of personnel at the *Advertiser* until her retirement and Julie had told her she hadn't been able to find digs she was happy in. 'I offered to take her in here, temporarily,' Miss Tysoe explained. 'Till she could look round to find somewhere she really liked. But we both found it worked well, her being here. I liked having someone around in the evenings and at weekends, and Julie liked living out of town; it was what she had been used to before she came to Millbourne. She wasn't a girl who wanted to go out much in her free time. So she stayed on.'

But they had never been close. Both tended to be self-sufficient, and Julie was not by nature a confiding girl. It was a satisfactory relationship of good-natured live and let live, with mutual benefits. There had never been any friction between them.

Lambert told her he now knew that Julie had stayed in a caravan for several days after leaving Calcott House. No, Miss Tysoe had no idea where Julie might have gone at the end of her caravan stay. She wasn't entirely surprised at Julie taking herself off on indefinite leave; she had been showing signs of restlessness for some time. She had made remarks about the *Advertiser* being small fry, Millbourne being a very provincial place, Honeysuckle Cottage being in a backwater.

From her years in personnel work Miss Tysoe had garnered a good deal of experience of young women and she believed she could read the signs. 'I think it could have been her twentieth birthday that sparked it off,' she hazarded. 'She seemed to feel it was some kind of milestone. When she first came to Millbourne she hadn't long lost her mother. She badly needed a breathing space to come to terms with adult life. And I suppose, coming more or less straight from school into a newspaper office, from a little village to a town, it all seemed new, interesting and exciting, being out in the world on her own, learning a job, earning money.

'But that was three years ago. By this time she must feel on top of her job, it can't be much of a challenge any more. She's probably beginning to want something livelier and more demanding. She might feel she's completed one stage of her growing up – after all, at twenty, she's no longer an adolescent. I imagine she's ready to spread her wings again, take a good look at her life and how she intends to spend it. She'll come back, I'm positive, when she's reached some decisions.'

'What about boyfriends?' Lambert wanted to know. 'A pretty young girl, she must surely have boyfriends.'

But Miss Tysoe was positive there was no one. Nor did Julie have any close girlfriend. There had been two girls at the *Advertiser* she had been friendly with at one time but both had left some time ago. As far as Miss Tysoe knew, Julie hadn't kept up with either of them, nor could she say where either was now living. She was sure Julie had made no special friend since then. 'Most of the young women at the *Advertiser* are married, with young families,' she pointed out. 'They have their own very busy lives to lead, apart from their jobs.'

Lambert asked if she could tell him the name of Julie's bank and she was able to supply it. She also told him Julie had a savings account with a building society, but she didn't know which one. Nor did she know if she had a post-office account.

Lambert asked if he might look through her things. She took him upstairs to a good-sized room, comfortably furnished as a bedsitter. 'She often stayed up here, reading or watching TV,' Miss Tysoe told him. She indicated a portable television set, well-filled bookshelves. 'If she wanted to join me downstairs, she was always welcome.'

Lambert went over to the bookshelves and stooped to read the spines. Old bound editions of the *Strand Magazine*, handsome copies of Edgar Allan Poe, Wilkie Collins, Conan Doyle, Rider Haggard, John Buchan, Dorothy Sayers, Agatha Christie. He picked out a book at random and opened it. An ornamental ex-libris plate bore a name and date written in faded ink: *Gilbert Michael Dawson. March, 1935.*

He picked out other books here and there. Some bore the same bookplate with dates ranging from the thirties to the sixties. Others carried more modern plates with Julie's name – written sometimes in a schoolgirl hand, sometimes in a more adult style, with more recent dates.

The room was very neat. 'That's the way she left it,' Miss Tysoe said. 'I've never had to clear up after her, she's always been tidy.'

Lambert glanced through the contents of the wardrobe, through drawers and cupboards; he opened the bureau. He found no bank books, no chequebook or credit cards. No letters or diaries, no personal papers of any interest.

But he did come across a folder of snapshots: Julie at various ages, exterior views of a cottage, a garden, a couple who were clearly her parents. Another woman, sitting beside Julie's mother in the garden under an apple tree, looked about the same age as Julie's mother. There were several snapshots of a freckle-faced, dark-haired lad of nine or ten, with a cheerful, open smile. And a few photographs of the Eardlows, taken some years ago when they were rather more hale and hearty.

Miss Tysoe could identify none of the photographs; Julie had never shown them to her. She had said little about her background and Miss Tysoe had never pressed her.

When Sergeant Lambert left, Miss Tysoe came limping out to the car with him. 'I'll be sure to let you know the moment I hear anything from Julie,' she assured him. 'And of course I'll let the Eardlows know too. I'm pretty certain in my own mind she's just gone off to think things out. She may decide to leave here altogether, find herself a job in London or some other city. After all, she has no ties, she can please herself.'

Lambert drove on into Millbourne. He called at Julie's bank and spoke to the manager. Julie had a current account with the bank; it hadn't been disturbed since the third week in May, the last two transactions being cheques drawn on the account, one dated May 15th, in favour of the estate agent from whom she had hired the caravan and the other, dated May 16th, made out to Calcott House.

Lambert went next to the *Advertiser* premises, a few doors from the bank. Mr Fielding was busy but when the sergeant's name and an indication of his mission were sent in to him he broke off at once and came along to reception. He shook hands with Lambert and took him into his office. On the way he mentioned the recent phone call he had received from the Eardlows. He was sorry they felt so worried. He was sure the anxiety was groundless, he had done his best to reassure them. Had the police found any genuine cause for alarm?

No, Lambert told him. They were merely looking into the matter, trying to discover if there was any need for concern, hoping very shortly to be able themselves to reassure the old couple.

In the office Lambert told Fielding he had traced Julie to a caravan a few miles from the hotel where she had gone after leaving Honeysuckle Cottage. She had left the caravan in the last week of May and there, for the moment, at least, the trail ended.

Fielding asked in what way he could be of use. His manner was friendly and helpful. The sergeant told him it would be useful to know Fielding's general impression of the girl, any idea he had about what might have led her to go off in this way, any guess at where or with whom she might now be. Perhaps, he suggested, Fielding might harbour some half-formed notion, too ill-defined to mention over the phone to the Eardlows, which might nevertheless be of use to the police.

Fielding shook his head with regret. No, he had no such notion. In the three years Julie had been with the *Advertiser* she had always been a willing and capable worker, punctual and accurate. She had progressed from the general office to telephone sales and was earning good money. He had thought her happy and satisfied in her job. She certainly hadn't come to him looking for some further opportunity, something with more challenge. If she had he would have taken her seriously, would have done his best to find her a suitable niche.

He was not aware of any trouble between Julie and any other employee. She was a quiet girl with a pleasant manner. The official position was that she was on indefinite leave, unpaid now as her entitlement to paid leave had run out. Her job was being kept open for her – within reason. When she went off in the second week in May Fielding had never imagined she would be absent as long as this, but he would make no attempt to fill her job permanently for another month or two.

Whenever she came back she would be listened to sympathetically. If it turned out that some illness had overtaken her, if she had suffered any kind of breakdown, then she would – if she so wished – be reinstated and her absence treated as sick leave, with backdated pay.

But if it should turn out that she had decided to leave permanently, had found herself another job, maybe, there would be no difficulty about that. She would be given any references she might require, very good references, too. She would be advised about pension rights.

As to what Fielding's own private guess might be, he admitted he still felt no real concern. He had employed a good deal of female labour for some years now; sudden departures, abrupt termination of employment, unexplained absences, brief or more lengthy, were by no means unknown. He smiled. 'Usually it's for some personal reason – when a reason is ever given. You learn not to ask too many questions; you don't want to find yourself involved in some emotional mishmash, drowned in floods of tears.'

On that score, no, he knew of no boyfriend among the *Advertiser* staff. 'But I would scarcely expect to know,' he added. 'I never concern myself with gossip, there's far too much work to be done. Audrey Tysoe – Julie's landlady at Honeysuckle Cottage; she used to run Personnel here till she retired – she'd be far more likely to know about anything like that.' He glanced at his watch. 'If there's nothing further, I do have an appointment.'

Lambert rose at once. He thanked Fielding for his time, his assistance. If he learned anything definite he would be sure to let Fielding know. Fielding promised to do the same.

Fielding shook hands, walked with him into the corridor. 'I don't for one moment think anything's happened to Julie,' he said with conviction. 'In my opinion she's a girl well able to take care of herself.'

On Monday morning Chief Inspector Kelsey returned from his conference in a worse state than ever. Late nights, smoke-filled rooms, food and drink far too abundant, too indigestible.

A great many matters clamoured for his attention. Very low on his list of priorities came the unknown whereabouts of Miss Julie Dawson. He listened with ill-concealed impatience as Lambert sketched in a brief account of his endeavours with regard to the missing girl. Towards the end of the sergeant's recital the Chief burst into a paroxysm of coughing. He reached into a drawer and laid hold of yet another bottle containing yet another lethal-looking mixture. He took an extra-long swig, totally heedless by now of all warnings on all labels.

He replaced the bottle in the drawer and sat leaning forward, gasping. No good, he thought, I'm going to have to give in. I can't go on like this. For once in his life he was going to have to do what the doctor ordered, remove himself from the scene for a couple of weeks. He didn't give a tuppenny toss where, just somewhere quiet and soothing, where he could let his mind go completely blank, let peace wash over him.

He became aware that Lambert had finished his spiel and was waiting for his response. The Chief pulled down the corners of his mouth. 'I can't see anything in it. She's a grown woman, not a child. She's able to please herself as to what she does, where she goes. I've decided to take some leave, I'm never going to feel right till I do. You can forget Julie Dawson. Drop the case.'

Lambert at once suggested that he should take some leave himself at the same time. He still didn't feel one hundred per cent right.

'Fine,' the Chief agreed without hesitation. 'Good idea. Better get started clearing up the odds and ends. Don't want to leave things in an almighty mess.' A thought struck him. 'Those relatives of the girl, what was the name? Eardlow, that was it. Better get over there to see them, have a word in person.' Old folk, easily overwhelmed by anxiety, justified or not; a letter or phone call would be too impersonal, would do little to calm their fears.

On Thursday afternoon Lambert managed to find an hour to spare for the Eardlows. This time he didn't let them know he was coming. He was quite certain he would find them both at home and the last thing he wanted was for the two of them to wear themselves out cleaning and polishing, preparing another elaborate tea.

And he did find them both at home, watching an old film on television. They searched his face apprehensively, fearful of what he might be about to disclose. He tried to reassure them, leave them in a hopeful frame of mind. They did their best to oblige him by assuming looks of buoyant optimism but he was far from sure that he had succeeded in his attempt.

'Don't forget,' he reminded them as he left. 'Let us know the moment you hear anything from Julie.'

By Friday afternoon Kelsey and Lambert had cleared their desks. The Chief had booked himself a cruise, a cancellation vacancy. He was due to board the ship on Sunday, not without deep misgivings. 'You'll love it,' they told him encouragingly in the police canteen. 'All those footloose, blue-rinse ladies. Six to one, the ratio, by all accounts.' It was not what he wanted to hear.

Sergeant Lambert had not as yet decided where to go. He would allow himself a day or two to unwind, think about it, decide between the attractions of Sussex and Wales.

His landlady had been delighted to learn he would be taking himself off. She had made immediate plans for having his room redecorated while he was away.

When he came in on Friday evening, relaxed and smiling at the thought of two weeks of utter idleness, she asked when he was likely to be off.

'All in good time,' he promised.

By the time he had washed and changed, eaten his meal, he had more or less decided on Sussex. It would be good to see his sister and her family again. Two or three times during the evening he picked up the phone. Once he got as far as beginning to tap out the number. But always something niggled at his mind, preventing him from going further, some little point of disquiet he couldn't identify. Always he replaced the receiver.

On Saturday morning he woke early to discover, the moment he reached consciousness, that the niggle had at last declared itself: what if it wasn't Julie Dawson but someone else who had returned the caravan keys to the estate agent? Someone who didn't know about the arrangement with the farmhouse, someone who cleared Julie's things out of the caravan, locking it afterwards. Someone who read the agent's address on the key tag, put the keys in an envelope, drove into Cannonbridge during the hours of darkness, slipped the keys in through the letter box.

He linked his hands behind his head and lay staring up at the ceiling. He could spend the first few days of his leave here, in his digs; use them to have another unobtrusive little ferret round on his own. He wouldn't be a detective sergeant on duty, just a holidaying member of the public. Nothing to stop him touring round the area; no law against chatting to folk here and there.

More than once in the course of Sunday his landlady permitted herself to display overt signs of irritation. Deep sighs, clicks of the tongue, shakes of the head. By evening she could contain herself no longer.

'I can't for the life of me think why you should want to hang round Cannonbridge when you're supposed to be on leave,' she burst out at him. 'Any ordinary normal human being' – by which she meant any citizen not in the police force – 'would be only too glad to get away from the place for a real break. Heaven knows it's no beauty spot.'

Lambert judged it prudent to offer no reply.

Shortly before ten on Monday morning he began his unobtrusive little ferret round by driving over to Calcott House.

The holiday season was advancing towards its peak. The car park was a good deal more crowded than on his previous visit, the number of guests had visibly increased, there was considerably more bustle.

As he came into the hall he saw the plump, pouter-pigeon figure of Mrs Marchant. She was standing chatting to a family party, her marmalade hair dressed higher than ever. Her sharp, darting eyes came to rest on him; he saw recognition wake in her face. She gave him a little fleeting nod and resumed her chat. He stood to one side, discreetly waiting till she was free. In the to and fro of the hall he caught here and there an American voice, the accents of France and Germany. After a few minutes the family party went off down the front steps and Mrs Marchant came over to him.

She smiled archly as she approached. 'I remember you,' she greeted him before he could open his mouth. 'You lunched here back in the spring, with Miss Dawson.' She made an apologetic movement of her head. 'I'm afraid I don't remember your name.' Lambert supplied it.

'It's about Miss Dawson that I'm here,' he told her.

She broke in before he could go further. 'I thought it might be.' She explained that after the phone call from the Eardlows she had questioned the hotel staff in a fruitless attempt to discover if anyone could offer a guess as to Miss Dawson's whereabouts. In the course of her questioning she had unearthed the fact that the lunch guest at Miss Dawson's table that Friday in the spring had been a policeman, a detective sergeant; Miss Dawson had confided as much to Iris, one of the waitresses.

'The Eardlows told me they were thinking of going to the police if they had no luck with their own inquiries,' she added. 'I take it Miss Dawson hasn't turned up yet?'

'No, I'm afraid she hasn't.' Mrs Marchant clearly took it for granted he was here on an official visit and he didn't correct this impression.

She apologized for the absence of her husband who had gone into town on business. She took Lambert into the office and sat him down but she didn't offer any refreshment. Her manner on the surface was friendly and helpful but on another level he was receiving with unmistakable clarity a totally different message: Say what you have to say and then clear off out of here. This duality in no way surprised him. He well knew that no hotel, guest house or similar establishment encourages the presence of police on its premises; nothing makes the clientele more uneasy.

He set about dispatching his business as speedily as possible. He asked if Mrs Marchant could remember anyone calling at the hotel asking for Miss Dawson during her stay, any phone calls or mail that might have caused Miss Dawson distress.

40

She shook her head. There had been nothing like that. There had been no trouble with any guest or member of staff, nor was she aware of any friendship Miss Dawson had struck up while she was at the hotel.

Lambert asked if she had mentioned the matter of Miss Dawson's present whereabouts to any of the guests. She looked horrified at the idea. She fervently hoped the sergeant had no intention of questioning any of the guests. She could assure him there was nothing to be gained by such questioning. The bulk of the guests at this moment were short-stay holiday-makers or overnight bed-and-breakfasters, none of whom had set foot in the hotel while Miss Dawson was there. The long-stay residents who had been at the hotel during Miss Dawson's stay had either left for good or were currently away on holiday or staying with relatives; one had been taken ill and had gone into hospital.

Lambert assured her he had no intention of even speaking to any of the guests, let alone attempting to question them. She gave a sigh of relief.

He asked if she knew where in Calcott village Miss Dawson had lived before she went to Millbourne but she shook her head. Miss Dawson had mentioned that she used to live in the village but she hadn't said where. Perhaps Iris, the waitress, might know, Lambert suggested; Miss Dawson might have chatted to her in the dining room. Would it be possible to speak to her?

Mrs Marchant considered. Yes, that would be all right. 'Iris works 10.30 to 2.30,' she told him. She glanced at her watch. 'She'll be in by now. She's never late, she lives just down the road. I'll go and get her for you.' She paused in the doorway. 'Was there anything else you wanted to ask me?'

Lambert told her no. 'Then I'll leave you to it,' she said briskly. 'I've a dozen things to attend to. I'm sure you won't mind seeing yourself out when you've spoken to Iris.'

And Iris, when she appeared a few minutes later, was able to give him Julie's old address in the village. She had not herself known the Dawson family. 'The cottage is quite some distance from where I live,' she told Lambert. 'You have to go right through the village and out the other side.' She gave him detailed directions.

She could offer no suggestion as to where Julie might be now.

41

Miss Dawson had often chatted to her while a meal was being served but she hadn't mentioned future plans. When she left the hotel Iris had told her she was welcome to drop in at her house for a cup of tea any afternoon if she found it lonely in the caravan. Miss Dawson did in fact drop in and they had spent a pleasant hour in casual conversation. Miss Dawson had said nothing that might throw any light on her intentions.

'Did she ever mention anyone she'd met while she was staying at the hotel?' Lambert asked. 'Some man who took an interest in her? One of the guests, perhaps? Maybe someone she'd known when she lived in the village? Or someone she chanced to meet while she was going round visiting different places in the area?'

'If you mean some sort of romantic interest,' Iris said, 'she never mentioned anything like that. She didn't seem much interested in that kind of thing.' She looked thoughtful. 'A pretty girl like that, you'd expect her to have boyfriends, wouldn't you?' She grinned. 'I did have a shot at getting her to open up, I'm nosy that way. But I couldn't get anything out of her. She was quite definite there wasn't anyone.' She grinned again. 'Could be, of course, there's someone she's not letting on about – for one reason or another.'

As Lambert came down the hotel steps he heard in the distance the put-put of a motor mower. He set off towards the car park. He didn't turn his head to look across the wide expanse of lawn to where Luke Marchant on a ride-on machine drove up and down the greensward in a beautiful, precise pattern.

CHAPTER 7

The cottage where the Dawsons had lived was the first of a pair of semi-detached dwellings in a quiet, pleasant lane just outside the village. Lambert rang and knocked but got no reply. He went round to the back, knocked and rang again, without success.

In the adjoining garden a woman was picking peas. She looked across as he went up to the fence to speak to her. A motherly, cheerful-looking woman in her sixties, with an air of capable common sense. She walked over to the fence. She had rosy cheeks, bright blue eyes; thick, wavy hair, a greying chestnut, coiled up on top of her head. Lambert recognized her – and the two gardens – from the snapshots in Julie's room at Honeysuckle Cottage. She was the woman sitting beside Julie's mother under the apple tree.

'You won't get any answer next door till this evening,' she told him. 'They're both out at work.'

He explained that he was a detective, trying to locate a young woman, a Miss Julie Dawson. She broke in before he could say any more. 'I know Julie Dawson. I've known her since the day she was born.' She looked up at him with concern. 'Why are the police trying to find her? Is something wrong?'

He told her briefly about the Eardlows, the police inquiry. 'I thought Miss Dawson might have called at her old home. She might have mentioned her plans to the people who live there now.'

'Julie did call here, back in the spring,' she confirmed. 'But it was to see me, not the people next door. She never knew them; they wouldn't be able to tell you anything. They're not from this village. They moved in next door a month or two after Julie left here, three years ago – these are rented cottages.'

Lambert asked if she could remember exactly when Julie had called to see her.

'She came more than once,' she told him. 'The first time was

43

at the end of April, she was staying at Calcott House for the weekend. Then she called again in May, when she came back to the hotel for a longer stay.' She paused. 'You'd better come inside. I'll make a cup of tea.' She gave him a friendly smile. 'My name's Norbury, by the way. I've lived in this cottage over forty years. I came here as a bride.'

He walked back round again and in through Mrs Norbury's gate. Her front garden spilled over with pinks, sweet william, love-in-a-mist, stocks, lilies; the air was full of perfume. She opened the door and took him along a passage into a comfortable kitchen with its windows open to the breeze.

'I was always fond of Julie,' she said as she made the tea. 'She was in and out of here a lot when she was a child. She was a bright, happy little girl, always lively and imaginative. I was very friendly with her mother, she was the same age as me – Julie's father was a lot older. He died about ten years ago, he'd been retired five years by then.'

She got out a tin of biscuits. 'Julie's mother died three years ago.' She sighed. 'I still miss her. Julie was only seventeen at the time. She'd left school a year before, she was halfway through a secretarial course. Her mother wasn't ill very long. It must have been a terrible shock for Julie when she died, though she seemed to take it quite well.

'She made up her mind what she was going to do very quickly. I thought she ought to take more time to think it over. My husband was alive then. He tried to advise her; he thought it most unwise to decide in such a hurry.' She shook her head. 'But there was no changing her mind. She knew what she wanted to do and she did it. There was no one to stop her, no aunt or uncle, no grandparents.'

She poured the tea and sat down opposite Lambert. 'She sold the furniture – there wasn't a great deal but there were some nice pieces. It gave her something in the bank to start her off. And of course she had what money her mother left. It wasn't a fortune but her parents had always been careful.'

She drank her tea. 'I suggested she moved in here with us, she could finish her secretarial course at the college.' She shook her head. 'She was very polite, very grateful, but she'd come to her own decisions. She was going to make a new start, leave the area, find herself a job, finish her secretarial course at evening classes.'

She pressed Lambert to biscuits. 'I must say she managed everything very efficiently. My husband tried to help but she would do it all on her own. In no time at all she was off. She told me she'd got a job in Millbourne, on one of those free newspapers.' She never heard from Julie after she left, never got a letter or a Christmas card. 'I must admit I was rather hurt by that, but I could understand it in a way. I think she was pretty well knocked sideways when her mother died, however little she tried to show it. I think she felt the only way she could get to grips with things, make a life for herself on her own, was to plunge right in, sink or swim by her own efforts. It was a brave thing to do, when you come to think about it, a girl just seventeen, all on her own. I don't know if I'd have had the gumption at her age, to do what she did.'

She poured more tea. 'I was really surprised, I can tell you, that day back in April when there was a ring at the door and there she stood, smiling at me. I'd never expected to see her again; I'd often wondered how she was getting on. I always felt sure she'd make out all right, she'd been so competent and independent after her mother died.'

She sighed. 'She didn't know about my husband, of course; she was very upset when I told her he'd passed away. She told me she was here just for the weekend. She said: "You'll never guess where I'm staying – Calcott House." I said she must be doing well if she could afford their prices. She laughed and said she'd always dreamed of staying there when she was a child – and she was enjoying it just as much as she'd imagined she would. She liked it so much she'd decided to come back soon for a longer break, a week or two.

'I told her she was welcome to call at any time and that Simon – he's my grandson – would be coming in May for two weeks, when the school would be on holiday. Julie had just missed him. He'd been staying with me over Easter; he'd gone back to school a few days earlier. Julie knew Simon from when she lived next door and Simon used to come here on visits with his parents. He's eleven, my one and only grandchild, my son's boy. His mother was killed in a road accident four years ago; my son's never had any thought of marrying again. He's an engineer. He's out in Turkey just now, working on a big construction project. He's got a two-year contract, he went out there six months ago. Simon's at a prep school. He's a boarder; he's very happy there.'

She took another biscuit. 'Julie did call again when she came back for a longer holiday. She'd left the hotel and moved into a caravan a few days before she called here. Simon had arrived from school the day before. Of course he'd grown a lot since the last time she'd seen him, she hardly knew him for a moment. But they got friendly again very quickly. Simon was laid up when she came.' She laughed. 'He'd gone running round the garden just after he got here. He climbed up into a tree and jumped down again.' She spread her hands. 'He twisted his ankle. That was a fine start to his holiday. The doctor said it wasn't a bad sprain but he'd have to rest it for at least a week. It was bandaged up and I put him on the sofa in the sitting room during the day.

'Fortunately he's never been a child that's easily bored so it wasn't too bad for him, he had his books and his woodcarving. That was my husband's hobby, woodcarving, he taught Simon a lot. After he died I kept all his tools, all his wood, for Simon. He's really quite good at it, when you think how young he is.

'And then, of course, there was Julie. She came to see him a few times. She played chess with him – she used to play chess with her father. I left the two of them while I got on with my chores or popped into the village. I used to hear them laughing together, as if they were both children. Simon really looked forward to seeing her.'

She fell silent for a moment. 'It made me remember the lad Julie was so friendly with when she was a child. He was the only close playmate she ever had. She didn't go to the village school; her parents sent her to a private day school in the town. Her father used to take her in every day, he was a clerk in an office. None of the other pupils in her class came from the village. The lad she was so friendly with, he went to the village school but he lived quite near here, and he was an only child too. He was the same age as Julie. They played together from when they were small. They were both full of fun and adventurous, though they never got up to any real mischief.'

She looked across at Lambert. 'One summer when they were about eleven years old, the lad went off to the seaside with his parents for a holiday. He got carried out to sea on one of those rubber floats and he was drowned. It was a terrible blow for

46

Julie. She couldn't seem to accept that he was dead. It was quite a time before his body was washed up and she'd half convinced herself he'd turn up again safe and sound, it had all been some silly prank.' She sighed. 'She never palled up again with any other youngster, not in the same way.'

She fell silent again, then she said, 'The second time Julie called here to see Simon – that was the very next day – I could hardly believe my eyes when I opened the door to her. She'd had all her beautiful hair cut off.' She pulled a little face. 'I made out I liked it short. I said I thought it suited her, but I didn't like it at all. I thought it was a terrible shame to cut it off. She was still nice-looking, of course, but nowhere near as pretty. It made her features look very sharp, and she'd left off all her make-up. She'd got jeans and a T-shirt on. She looked just like a mischievous lad or one of those actresses playing Peter Pan. She didn't say why she'd done it and I didn't ask her.' She moved her head. 'But it did just cross my mind it could have been on account of Simon. He's the same age now as that other lad was when he was drowned. I did wonder if she was making believe she was a child again, making believe Simon was that other boy come back to life.'

She stood up and began to clear the cups from the table. 'Julie called again early the next week.' She cast her mind back. 'That was on the Tuesday. I remember because I popped into the village while she was here, to go to the butcher's – I always go to the butcher's on a Tuesday.' She consulted a wall calendar. 'May 23rd, that would be.' She returned to the sink and began to wash up the cups. 'That was the last time she called.'

'Did she say it was going to be the last time?' Lambert asked.

'No, she didn't. I knew she'd have to move out of the caravan on the Saturday. She didn't actually say she'd be going back to Millbourne, back to her job, after she left the caravan. I just assumed that's what she'd be doing.'

'Did Simon expect her to call again?'

'Yes, he did. When the days went by and she didn't come, I asked him if she'd said anything definite about calling again. He said no, she hadn't.' She consulted the calendar again. 'He was here another ten days after the last time Julie called. He went back to school on the Friday, June 2nd. His ankle was fine by then.'

Lambert asked if she knew of any boyfriends Julie might have, back in Millbourne, but she shook her head. Julie had said nothing about any boyfriend. She had never had boyfriends as a teenager when she lived next door.

Nor had Julie made any mention of any problem she might be having. She hadn't appeared in any way worried, she seemed to be enjoying her break.

'Would you say she's the type who might decide to take off for somewhere new on the spur of the moment?' Lambert asked.

'Yes, I could easily imagine her doing that,' Mrs Norbury answered without hesitation. 'If she got bored with her life, wanted something different. I could imagine her just deciding to go, turning her back completely on the old life. After all, that's more or less what she did after her mother died.'

He asked if she had any objection to his visiting Simon at his boarding school, in case Simon might have any clue to offer.

'No objection at all,' she assured him. Would he like her to ring the headmaster now, to explain? To say he would be calling with her agreement.

'That's very good of you,' Lambert said. 'I'd like to go tomorrow if that's all right with the school. But I'd rather Simon wasn't told I'm coming.'

'Yes, I quite see that,' she agreed. 'Better not give him time to start using his imagination, working up some tale that could be half moonshine. And best not give him time to start worrying about it, come to that.'

She took him into the sitting room and rang the school. The headmaster was most cooperative. He would expect the sergeant tomorrow. It would be least interrupting to Simon's timetable if Lambert could call in the early afternoon.

'Simon's flying off to Turkey tomorrow week, to join his father,' Mrs Norbury said when she had replaced the receiver. 'He's spending the whole of the summer holidays out there. He's looking forward to it tremendously. It's the first time he's flown anywhere on his own.'

She walked over to a handsome set of bookshelves, one third filled with books neatly ranged. 'My husband made this set of shelves as a Christmas present for Simon, the year before he died.' She ran a hand lovingly along the silky wood. 'Simon's always loved books. He goes poking round second-hand shops and market stalls, looking for them.'

Lambert scanned the shelves: Jules Verne, Marryat, Conrad, Jack London, Zane Grey, Edgar Wallace, bound copies of the *Rover* and the *Champion*. Shades of his own boyhood returned for a moment. 'Quite a collection he's got there,' he said on a fleeting note of envy.

'Julie and Simon had a good long natter about books,' Mrs Norbury said. 'Julie read a lot as a child – she got that from her father. His hobby was books; he had hundreds of them. Not first editions or anything grand like that, just old books he'd picked up over the years. Most of them went to a dealer after he died. Julie kept the ones she liked best and some of her father's favourites.'

She picked up some small pieces of carved wood from shelves set in a niche by the fireplace. 'Simon made these. Not bad, are they, for a young boy?' She indicated a tiny fieldmouse. 'He was only nine when he made that.'

She picked up another piece. 'This is one he made this last time, when he was laid up with his ankle.' A little retriever puppy, lovingly fashioned, a mellow, golden shade of wood. She passed it to Lambert.

'He has quite a gift,' Lambert said.

'It's made from pine,' Mrs Norbury told him. 'A beautiful piece of wood. It was the colour decided Simon to make the puppy out of it, just right for a golden retriever.'

He handed the puppy back to her and she replaced it on the shelf.

'He made some lovely little good-luck charms, too, out of the same wood, to take back to school for the boys – and Matron.' She smiled. 'Matron's quite young. And pretty. He made a special one for Julie, a four-leafed sprig of clover. He took tremendous care over the finishing. Julie was delighted with it. She said she'd always carry it, it was certain to bring her luck.'

She came out to the car with Lambert when he left. 'I really don't think the Eardlows need worry about Julie,' she said as he switched on the engine. 'She left here three years ago and there was never a word from her, then one day she rang my doorbell.' Her tone was buoyant, confident. 'I'm sure that will happen again one day, and probably sooner rather than later. The bell will ring and there she'll be, on the doorstep, smiling at me.'

CHAPTER 8

The preparatory school where Simon Norbury was a boarder lay a good hour's drive from Cannonbridge. Lambert left his digs shortly after breakfast – and wasn't at all sorry to leave. His landlady's eyes constantly searched his face for any sign that he had reached a decision about where he was going for his holiday and when he would be setting off.

It was a warm, sunny day. The grass glittered on the breezy commons, rosebay willowherb flowered along the banks. He enjoyed a leisurely drive, stopping from time to time for a snack, a spot of sightseeing.

It was almost 1.30 as he approached the school, an Edwardian mansion set at the head of a long avenue of lime trees breaking into blossom. Lunch was over. In the relaxed, end-of-term atmosphere, all examinations finished, lessons were confined now to the mornings, the afternoons being devoted to cricket, to a series of house matches.

The headmaster, a young, energetic man, was shut away in his study, composing a moving appeal for funds to be sent out to all the parents, in the hope of raising enough to update all the school's computer equipment. When Lambert tracked him down he dispatched a passing pupil to the changing rooms to winkle out young Norbury.

Simon came hurrying along a few minutes later. He wore cricketing gear; a dark-haired, athletically built lad with a confident grin, a face plentifully sprinkled with freckles.

The headmaster made the introductions, presenting Lambert as a sergeant with the Cannonbridge police – no mention made of his being a detective – who was here now with the permission of Simon's grandmother to ask him a few questions, in case he might be able to help them in one of their inquiries.

Simon looked mightily intrigued; his face glowed with pleasurable importance. 'You can take Sergeant Lambert out into the grounds,' the head added. 'Find somewhere quiet to sit down and have your chat, then you can get off to the cricket.'

As they went along the corridor Lambert inquired about Simon's ankle.

'It's fine now, thank you.' Simon looked up at him with lively curiosity. 'Are you a friend of Gran's?'

'No, I can't say I am,' Lambert admitted. 'I met her yesterday for the first time. We had a good long chat. We're trying to get in touch with a young woman called Julie Dawson; her relatives are anxious about her. She seems to have gone off somewhere without telling anyone where she was going. Your grandmother tells me you know Julie, she came to see you in May, while you were staying in Calcott.'

Simon nodded. 'That's right.' A question burst from him. 'Are you a detective?'

'Yes, I am.'

'Are you the detective Julie met? She told me she'd met a detective sergeant the last time she'd stayed at Calcott House. She'd never met a detective before.'

'Yes, that's me,' Lambert confirmed.

Simon's eyes darted over him as if expecting to discover some extraordinary attributes.

'A person couldn't tell you were a detective by looking at you.' His voice held a strong note of disappointment but a moment later he added as if a more favourable thought had struck him, 'But I expect that's the idea?'

'Something like that,' Lambert acknowledged.

They came out into the soft, sweet air. From every direction boys in cricketing gear, singly or in groups, hurried towards the playing fields, an occasional master among them. The air was full of excited chatter.

Simon gazed after them with an expression of longing. 'I don't suppose it'll take very long, whatever it is you want to ask me,' he suggested hopefully.

'Not if we get started right away,' Lambert told him briskly. He spotted a wooden seat beside a stretch of lawn. 'We'll sit down over there, then we can get on with it.' Simon almost broke into a run in his eagerness to reach the seat and get the whole thing over with.

They sat down. From the seat, fortunately, there was no view of the playing fields. 'Your grandmother told me you got on

51

well with Julie,' Lambert began at once. 'I thought maybe when you were chatting she might have given you some idea where she intended going after she left the caravan.'

Simon shook his head. 'I don't know where she went, she never said anything. Did Gran tell you I'm flying out to Turkey a week today? My father's working out there. I've been looking up all about Turkey in the school library, maps and everything. I reckon I know more about Turkey now than any of the masters.'

'Did Julie ever mention any problems she had?' Lambert managed to get in. 'Any troubles or difficulties? Back in Millbourne, perhaps?'

Again Simon shook his head. 'She never talked about anything like that. She didn't seem worried about anything. She was always in a good mood, she laughed a lot. My father says there'll be other British children flying out for the holidays. Some of the mothers will be out there too, they're going to arrange trips and picnics for us. It's not far from the sea, we'll be able to swim and sail. There'll be all sorts of things to do.' He gave a wide grin. 'I'm really looking forward to it. None of the other boys in my class has ever been to Turkey. I've asked every single one and I'm the very first. Have you ever been to Turkey?'

'No, I haven't.' Lambert kept a grip on his patience. 'Nor am ever likely to go. Now do try to think. Is there anything at all you can remember that might give us a hint? Even something that might not seem very important. Please try to give your mind to it, you might recall something.'

Simon dragged his thoughts back from the bazaars and mosques, the fig trees and the roses.

'Just the letter, I suppose,' he said after a moment. 'I don't know if that would be any use. I don't expect so. It was just a game.'

'Letter?' Lambert echoed sharply. 'What letter?'

From the playing fields came a wave of clapping and cheering. Simon jumped as if galvanized; his head jerked round.

'What letter?' Lambert asked again.

Simon moved his shoulders. 'Just a letter she found.'

'Where did she find it?'

'In the hotel, when she was packing her things to go to the caravan. She opened a drawer in the bureau and she pulled it too hard; it came right out. The letter was in the space underneath; it had slipped down from the drawer.'

'Do you know what was in the letter?'

'No, I can't remember. But I've got the letter upstairs in the dormitory with my things. She gave it to me, for safekeeping, she said. She'd made a copy of it for herself.'

'When did she tell you all this? When did she give you the letter?'

'She told me about the letter on the Saturday, that was the second day she called. It was the next time she came, on the Tuesday, that she gave me the letter to put away somewhere safe, in case anything happened.'

'What did she mean by that? In case anything happened?'

'I don't know.' Simon frowned. 'I suppose she meant she could have lost it.'

'Would you mind fetching the letter?' Lambert asked.

Simon sprang up and sped off, returning shortly with equal speed. He handed Lambert an envelope and dropped down again beside him.

'The name on the envelope,' he explained, 'the lady it's addressed to, Julie said that was the name of the lady who'd had the room before her at the hotel.'

Lambert scrutinized the envelope. Plain, white, very ordinary quality. Addressed to Miss O. Hammond, at Calcott House. The postmark gave the date, March 31st, and the post town, Yelmerton – a market town some twenty-six miles from Calcott.

The envelope had been neatly slit open across the top. Inside was a single folded sheet of white writing paper of the same indifferent quality. Lambert unfolded it, ran his eye over it.

It could scarcely be dignified by the name of letter; it was no more than the briefest of notes, written in black ink, in a large, bold hand. No date, no address, no greeting, no heading or preface of any kind. Just three words – one of them not even a complete word – dashed across the page in a forceful, slanting line, with a couple of initials underneath by way of signature:

Enc. usual cheque.
H.J.

A storm of cheers and clapping rose from the playing fields as Lambert turned the envelope over. On the back, in blue ink, in a markedly different hand, cramped and convoluted, some scribbled jottings: a couple of small addition sums with initials or what could be abbreviated names alongside the figures – some of which had been crossed out; what appeared to be, from the use of query marks, a number of questions. Some words ringed round, ticked, underlined, followed by exclamation marks.

'Why did Julie want you to keep the letter safe?' Lambert asked. 'Why did she make a copy of it? Did she think it was important in some way?'

Simon gazed uncertainly up at him. His manner was tinged with embarrassment. 'I didn't know if she was serious or just fooling about to pass the time. It was like a story she was making up as she went along.'

'What kind of story?'

Simon reddened, he wriggled his shoulders. 'It sounds silly now.'

'Never mind that. Tell me.'

'It sounded all right at the time,' Simon protested. 'Sort of fun and jokey.' He made a face, let out a noisy sigh. Then he said in a defiant rush: 'She said she thought Miss Hammond could be running a nice little business.'

'What kind of business?'

Simon hesitated again. He rolled his eyes at Lambert, a deprecating, upward glance, distancing himself from the unfathomable follies and machinations of the adult world. He clicked his tongue, ground out between his teeth a single word in reply: 'Blackmail.'

CHAPTER 9

'Blackmail?' Lambert echoed.

Simon squirmed and grimaced. 'I told you it sounded silly, but that's what she said. I didn't think she could be serious. If she was, she'd have got onto you, told you about it. I asked her if she was going to and she said no, you'd only think it was an excuse to get in touch with you again.'

'Did she say she'd done anything about the letter? Or intended doing anything?'

'She said she thought she'd managed to work out what some of the scribbles meant. She said you could learn quite a bit from phone books and Yellow Pages. And from old newspaper files. And gravestones in churchyards.'

'Did she mention going to see anyone? Any place she'd been to? Or intended going to?'

'She said she'd had a prowl round and she'd found out one or two things but she had a lot more to do. The next time she called – that was on the Tuesday, the last time I saw her – I asked her if she'd found out any more and she said yes, heaps, but she still hadn't finished working out what all the scribbles meant.'

Again Lambert asked if she'd made mention of names or places but Simon shook his head. 'She said she'd talked to the people she'd found. She looked pleased when she said that, as if she thought she'd been very clever. She said she'd made up some story as an excuse for calling. She made up a different story every time, anything that came into her head that she thought that particular person would swallow. She said that was the really exciting part.'

He looked up at Lambert. 'I asked her if any of them were suspicious but she said no, everyone was very nice to her. They all talked to her, gave her things to eat or drink.'

'Did she discover any proof that Miss Hammond was black-mailing anyone?'

As Simon opened his mouth to reply there came a fresh explosion of cheers, a rain of clapping. Simon jumped up, subsiding again with a look of frustration. Lambert had to repeat his question.

Simon gave vent to another noisy sigh. 'She said she'd found out some things about Miss Hammond, about places where she'd worked. She was pretty sure Miss Hammond was doing some blackmailing; she'd probably been doing it for a long time.'

'Nothing more definite than that?'

'She said she could see where serious crimes could have been committed and Miss Hammond could have known about them, being a nurse on the spot. She was sure Miss Hammond had never helped to commit any of the crimes herself but she knew they'd taken place and she turned a blind eye to them. Then later on she was able to blackmail the people who had committed them.'

'What kind of serious crimes did she think had been committed?'

He looked uncomfortable. 'Murder,' he answered after some hesitation. 'She thought there'd been more than one murder. And destroying a will.' His tone grew defensive. 'There were some others too but I've forgotten them. It's weeks ago now, I can't remember everything she said.'

He looked up at Lambert. 'I could never tell if she was serious or if it was all a game. She never said anything about any of it to Gran and she made me promise not to say anything either. I thought if it really was serious she wouldn't just be telling me about it.'

Lambert pressed on. 'Did she say she had any proof that any of these serious crimes had ever been committed?'

'I asked her that,' Simon said at once. 'She said she didn't have any real proof, not the sort of proof you'd have to have in a court of law, but she felt in her bones it could all have happened the way she thought it had. I said if it was me, and if Miss Hammond really was a blackmailer, I'd be afraid of going round asking questions. If people really had committed serious crimes, they weren't going to be very pleased if they thought Julie was onto them. But she said it was Miss Hammond who should be afraid – of being found out as a blackmailer. She

56

wasn't at all afraid herself; she said she wasn't the sort of person who could easily be put off. If she thought she was on to something she'd hang on like a bull terrier.

'I asked her if she was going to let Miss Hammond know what she suspected. She said she might drop a few hints. It might be exciting to play cat and mouse with her, see if she could trick her into admitting anything. I said surely that could be dangerous but she said it would be part of the fun.'

'Did she say if she'd actually been over to the cottage to see Miss Hammond?'

Simon screwed up his face. 'I can't remember her saying that. I remember her saying she was going to go over but not that she'd actually been.'

'Do you know if she intended going back to have another talk with any of the people she'd come across?'

'She did say two or three places seemed very interesting, it would be worth going back. I said she really must be careful what she said, a second visit might start folk wondering what she was up to. But she just laughed and told me not to worry about her, she could always think up another good tale; no one would guess what she was up to.'

'Did she ever say what she made of the scribbles on the envelope?'

'Yes, she did. She explained it all to me.' He screwed up his face again. 'She said she was sure Miss Hammond had been getting money regularly from different people and now she was going to make them all pay more. That was because she'd bought a cottage and it was going to cost a lot to do up – and to run it.' He bit his lip in an effort to recall. 'She said everyone was going to have to make an extra one-off payment and on top of that, they would all have to pay more every month.'

'Did she think Miss Hammond had got as far as asking these people for the extra money?'

He frowned more deeply. 'She said going by the date stamp on the envelope and some of the scribbles, she guessed Miss Hammond had just about got round to asking for the extra.' He turned his head longingly towards the playing fields but Lambert still wouldn't let him go.

'Were you surprised when Julie didn't come back again to see you after the Tuesday?'

Simon shrugged. 'No, not really. She's not the sort that always means what she says.' He went on in a rush: 'If you really want to know what I think, I think all that blackmail stuff's a load of rot. She told me she always liked reading about blackmail in books, it always made a good story. I think she just liked to imagine the letter was something to do with blackmail, it stopped her getting bored. She was just playing at being a detective.'

'If you do remember anything else,' Lambert urged, 'anything of any possible use, no matter how trivial or silly it may seem, I'd be very grateful if you'd get in touch with me. Don't for one moment think you'd be wasting my time. I won't in the least mind if it turns out to be nothing at all.' He wrote down the address and phone number of his Cannonbridge lodgings.

Simon took the piece of paper from him without so much as glancing at it. 'Yes, sure,' he promised glibly. 'I'll do that.' His face was alight with hope and joy. 'Does that mean you've finished with me?'

'Yes, it does. I'm sorry I kept you from the match. I hope you enjoy what's left of it. I'm very grateful, you've helped a lot.' He held out his hand.

Now that escape was in sight Simon found his manners again. He shook hands courteously. 'I hope you find Julie. It was very interesting meeting you.'

Lambert opened his mouth to say, 'You'd better put my address in your pocket or you'll lose it.' But it was too late. Simon had gone like a bullet from a gun, towards the shouting and the cheering, the piece of paper still clutched – for the moment at least – in his hand.

On Tuesday evening Lambert's landlady began a determined attack, appealing to reason, fair play, the good of all concerned.

'You did actually say you'd be going away and on the strength of that I did more or less arrange with a decorator to do your room. If I have to cancel it there's no knowing when I can get it done again, and it's hardly fair to the man.'

But Lambert stood firm. He would let her know the moment he reached a decision.

He hadn't got where he was – wherever that might be – by yielding to pressure from landladies, he told his image grimly as he shaved on Wednesday morning. He certainly wouldn't allow himself to be ejected from the house one instant before it suited him.

Over his breakfast cereal he took out the white envelope again and studied the jottings, pondering, cogitating. Come over and see the cottage, Olive Hammond had invited him. Drop in any time. Take me as you find me.

I could nip over there this morning, he thought. Have a little chat with her. He cast his mind back and managed to dredge up enough of what she'd told him about finding the place.

His landlady brought in a large, succulent kipper, freshly made toast, a jug of steaming coffee. 'I expect you'll be phoning your sister after breakfast,' she said cheerfully as she set down the tray. 'Or your friends.'

Lambert met her eye resolutely. 'No, not yet. I'm still thinking about it.' He picked up his knife and fork. 'I must say this looks very good.'

After his excellent breakfast and an unhurried read of his newspaper he set off for Olive Hammond's cottage. He drove without haste under a cloudless sky. At first the countryside looked reasonably prosperous and well tended but after a few miles his road began to take him past neglected orchards planted long ago, straggling hedgerows untrimmed for many a year, rabbits and jackdaws feeding together on sour old pastures over-run with brambles, nettles, rusty docks, purple thistles. Scarcely a dwelling to be seen.

He rounded a bend and saw some way ahead, on his right, a massive, spreading oak. 'You can't miss the turning to the cottage,' Olive had called after him as he pulled out of the hotel car park. 'You'll see a big oak tree.'

A pair of magpies strutting about the lane rose up as his car approached. He drove slowly along between high banks thick with cow parsley, daisies, dandelions, pink and white bindweed. From the topmost branches of the oak came the raucous cawing of rooks.

After a quarter of a mile or so he came upon the cottage, set back a little way, the wooden gate closed. He got out and opened the gate. He stood for a moment, listening. He could hear nothing but the chirruping of birds, the distant clamour of the rooks.

He couldn't risk leaving his car where it was even for the brief time it would take to discover if Miss Hammond was in; the lane was too narrow for that. He got back in and manoeuvred the vehicle through the gateway and onto a square patch of ground rank with tall weeds and seeding grasses.

He got out of the car. Still no sound from the cottage. But he would go through the motions all the same. A crumbling brick path led to the front door. There were signs of recent effort in the garden: clipping, hacking, clearing, even a little planting. But the plants and cuttings had shrivelled and withered from lack of water.

Nothing on the doorstep, nothing sticking out of the letter box. An attempt had been made to restore the brilliance of the brass of the doorknob, the bell, letter box, lion-head knocker; their last polishing, Lambert judged, had been several weeks ago.

He rang and knocked; no reply. He walked round to the back. None of the windows was curtained. The panes looked fairly clean; they certainly no longer bore the grime of years.

No reply at the back door either. He wandered round the sizable rear garden. Again, for the most part, bearing all the marks of long neglect, and again, here and there, signs of recent work, digging and planting, plants and cuttings all dead.

There was no garage. A dilapidated, three-sided shed, large enough to accommodate Olive's little Volkswagen Beetle, stood empty. A few yards away was a somewhat more modern structure – though still, in all probability, a good fifty years old: a small, locked shed. A new padlock. No windows.

I won't be taking a holiday this year, Miss Hammond had told him in the hotel car park. I'm devoting all my time to the place.

He returned to the house and walked all round it, trying doors and windows. All well secured. He cupped his hands round his face and peered in. Everything neat and clean. Sparsely furnished with old pieces. Inside one window a dead plant in a pot. Flower vases here and there with faded tulips, withered sprays of forsythia and flowering currant.

In the kitchen a vegetable rack holding shrivelled carrots, green-sprouting onions. A bowl of rotting apples. In the sitting room an easy chair and footstool. A table drawn up beside the chair, with a few books, a folded newspaper, portable radio, all tidily arranged. A knitting bag on the lower shelf of the table.

At the far end of the room a birdcage on a stand. He could discern no sound or movement from the cage. He turned from the window and looked about the garden. Under a hedge he found a small pile of old bricks. He picked up a couple and took them across to the window. He raised himself up on the bricks, standing on tiptoe, in an attempt to peer down into the distant recesses of the cage.

He could just make out a little heap of green feathers, a pair of tiny legs sticking up into the air.

CHAPTER 10

Lambert got back into his car and drove out again into the lane, closing the gate behind him. He headed in the direction of Calcott village, watching out for any other habitation. It was three quarters of a mile before he spotted a dwelling some distance ahead on the left, a couple of hundred yards down a lane.

He reached the lane and turned into it. It was even narrower than the lane leading to Olive Hammond's cottage, the banks smothered in rank weeds, the rutted surface thickly grass-grown. A mangy-looking cat was stalking something in the hedgerow.

A tall screen of thorny berberis obscured his view of the dwelling. A few yards beyond it he could see an opening into a field where he might leave the car. He glanced at the cottage as he went past. His immediate impression was far from favourable: a small, squat abode, largely covered with ivy, crouched in a rampant garden.

He left his car in the field and walked back along the lane to the dwelling. He paused by the little gate; it was broken, fastened up with a length of fraying rope. Not a lick of paint had touched gate or cottage for many a long day. The roof had been patched at some distant time with a sheet of corrugated iron now covered with rust. Under the eaves tiny windows caked with ancient dirt, closed against any chance whisper of fresh air, peered out from the ivy. Rotting frames, a broken pane roughly boarded over. A vast old wistaria clothed a side wall, hung with huge trusses of mauve blooms.

This is a total waste of time, Lambert told himself. There's no way a woman like Olive Hammond would come calling at a dump like this. But even as the thought formed itself his fingers were busy unfastening the rope. If there was one thing his time in the force had taught him it was this: you simply never could tell.

He had no sooner set foot on the crunching cinder path than a furious barking erupted inside the dwelling, persisting unchecked as he made his way towards the front door, past an old iron pump, a gnarled apple tree draped with purple clematis, crimson hollyhocks rearing up along the rickety fence.

He lifted the doorknocker and gave a double rap. The barking increased in frenzy. A man's voice loudly cursed the dog. The barking ceased abruptly.

The door swung back, disclosing a big, heavily built man with a deeply lined, mahogany-coloured face and several days' growth of beard. He wore an ancient, collarless shirt of striped flannel fastened at the neck with a brass stud; his corduroy trousers, stained and shapeless, were secured, like his gate, with a length of fraying rope. His left hand gripped the collar of the straining cur at his side.

He cast a surly, suspicious look at Lambert. 'What do you want?' he demanded. At his hostile tone the dog tried to leap forward, baring his fangs, but his master jerked him powerfully back; he subsided, growling.

No, I can't altogether see Olive Hammond cultivating this curmudgeon as a bosom pal, Lambert thought, however lonely or isolated she might feel.

He apologized for disturbing the householder and explained that he was trying to contact a Miss Hammond. 'She lives over there.' He waved a hand in the direction of her cottage. 'She moved in a couple of months ago. You appear to be her nearest neighbour. There's no one about at her cottage; it looks pretty deserted. I wondered if you'd seen her recently, if she'd spoken to you, if you have any idea where I might get in touch with her.' During the whole of this speech the householder's fierce, bloodshot eyes never for an instant left Lambert's face. The beast at his side likewise kept his savage stare trained on the intruder, his growl temporarily maintained at a simmering level.

When Lambert ceased speaking the householder didn't immediately reply but raked Lambert from head to foot with a gaze that was far from overflowing with goodwill and helpfulness.

'I mind my own business,' he averred grudgingly at last. 'I let other folk be and I expect them to let me be.'

I don't doubt you find them most cooperative in that regard, Lambert said to himself. Aloud he came back with honeyed words: 'And a very good policy, too. It's just that I have urgent business with Miss Hammond; I'm anxious to track her down. Have you seen her at all since she moved in?'

Another pause while the householder considered all the varied implications of the query, then he reluctantly conceded, 'I did see her moving in. She had a little van and two men. And I seen her little car, one of them foreign Beetle efforts, a couple of times after. I've never spoken to her nor she to me, never been any necessity nor wish.'

'Do you by any chance remember when was the last time you saw her?'

The look grew deeply suspicious again. 'You want to know a lot.' The dog, sensing a raising of the emotional temperature, increased the volume of his growl.

Lambert judged it wise to maintain a docile, unchallenging stance. It appeared to work.

'Can't be sure,' the man came out with in a marginally less truculent tone. At his side the level of growling diminished. 'Weeks ago, must be, last time I seen her, can't say nearer than that. I dare say she's gone off on holiday – abroad, as likely as not, gallivanting anywhere that takes her fancy. Folk never satisfied these days unless they're rushing about all over the place. Home ain't good enough for them.'

At this juncture, by sheer chance, Lambert made a cardinal error. As he digested the information in silence he inadvertently moved his head, first to one side, then the other, his abstracted, unseeing gaze travelling across the face of the dwelling and back again. The householder sprang instantly into action.

'So that's your game!' He reached down behind the door and snatched up a stout cudgel. He lunged forward. 'Sizing up the place for a break-in!' The mongrel sprang into the air, all but leapt free.

Lambert jumped back, raised a pacifying hand; it served only to inflame the ferocious pair.

'Spying on honest folk! Watching their comings and goings! I've half a mind to set the dog on you!' He brandished his cudgel. 'Do you want a taste of this? Go on! Clear off or I'll call the police.'

At this last threat – the most powerful in the circumstances that he could have uttered – Lambert swiftly decided to call it a day. A fresh explosion of curses and growls pursued him down the path and out through the gate. He paused just long enough, from indelible training and habit, to secure the gate behind him.

The curmudgeon and his straining henchdog remained implacably at their posts till he had got back into his car, reversed and driven past again between the unruly hedgerows, into the brilliant noonday.

He pulled up at the first lay-by and sat for several moments gazing out through the windscreen, then he took out the envelope Simon had given him. He scrutinized the jottings again, looked at the letter, then he put the envelope back in his pocket. He remained for some time leaning back against the upholstery with his eyes closed, sunk in thought.

At last he roused himself and drove off, towards Calcott. A couple of miles short of the village he pulled up by a pretty stretch of river with anglers strung out along the banks.

There was a tiny hamlet close by, no more than a small general store and a cluster of dwellings, one of them displaying a board offering fishing bait, refreshments, light lunches.

He sat on the river bank in the shade of a willow, listening to the far-off, hypnotic pulsing of some agricultural machine, watching the dragonflies hover in the shimmering air, a kingfisher swoop in a brilliant, blue-green streak. At lunch time he ate a delicious wedge of cold mushroom quiche, followed by raspberries and cream, in the parlour of the fishing-bait cottage, then he strolled about the hamlet.

When his watch showed 2.15 he got back into his car and drove to Calcott House, parking discreetly to one side of the entrance where he could keep an eye on the gates.

Shortly after 2.30 he heard the sound of footsteps on the gravelled drive and a minute or two later Iris came out through the wicket gate.

Lambert got out of his car and went across to intercept her. She halted in surprise at the sight of him.

'Sergeant Lambert!' She flashed him a wide smile. It vanished abruptly as a look of concern crossed her face. 'Has something happened? Has there been an accident?'

He hastened to reassure her. 'I happened to be out this way and I remembered you finished work around this time. I'd appreciate a chat about Miss Dawson, if you can spare the time.' He smiled. 'You might be able to fill me in on a few points. I'd rather talk to you than to the Marchants. The last thing they'd want to see is my face, frightening the guests, getting the place a bad name.'

She jerked out a hand, dismissing the Marchants and their foolish notions. 'Yes, of course I can spare the time. I liked Miss Dawson; I don't like to think of her folks being worried about her. If there's anything I can tell you that would put you on the right track, I'd be only too happy.'

'That's very good of you,' he told her warmly. 'I take it you're off home now?' She nodded. 'If I might come along with you,' he suggested. 'I won't keep you long, I'm sure you have a lot to do.'

'That's all right,' she said airily. 'No great rush. The kids won't be in from school for another hour or two and my husband never gets home till turned six.'

They walked across to his car and she gave him directions. A few minutes later they halted in front of a semi-detached house in a group of modern dwellings near the green. The windows sparkled, the curtains were fresh and clean, the front garden a brilliant, disciplined show of colour.

Iris giggled as they walked up the path to the front door. 'This is going to set tongues wagging – me taking a handsome young man into the house in the middle of the afternoon.' She got out her key and let him in.

In the hall she set down her holdall. 'You go along in, make yourself at home.' She nodded towards a door on the right and Lambert went obediently along into the sitting room.

Iris leaned forward and closely scrutinized her reflection in the hall mirror. She turned her head this way and that, patted into place her frizzed, bleached hair, took a lipstick from her bag and carefully renewed the pillar-box red.

When she was satisfied with the results she went briskly off towards her immaculate kitchen, filled the kettle and plugged it in, whisked out a tray, set it with a spotless cloth, gleaming cups and saucers.

She went back along the passage and stuck her head briefly into the sitting room to say, 'I'm making a cup of tea, I won't be a moment.' Lambert was standing in front of the sideboard, picking up and examining ornate silver cups and trophies from a proud display. 'Beautiful, aren't they?' she said with fond pride. 'They take a bit of cleaning. They're my husband's. Swimming. Running. Cross-country. Sports mad, my husband. Grass widow in the evenings and at weekends, that's me.' She went rapidly back to her kettle. Lambert followed, to bring in the tray.

Back in the sitting room he set the tray down on a table in front of the sofa. He took his seat in an easy chair by the window. Iris poured the tea and held out a cup to Lambert. He went over and took the cup, turned back to his chair.

'Don't you think you'd be more comfortable here?' She patted the sofa beside her, looked up at him with a smile there was no mistaking.

'I'm all right here, thanks, this chair suits me fine.' He sat down again. He kept the tone of his voice, the expression on his face, easy and amiable. His position at this moment with regard to the Dawson inquiry was tricky enough without going out of his way to look for further complications.

Iris appeared not the least whit abashed. 'Well now,' she said with relish. 'Fire away. Anything you want to know, ask me.'

'When I spoke to you a couple of days ago at Calcott House,' Lambert said, 'you told me Julie Dawson dropped in on you here one afternoon. I'd like to ask you a little more about that. Can you remember exactly when it was that she called? And exactly what she talked about?'

Iris cast her mind back. 'She called the very next day after she left the hotel. I remember that because I was surprised – I hadn't expected she'd call quite so soon. We talked about Calcott House, mostly. She seemed fascinated by it, wanted to know all about the history of the hotel, all about the residents, the different owners.

'I've worked there a long time, ever since I left school, on and off. I used to chat a lot to the old residents, the ones who were there years ago, so of course I was able to tell her pretty well all she wanted to know.'

She waved a hand at the table. 'Do help yourself to biscuits or those little fancies. Don't wait to be asked.'

Lambert went over and took a small iced cake. Iris watched with detached, good-natured amusement as he returned to his chair. Had your fingers burnt? her look asked. You don't know the half of it, his equally eloquent look told her in reply. I make sure I don't get them burned again. They understood each other very well.

Lambert explained that he still hadn't the faintest notion of

Julie's present whereabouts. 'I thought she might have gone over to see Miss Hammond,' he added. 'She might have mentioned her plans to Miss Hammond.'

Iris nodded. Her manner was as comfortable and relaxed as if they had been old friends. 'Julie did say she intended going over to the cottage. She asked me if Miss Hammond had been back to Calcott House at all, if I'd seen her since her move, if I knew how she was settling in.'

She moved her shoulders. 'I told her I hadn't laid eyes on Miss Hammond since she left the hotel. I hadn't heard anyone say she'd been back for a visit.' She laughed. 'And I hadn't heard anyone say they'd been over to the cottage. She'd certainly invited everyone.' She laughed again. 'Including me! As if I'd go!'

She gave Lambert a shrewd look. 'It's my opinion she got cold feet when she realized she'd actually be living out there all on her own, not a soul to talk to; that's why she started issuing invitations all round. She still kept on about how much she was looking forward to the move, how she was going to enjoy living in the country, but it seemed more like whistling in the dark to me, keeping her courage up.'

'I've just been over to the cottage myself,' Lambert explained. 'I wanted to ask Miss Hammond if she'd seen Julie. But I couldn't find her. It looked to me as if she hadn't been there for some time. I got the strong impression she'd left in a hurry.'

'Could be she just got fed up being in the cottage on her own,' Iris suggested. 'She might have gone off on a holiday on the spur of the moment, woken up one morning and decided she must have a break, somewhere more civilized.'

She grimaced. 'It wouldn't surprise me if she put her precious cottage on the market and went back to living in a hotel or bedsit somewhere – she might even come back to Calcott House.'

She took a biscuit. 'When Julie was leaving here that day I told her to drop in again, any afternoon. She said she'd love to but she never did.' Something else came back to her. 'About a week later, when I was leaving the hotel one afternoon, I spotted Luke Marchant in the garden. I went over and asked him if Miss Hammond had been back to cadge plants and cuttings from him, if he knew how she was getting on.'

She smiled. 'He gave me short shrift, as usual, but he did manage to spare me a few sentences. He said he hadn't laid eyes on Miss Hammond since she'd left. She'd never been back for any plants; he didn't know anything about her.'

She ate her buscuit. 'People will get these romantic notions about country life. Miss Hammond always had this vision of a pretty cottage, a snug little place of her own by a babbling brook. I know because she told me so this last Christmas.

'She's never been one to talk about herself, not in the usual way, but it was Christmas Eve and the residents and staff were putting little gifts for each other under the tree. She'd had a drop of sherry more than she normally took; it must have loosened her tongue. She started telling me about Christmases when she was a child. She got quite sentimental – for her.'

Iris mentioned a town of no great size some twelve miles from Calcott. 'She told me she was born on a council estate there. She lived there till she was thirty. She hasn't any family left now. I told Julie that, in case it might be some help to her in getting in touch with Miss Hammond.'

She poured more tea. 'Miss Hammond said the town wasn't much of a place, she was glad to get away. It was just at times like Christmas and New Year she started feeling sorry for herself. The only relative she's got now is some old cousin in Hampshire, some old chap pushing eighty, living on his own in a flat. She went there once or twice for a visit while she was at Calcott House.' She inclined her head. 'I suppose she could be there now. He might have been taken ill; she might have gone there to nurse him. It could all have happened in a rush.'

Lambert asked if she knew the old man's address, but she was sorry, she didn't.

He asked if Miss Hammond had had any special friend, at Calcott House or elsewhere, if she had much social life.

'Julie asked me that,' Iris recalled. 'I told her Miss Hammond never had any friends come to the hotel for lunch or dinner, not like the other residents – some of them have lots of visitors. She went walking a lot, or driving round in her little Beetle. Reading, knitting – she was always knitting herself jumpers and cardigans. And shopping, of course.' She laughed. 'She always made a song and dance about any bits of shopping she did, as if it was some big deal.'

She looked reflective. 'I don't think any of the other residents liked her all that much. She never joined in a game of cards. Some of them play bridge night and day, but not Miss Hammond. I used to feel sorry for her sometimes. I used to think maybe she'd retired too early, she'd have done better to stay on at work for another few years. She didn't really have enough to occupy her, and she'd been used to a busy life. I thought sometimes that might have been her real reason for buying the cottage, to give herself something to do, something to thin. about.'

'Do you happen to know of anyone Miss Hammond knew with the initials H.J.?' Lambert asked.

She flashed him a startled look. 'That's another thing Julie asked me. I'll tell you what I told her. I don't know about the *H* but there was someone whose surname began with a *J*. Miss Hammond hardly ever got a phone call but she did get a few calls in a bunch, not long before she left the hotel. I particularly noticed; it was so unusual for her. The calls were all from the same woman; I got to recognize her voice. Her name began with a *J*. It was Jerrom, Miss Jerrom. The first time I took the call, when I asked who I should say was calling, she said: '"Tell her it's Miss Jerrom, from Greenfield."'

Back in his car Lambert made once more for the nearest lay-by. He had no sooner pulled up than he was assailed by a sharp fit of coughing. When it had subsided he took from his pocket the envelope Simon Norbury had given him. He looked again at the post town and the date stamp: Yelmerton, March 31st.

He studied the note inside, signed H.J. The initials H.J. also figured in the jottings on the back of the envelope. *J* for Jerrom?

He put the envelope back in his pocket and switched on the engine. A visit to the public library in Cannonbridge would seem to be indicated. Better get cracking – the library closed at five.

The reference room was almost empty when he arrived. He went immediately to the shelves where phone books covering the entire country were ranged. He found the book covering the Yelmerton area, took it to a table and sat down.

The name Jerrom didn't appear to be very common. There were eight entries listed, only two clearly female: a Mrs W. and a Miss H. He stabbed his finger down at Miss H. – her address was given as Greenfield, Bowpatch. He consulted the area map at the front of the book: Bowpatch was shown as a hamlet a few miles from Yelmerton.

He closed the book and sat pondering. The initials H.J. on the letter. The Miss Jerrom who had phoned Olive Hammond at Calcott House. Miss H. Jerrom in the phone book. Were they all three one and the same?

The H.J. of the letter might not be a woman. The J might stand for any one of a hundred surnames. Greenfield was by no means an uncommon name for a rural property.

The Miss Jerrom who rang Olive Hammond need not be listed in any phone book; she might not be the head of the household, in whose name a phone would be listed. Or the house where she lived might not be on the phone; she could have been speaking from a call box. She might not live in the Yelmerton area at all; she could have rung Olive Hammond from the wilds of Cornwall or the north of Scotland.

What it amounts to, he concluded, is that the chances of Miss H. Jerrom of Greenfield, Bowpatch, being the same person as the H.J. of the letter are so slim as to be practically nonexistent.

The conclusion left him feeling remarkably cheerful. What a load of codswallop it all was. Common sense spoke out loud and clear: Forget the whole pack of nonsense. Give your landlady a break, ring your sister, pack your traps and clear out, down to Sussex. Spend the next ten days getting really fit, relaxing, enjoying yourself.

He picked up the phone book and pushed back his chair. All at once he was assailed by a flash of memory: Julie Dawson standing in the hall at Calcott House, looking up at him with a hesitant, unguarded gaze. 'Will I be seeing you again?' she had asked.

He drew a long sigh. No use, he couldn't just turn his back on it. It wasn't going to be Sussex. It was going to be Bowpatch.

Might not be too bad. He'd driven through that part of the county once or twice. Good walking country, far enough from Cannonbridge to give him some sense of change. Sure to be tourist attractions within striking distance, something to do and see. He should be able to put together some sort of holiday.

He stood up and put the phone book back on its shelf. Yes, that's what I'll do, he told himself with finality. I'll go over to Bowpatch tomorrow morning, find somewhere to stay.

As he turned to the door he had a sudden odd sensation for a moment, as of having responded to some far-off, tenuous appeal, having answered a distant, muted cry.

71

CHAPTER 11

Lambert's landlady was on the alert as he entered the house. Her gaze went at once to his face, searching for signs of decision. Before she could start in on him again he raised a quelling hand. 'I'm off tomorrow out of your way.'

She gave a cry of joy and struck her hands together. Unconcealed delight shone from her face. 'That's marvellous!' She pulled herself up. 'Not that I want to be rid of you, of course.'

He let that pass. 'I thought I'd come back Friday of next week. That should give you enough time to get the room done.' And give him a day or two to get himself together before going back to work the following Monday.

'That'll do fine,' she assured him.

He had a request to make. 'I'd like you to send on any mail that comes for me. I'll phone you with my address as soon as I've sorted out somewhere to stay.'

That jerked her eyes open. 'Somewhere to stay? Aren't you going to your sister? Or your friends?'

'No, I'm not.'

'Where are you going? Abroad?'

'Not exactly abroad. I'm going to Bowpatch.'

'Bowpatch?' she shrieked in incredulity. 'You don't mean that tinpot little place –'

'Yes, I do mean that little place.'

She almost choked with unasked questions. But she hadn't been his landlady all this time for nothing. He had trained her long and with some degree of success. She managed to swallow her questions.

'If you'd be good enough to put any mail in another envelope before you send it on,' he pursued. 'Don't address it to "Detective Sergeant Lambert", whatever you do, just plain "Mr".'

She gave an abstracted nod, staring after him as he went upstairs to pack.

It didn't take him long. Walking gear: stick, lightweight back-pack, binoculars, casual clothes, comfortable footwear, something waterproof in case the weather turned nasty. Walking gear carried an invaluable bonus: everywhere it disarmed suspicion.

A person couldn't tell you were a detective by looking at you, Simon Norbury had said. Lambert intended to make it even more difficult for a person to tell. He considered his hair in the mirror. It was already overdue for its usual cut. If he let it be, if he remembered not to hold himself quite so upright, if – most difficult of all to bear constantly in mind – he allowed his gaze to rest more lightly on folk, not automatically subject them to the professional laser-beam glance of the policeman, there might be a sporting chance of passing himself off as one of his landlady's ordinary normal human beings.

The hamlet of Bowpatch lay deep in the countryside. Lambert drove there next morning under a sapphire sky laced with drifts and puffs of snowy cloud. The hedges sported a fine show of dog roses, pale pink bramble blossom. The banks spilled over with creamy meadowsweet, a tangle of wild flowers, nodding heads of grasses heavy with pollen.

When he reached a signpost showing Bowpatch half a mile away, he decided to make a preliminary sweep of the area. After fifteen minutes of crawling through narrow byways, picking his way along cart tracks, reversing in field entrances, surveying the terrain from all points of the compass, he came upon the signpost again. This time he followed its directions, shortly finding himself in what was clearly the centre of the hamlet.

A couple of wooden benches beside a small green, tidily kept. A dozen houses of varying ages and sizes, all well maintained, with attractive gardens. In the course of his drive round he had spotted a further score or so of scattered properties. The area appeared generally prosperous.

No sign of any church, school, hall or pub. A notice in the window of one of the smaller dwellings by the green indicated that it was a post office. He left his car by the side of the green and walked across.

At a counter in the front room a grey-haired woman with a sharp, shrewd face was serving a doddery old man; it took his trembling fingers some time to deal with the postage stamps, his purse, his change. Lambert glanced about as he waited.

Shelves ranged along one wall carried cigarettes and confectionery, a few staple lines of groceries and tinned foods.

When the old man finally tottered out with his stick, Lambert bought a bag of potato crisps, a bar of chocolate, a packet of biscuits to show goodwill, then he asked the postmistress if there was anywhere in Bowpatch offering holiday accommodation. He was taking a short break from a desk job; he wanted somewhere quiet as a base for walking, touring, sightseeing. Nothing too grand or expensive; bed and breakfast or half board would suit him very well.

The postmistress didn't answer at once. She first surveyed him carefully and keenly. What she saw must have satisfied her for her expression lightened somewhat.

'I believe I know somewhere.' She gave a judicial nod. 'Mrs Inskip. Her husband works on one of the farms, they live in a farm cottage. Should suit you nicely. No young children to bother you. Mrs Inskip's children are grown up and gone away. She started doing a bit of bed and breakfast a couple of years back. You won't find any fault with her cooking.' She came to the door and gave him directions. 'You can say I sent you,' she graciously allowed.

The cottage stood alone on farmland a few minutes' drive from the central green. Lambert left his car a short distance away in order to make a discreet inspection of the dwelling on foot before committing himself so far as to press the doorbell.

His survey was eminently satisfactory. Well maintained, snug, orderly. The front garden pleasing to the eye; every inch of the back garden productively disposed in a thoroughly workmanlike fashion. A neatly lettered card in the window offered holiday accommodation.

He opened the front gate and strode with confidence along the path to the door. His ring at the bell was answered by Mrs Inskip, a little brown sparrow of a woman with quick, bobbing movements. Gentle brown eyes in a sweet-tempered face, feathery tendrils of peat-brown hair escaping from a bun, a shy, charming smile that knocked ten years off her age. I'll be all right here, he told himself with certainty before a word had been uttered on either side.

He embarked again on the tale he had given the postmistress. If Mrs Inskip had in any way pressed him about the exact nature of his desk job he would have responded with some reference

74

to local government. But he could see at a glance she wasn't the kind to pry and probe.

She showed him a bedroom overlooking the back garden; it was airy and sunny, agreeably furnished, provided with a radio and television set, a selection of books. 'But you'd be very welcome to join us downstairs in the sitting room any time you want,' she assured him warmly. She always supplied a substantial cooked breakfast, evening meals by arrangement, a traditional lunch on Sundays. Nothing foreign or fancy; good, plain, English cooking and plenty of it.

Lambert settled terms and took the room. 'I'm sure you'll find it quiet enough for you,' Mrs Inskip said. The nearest pub and general store were in the next village. Most folk did their shopping in Yelmerton, four miles away. She showed him where he could leave his car, then she brought him a tray of tea and left him to unpack and settle in. He pondered his next step as he drank his tea.

First, phone his landlady to give her his address, then try to discover the whereabouts of Greenfield. He hadn't spotted any property bearing that name during his drive round. Better do it on foot, get started in his character of dedicated walker – and draw far less attention to himself than dodging about the narrow lanes in a car. He had noticed isolated dwellings in various directions that probably belonged to the Bowpatch postal district. He might not succeed in locating Greenfield today but he could go on combing the area until he did come across it. One thing he assuredly was not going to do: he wouldn't ask Mrs Inskip or the postmistress where Greenfield was.

He put on his walking gear and set off, not forgetting to take with him his supply of goodies from the post office. He couldn't rely on coming across any ready source of food and it was a long time till 6.30, when Mrs Inskip served the evening meal, immediately after her husband came in from work. I'm going to enjoy this, he thought, remembering not to throw his shoulders too squarely back. I'll be as fit as a flea in a day or two.

By 5.30 he was feeling far from fit. He had long ago consumed the last of his goodies and was now ravenously hungry. His feet were tired, he was tired. He no longer needed to remind himself not to square his shoulders, he was reduced to ambling along with a pronounced slouch, his resemblance to an ordinary normal human being by now very close indeed.

75

He had covered, he reckoned, about three quarters of the territory and had come upon nothing to suggest such a property as Greenfield even existed. A few householders inhabiting particularly inaccessible retreats had been considerate enough to place at some convenient spot, a quarter or half a mile nearer civilization, a board giving the name of the property and its distance away, thus saving Lambert several fruitless tramps up hill and down dale.

He'd have to abandon his quest until tomorrow; time he was getting back to the Inskips'. At his present pace he would just about get there in time to clean himself up before sitting down at the table. It would never do to get back late on his first evening, that would create a very bad impression.

But he might just sit down for ten minutes first, to rest his feet and get his breath back. He found an old tree stump and slumped down on it. He closed his eyes in sweet relief. The only sounds were the twittering of birds and the relentless barking of a distant dog. He was careful not to allow himself to drift off into a doze. After his ten minutes were up he forced himself onto his feet again, pleased to discover he felt considerably more lively.

Ahead of him rose a small hillock. It occurred to him that if he were to make one last effort, scramble to the top of the hillock, he should be able to get a good long view, maybe spot a few more dwellings.

Having made up his mind, he took the incline almost at a run and sure enough, once at the top, he found himself with a fine panoramic outlook. Two properties lay within his field of vision: a farmhouse with outbuildings, a long way off, and a bungalow a good deal nearer.

He took out his binoculars and scanned the front of the bungalow. He could see no one about. On the entrance gate was a wooden nameplate. He could just make out the plain black lettering: GREENFIELD.

The enticing aroma of roast lamb floated to Lambert's nostrils as he hurried up the garden path to the Inskips' front door. He was after all in good time. Inskip opened the door to him, gave him a friendly greeting. A tall, broad man, weathered by wind and sun; a sensible, good-natured face. He shook Lambert's hand in a mighty grip.

Lambert could certainly find no fault with Mrs Inskip's cooking. The lamb, tender and succulent, gave way to a cherry tart and rich yellow cream. The talk, what there was of it, was easy and unforced. All three of them were united in a serious regard for food, a recognition of the fact that the purpose of the occasion was the appreciative dispatch of a magnificent meal, and not an endless flow of idle chatter.

The Inskips did speak fitfully of the local countryside, places of interest that Lambert might visit, the state of farming in the area, changes they had seen. By the time he rose from the table he felt immeasurably refreshed. He watched television in the sitting room for an hour or so, giving the roast lamb time to settle. Inskip had departed to labour in his garden but his wife sat with Lambert, watching the screen in companionable silence, knitting for a grandchild.

A feeling of great peacefulness washed over Lambert; the rhythmic click of the needles began to exert a profoundly hypnotic effect. It was as much as he could do, when a silvery chime from the mantel clock announced 8.30, to act upon the resolution he had made at the top of the hillock.

He got slowly to his feet. 'I think I'll take a stroll round before bedtime,' he told Mrs Inskip. 'Nothing very strenuous.'

She gave a nod. 'You'd better have a doorkey. You might be out later than you intend and we might have gone to bed.' She found the key and handed it over. 'If you want anything before you go to bed, any evening if I'm not about, you can always make yourself a hot drink in the kitchen, anything you fancy. Take what you like from the cake and biscuit tins, there's always plenty there.'

He set off at a leisurely pace and was pleased to find he had calculated well, the light was beginning to fail as he came within sight of Greenfield.

The bungalow looked seventy or eighty years old. It occupied a corner site of considerable size some distance along a lane, at a spot where the lane turned sharply, almost at a right angle.

He halted a few yards from the bungalow and surveyed the property. No sign of anyone about. The curtains were closed; the lights were on in a room at the front.

The hedge bordering the lane was neatly trimmed to a height of some four feet but along the other three sides a mixture of boundary trees and shrubs had been allowed to grow

77

unchecked. He approached the gate and stood looking in. The garden was well kept. A wide verandah ran along the front of the bungalow. Double doors at the back of the verandah led inside. Scents of stocks and tobacco plants rose up from the flower borders. His ear caught a thread of music from a radio.

He followed the bend of the lane a little way and stood in the darkling light glancing along the line of boundary trees. At the far end he could descry a second, larger gate. Another light appeared in the bungalow, then another, in the rear quarters.

As he turned and set off again, back towards his bed, a single star woke in the sky. From some nearby wooded slope came the echoing call of a night bird about its hunting.

CHAPTER 12

Lambert slept long and soundly. When he opened his eyes he was at once enveloped in a beautiful, deep, velvet silence, so far removed from the rattles and clamours of a Cannonbridge morning that he might have been on another planet.

And he did definitely feel better, though not yet one hundred per cent; the last descendants of the bug still seemed to lurk about his system.

Behind the closed curtains it was already broad day. He yawned and stretched his way luxuriously out of bed. When he finally went downstairs he was met by Mrs Inskip's shy, charming smile. Inskip had long ago left for work.

Mrs Inskip asked how he had slept. 'I didn't bring you a cup of tea,' she explained. 'I didn't know whether to or not, not having asked you last night, but I decided you might not thank me for waking you on your first morning.'

'That's all right,' he hastened to assure her. 'You needn't bother with tea any morning. If it's all right with you, there's nothing I'd like better than a chance to sleep as long as I can. I don't often get it.'

She brought in a breakfast even more substantial than that served by his landlady in one of her most manipulative, wheedling moods. He ate every last crumb. When Mrs Inskip appeared to clear the table she asked if he would have liked more. He laughed as he shook his head. 'Any more and I wouldn't be able to put one foot in front of the other.' And he had some nifty footwork in mind for this morning.

He put on walking gear again but this time he set off in his car. He left it parked under overhanging trees at some distance from Greenfield, out of sight of the bungalow; a circuitous route would bring him back to the same spot.

He set off at an unhurried pace. The trees massed along the boundary blocked his view of the front of the bungalow until he was right up to the property and could see in over the hedge.

Someone was sitting in a wheelchair on the verandah, a middle-aged woman, small and slightly built, with short, wavy hair, faded blonde. Her small-featured, childish face was still pretty.

She hadn't seen Lambert. She was trying to do a jigsaw puzzle on a table mounted on castors that had been placed in position over her knees. From her petulant expression, the irritated movements of her head, she wasn't having much success.

As Lambert walked slowly, silently along, the woman suddenly flung down the pieces she was holding. She thrust the table forward, scattering the puzzle in all directions. An instant later she looked alarmed at what she had done and began to snivel.

She leaned down sideways, trying to gather up the nearest pieces, her face strained and contorted. She overreached, the wheelchair started to tip. She threw herself back, bouncing the chair onto an even keel. But again she leaned down, stretched out her hand, again the chair rocked precariously.

'Hold on!' Lambert called. 'You'll tip yourself over!'

Her head jerked round; she threw him a look of surprise, tinged with fear. He went swiftly in through the gate, speaking as he approached in an easy, reassuring voice. 'It's all right, don't be alarmed. I only want to help you. I'll pick up the pieces for you.'

Her face relaxed. She sat back, upright again. The chair steadied. He reached the verandah and hastened up the steps. He gave her a friendly smile as he restored the table to its position. He dropped to his knees and began picking up the pieces, talking all the while in a soothing tone, as if to a child.

A smile stole over her features, an innocent, trusting smile, gentle and playful. She took the pieces from him as he collected them, stacking them tidily before her on the table. Her smile took on a conspiratorial air. He saw that the sleeve of her cardigan was neatly darned. Her hair was freshly washed, carefully brushed. At close quarters he saw it was touched with grey. Her skin was smooth and pink, her eyes the colour of cornflowers. Her blouse and slacks, like the cardigan, were far from new and could never have cost much, but they were very clean, in good order.

He stood up and walked about the verandah, stooping for stray pieces. The woman began to sing a little droning tune he recognized as a nursery rhyme. He turned his head and glanced at her; she looked pleased and absorbed, arranging the pieces.

As he gathered up the final strays his ear detected a sound from inside the bungalow, a chink and rattle, footsteps, movement. The verandah door opened and a woman came out, carrying a tray. She turned to close the door and caught sight of Lambert. She froze, staring at him in silence with an unsmiling, questioning look. A tall, thin, bony woman, wiry and sinewy, her skin deeply tanned, lined and leathery. Straight hair, very dark brown, almost black, pulled back without ceremony and secured in the nape of her neck. She wore a shirt and jeans, clean and mended. She had the look of a frontierswoman in the old American West.

Lambert straightened up. He smiled apologetically, holding out the pieces of the puzzle. He launched into an explanation, unhurried and amiable. She stood in the same rigid posture, listening.

When he had finished he handed the remaining pieces of the puzzle to the woman in the wheelchair. She received them with a smile of mingled gratitude and pleasure; she set about adding them to her stack.

The other woman moved forward, putting her tray down on a bench. 'I must thank you for helping my sister.' She had a light, clear voice, rather pleasant. 'My sister doesn't speak,' she added. 'I'm afraid she often gets frustrated.' She smiled slightly. 'That can lead to tantrums.'

'Very understandable,' Lambert said.

She ran her eye over him. 'Are you on holiday?'

'Yes. I'm doing a bit of walking.' He moved to leave. 'I'll be on my way.' She gave a little nod but the woman in the wheelchair put out a hand and touched the sleeve of his jacket. An expression of some distress showed in her face. She looked up at her sister and then across at the tray and back again to Lambert. Her meaning was plain.

'We were just going to have a drink,' the bony woman told Lambert, again with a faint smile. 'Won't you join us?'

'It's very kind of you, but I won't, if you don't mind.' He didn't particularly want to shoot down on top of his vast breakfast a tumblerful of some unidentified beverage. 'I'll be getting along.' He took another couple of steps but again the woman in the wheelchair put out a hand to detain him, again her face showed distress.

The bony woman looked at Lambert, now with an open smile.

'I'm afraid nothing will please Cicely – my sister – but that you should have a drink with us.' She smiled again. 'I don't think you'll find it too bad.' She gestured at the tray. It held a glass jug filled with some pale, cloudy liquid; sprigs of mint floated on top. 'It's a herbal drink, freshly made. And iced.'

Lambert knew when he was licked. 'I can't disappoint your sister,' he said. 'I should like some very much, thank you.' Cicely clasped her hands before her face, smiling in delight.

'I'll fetch another tumbler.' The bony woman went back inside. Lambert crossed to the table and picked up the puzzle box which was lying on the ground beside the wheelchair. He studied the picture on the lid. It showed a group of children on the seashore, shrimping, building sandcastles, running races, swimming. Rocks and waves, striped bathing tents, a mass of detail. No wonder the poor creature got temperamental, he thought. It looks pretty difficult to me. It'd take me the best part of a week to finish. Beside him Cicely tilted her head back, smiling up at him with unbounded trust.

The bony woman came out again with the tumbler and he replaced the box on the ground beside the wheelchair. She poured the drinks. Lambert manfully raised his glass to his lips. To his surprise it was delicious, with a subtle flavour, lemony, minty, faintly honeyed. 'That's beautiful,' he acknowledged. 'If you ever went commercial on that, you'd make a fortune.'

She was clearly gratified. 'One of my mother's recipes. Elderflower, lemon verbena, peppermint.' She didn't offer him a seat and she didn't sit down herself. She embarked on a little desultory conversation about his holiday. He told her he worked in Cannonbridge, throwing in this time for good measure a passing reference to local government; he was trying to get some fresh air and exercise, a break from his desk job. He was staying in Bowpatch, with the Inskips. He saw the name meant nothing to her. 'It's a farm cottage,' he enlarged. 'Over that way.' He gestured out across the fields.

She smiled deprecatingly and shook her head. 'I'm afraid we don't go about much locally. I'm kept very busy here.' Her gaze rested on her sister with fond affection. 'There's always more than enough to do.' He wondered briefly which of the two women was the older; he found it difficult to determine.

He drained his glass. The two women had by now finished their drinks. The bony woman picked up the tray. 'I'll take that in for you,' he offered automatically. She hesitated, then gave a little smiling nod and handed him the tray.

She went indoors ahead of him. The hall led into a central passage running the length of the dwelling. The back door stood propped open by a large stone to admit a cooling breeze, revealing a vista of kitchen garden, and beyond, a thick, crosswise belt of trees.

He followed her along the passage, flashing a rapid look to right and left as he went, taking swift snapshot impressions. Some of the doors were open to the currents of air, one or two were closed.

A sitting room on the left. Heavy, old-fashioned curtains, looped back with ornate gold tassel. Antique furniture, some handsome pieces. Framed watercolours on the walls.

More watercolours in the hall, along the passage. The first door on the right closed, the next slightly ajar; he couldn't get a peek inside.

Large bedroom on the left, two single beds, more watercolours. Closed door on the right, an inset panel of wire gauze high up; plainly a larder.

Door ajar on the left, a glimpse of tiles and chromium; clearly the bathroom. Just outside the back door, to the right, the edge of a carport, the rear end of a vehicle.

They reached the kitchen, a sizable room, bright and airy. She stood aside to let him enter and set down the tray. 'Thank you,' she said. 'Very kind of you.' Everything clinically clean, orderly; fixtures and fittings maybe twenty years old.

She turned to lead the way back down the hall. This time he riveted his attention entirely on the watercolours.

All clearly by the same highly skilled hand. Landscapes, village scenes, none of them very modern. Strikingly beautiful composition, colours delicate and subtle, a strongly individual style, at once romantic and truthful.

The largest picture, the one facing him on the wall of the sitting room, showed a large Victorian house, a garden dominated by a massive cedar of Lebanon. Children playing on the lawn, women taking tea on the terrace, dressed in the fashion of the 1920s. High summer, sunshine and flowers.

He halted for a moment by the front door. A much smaller picture on the wall to the left. A country church with a square tower. Tall cypresses, massy yews.

83

He managed a good snapshot flash at the signature and date in the bottom right-hand corner: *Blanche Kinnaird 1911.*

They came out into the shade of the verandah. Cicely was already at work again on her puzzle, seeking out straight-edged pieces to make a start on the border. She looked up with a sunny smile as he went over to say goodbye.

He let himself out through the front gate and turned to wave but neither woman was looking in his direction. Cicely was absorbed again in her puzzle and her sister was standing beside her, leaning down to select a piece.

He closed the gate and set off towards his car. The moment he had passed the end of the hedge and was out of sight of the verandah he stopped to jot down the name and date he had seen on the picture in the hall.

He reached his car and got in. There was an art gallery he knew; he had had dealings with the owner two or three years back, after a robbery at the premises. He had liked the owner, an amiable man, very knowledgeable, highly respected in the trade. The gallery was in a large, prosperous, arty-crafty village on the well-heeled tourist track, the best part of an hour's drive from where he found himself now.

He consulted his watch. He could go over there right away, see if he could get a word with the gallery owner, have a stroll round the village, find himself a decent lunch, get back to the Inskips' in nice time for the evening meal.

He switched on the engine and set off. His best plan would be to get onto the Cannonbridge road, straight through the town and out the other side.

In the centre of Cannonbridge he had to halt for the traffic lights. He glanced idly out at the passers-by, the shoppers, strollers, ambling pensioners, scurrying housewives.

A familiar figure suddenly halted his wandering eye: his landlady standing on the pavement outside a butcher's, trapped by a gossiping acquaintance, her eyes roving about as she kept up a polite succession of smiles and nods. All at once her gaze lighted on Lambert's car. Her head jerked up, she flashed a glance at the driver's seat, her eye met Lambert's. Her mouth fell open in a look of profound astonishment.

He had just time to raise a hand in salute, give her a cheery grin before the lights changed and he was off again and away.

CHAPTER 13

It was well past midday by the time Lambert reached his destination. There was a good sprinkling of visitors in the gallery. In the corner of one of the rooms he spotted the owner in conversation with a stout, dapper gentleman. He strolled up and down nearby. After a minute or two the owner became aware of his presence and glanced across at him. Lambert caught his eye and held it. He saw recognition begin to dawn. A few moments later the owner excused himself and came over.

'Sergeant Lambert!' He held out a hand. His eye noted Lambert's less than military haircut, his holiday rig. 'I didn't know you at first. Have you come to buy pictures or to make an arrest?' He permitted himself a microscopic movement of his head in the direction of the stout gentleman. 'I'm tied up at the moment. A big fish on the hook. Dutch.' He rolled his eyes. 'Very, very rich. I may have sold him half a dozen pictures but there's nothing signed and sealed as yet, he could still slip the line.'

'Then I won't keep you,' Lambert said. 'I've come to ask a favour, pretty straightforward.'

The owner waved a hand. 'Ask away.'

'I want to know anything you can tell me about a painter in watercolours, Blanche Kinnaird, painting around 1910, 1920.' He saw the name immediately rang a bell.

'No trouble,' the owner assured him. 'I'll look up the books as soon as I get a moment.' He massaged his chin. 'Could you come back later this afternoon? Around five, say?'

Lambert left the gallery and set off on a tour of the village. Much as he would have liked to treat himself to a magnificent lunch in one of the topnotch hostelries, he knew full well that the size of the bill, pitched at pockets far deeper and better lined than those of a detective sergeant, would effectively cancel out whatever pleasure he had taken in the meal. So, after he had been up and down the main thoroughfare, he began the serious business of looking for somewhere to eat among the side streets and alleyways.

He traced a particularly alluring waft of cooking odours to a modest, dual-purpose enterprise. The ground-floor shop offered locally made craft items, the upstairs dining room served a limited range of classic English dishes.

His nose hadn't led him astray. When he rose from his table an hour later and made his way downstairs his mood was expansive and cheerful, after a first-class meal very reasonably priced. He wandered round among the craft offerings, also reasonably priced. He might buy some little knick-knack to take back to Cannonbridge for his landlady.

He prowled among the racks and cabinets and came upon a stand of children's jigsaw puzzles fashioned in the shape of animals, the pieces of a sensible size, small enough to provide a challenge but not so small as to ensure frustration and failure. They were cut from unstained woods, the effect of colour, shading, texture, arising entirely from a careful juxtaposition of different timbers, different grains, natural markings. Beautifully designed, painstakingly made, meticulously finished; no two alike, each an individual work of art. Kitten, fox cub, rabbit, badger. He stood admiring them. He had known at once he would buy one for Cicely in her wheelchair. The question was: which one? Monkey? Kangaroo? Panda? He went on looking.

That's it, he decided instantly when he came to a squirrel holding a tiny nut between its paws; that's the one she'd choose herself. He had it giftwrapped in bright paper decorated with nursery-rhyme characters, tied up with pretty pink satin ribbon finished with an ornate bow. He smiled at the notion of handing it to her, seeing her delighted smile, watching her undo the wrapping.

He found no difficulty in amusing himself for the rest of the afternoon; there was something of interest round every corner. Promptly at five he walked into the art gallery again. An assistant took him along to the office where the owner awaited him. He had the air of a cat that had got at the cream. He couldn't stop smiling as he greeted Lambert.

'Come in! Come in!' He wrung Lambert's hand. The Dutchman had bought not six but ten paintings, all of fine quality.

'Sit down! Sit down! I've looked up your Blanche Kinnaird for you.' Reference books lay on his desk with slips of paper between the leaves. He had a tray brought in and set about dispensing China tea along with the results of his researches.

Not once in all his years at the gallery had he ever handled a watercolour by Blanche Kinnaird. That wasn't because her work was of inferior quality; on the contrary, it was of very high quality indeed. He would be cock-a-hoop if someone were to walk in through the door at this moment with half a dozen of her paintings to sell.

For many years Blanche's work had suffered an eclipse but modern taste had caught up with her again and she was now highly regarded. 'One or two of her paintings came onto the London market a few years back,' the owner told Lambert. 'They made good prices but nothing compared to what they'd make today.' Since then the Japanese and Americans had discovered Blanche; they would happily snap up any of her work they could lay their hands on.

To the best of his knowledge the bulk of her paintings were still in private hands and were never now exhibited. It consisted for the most part of rural landscapes with a small body of flower and plant paintings.

He threw out a hand. 'It's not unknown for relatives in these cases to have a stack of paintings stashed away in the attic. Never give them a thought, haven't the faintest notion they could be worth a small fortune.' He made a face. 'Gives you the shivers to think of it.'

Blanche Kinnaird's landscapes all depicted the same area: the village and countryside around the parish of Pennyhill. 'That's a few miles from here,' the owner said. He had paid more than one visit to the village in recent years, trying to winkle out paintings, but had had no luck. Nor, as far as he knew, had any of the other dealers who had gone there, hot on the trail.

Blanche had been born in Pennyhill and had lived there the whole of her long life. The only child of a well-to-do businessman, she had married a local cleric who succeeded to the living of Pennyhill, in those days a very substantial benefice. Pennyhill church, churchyard and vicarage figured in many of her paintings.

The owner didn't inquire why Lambert was interested in Blanche's work and Lambert didn't volunteer the information.

He got back to Bowpatch with just enough time to wash and tidy himself before supper. Mrs Inskip looked round the kitchen door as he hurried into the house. A savoury smell of roast duckling, sage and onion stuffing, floated into the hallway. 'There you are,' Mrs Inskip said. 'I thought you were going to be late. I was wondering whether to put the meal back a bit or keep yours warm in the oven.' He promised he would always phone if he was going to be late.

Her bright, birdlike eyes rested on the gaily wrapped parcel he was carrying. He glanced down at it. 'I'll tell you about this, and the reason I bought it, over supper. I think you might be interested.' He went swiftly upstairs and she turned back, intrigued, to her pots and pans.

She was dishing up when he came downstairs again. Inskip was carrying a tureen of soup into the dining room. 'It's a jigsaw puzzle in the parcel,' Lambert told Mrs Inskip as he sat down at the table. 'A child's puzzle, made in large pieces, but I didn't buy it for a child. I bought it for a grown woman, here in Bowpatch.' They both looked at him with sharp interest. 'Miss Cicely Jerrom, at Greenfield, the bungalow over there.' He gestured out.

'Do you know those two Jerrom women?' Mrs Inskip asked in astonishment.

He laughed. 'I can't say I know them, I just came across them.' He explained how he had been walking by and had seen the wheelchair about to tip over; he sketched in his encounter with the sisters and told how, later in the day, he had spotted the puzzles in a craft shop.

'Do you mean to tell me,' Mrs Inskip demanded, her shyness dispelled under the thrust of curiosity, 'that Hilda Jerrom – Hilda's the name of the other sister; I was going to say the older sister but that would only be guesswork on my part, I don't know which of them is the older – are you telling me Hilda Jerrom let you inside the house and gave you something to drink?' She was mightily impressed. 'That's more than can be said for anyone in this village.' She craned forward. 'What's the bungalow like inside?'

'Very pleasant.' He didn't go into details.

'I've never once seen Hilda in the post office here in Bowpatch,' Mrs Inskip went on. 'But I do sometimes see the two of them in Yelmerton, shopping. Hilda always takes her sister with

88

her; she never leaves her at home on her own. She's very good to Cicely, very kind; you can tell that just by seeing the two of them together. Hilda drives an old station wagon; it's been fixed up so it can take a wheelchair. She takes her sister all round the shops with her. You never see Cicely trying to manage the wheelchair on her own, like other disabled folk; it's always Hilda pushing her. Cicely just sits back and enjoys herself, like a child.' She shook her head. 'Poor soul. Sometimes she looks just like a little girl.'

She drank her soup. 'I never stop to speak to them. I don't think they'd like it. When they first came here – that must be ten years ago now – someone from the Women's Institute did go to see them, to ask if they'd like to join. The Institute is in the next village from here; Bowpatch isn't big enough for one of its own. But they didn't join; they weren't interested.'

She sighed. 'I did think once, years ago, of calling at Greenfield myself, offering to help in any way I could, maybe sit with Cicely if Hilda wanted to go somewhere on her own.' She moved her shoulders, sighed again. 'But you don't like to intrude if folk don't seem to want it, so I never did call round. I don't know whether I did right or not.'

'You did right,' her husband put in with conviction. 'You wouldn't have got much of a welcome if you had gone round.' He turned to Lambert. 'Hilda's a very handy sort of woman. She does all the repairs; anything that's needed in that line at the bungalow, she tackles it all herself. She's as good as any man.

'I see her sometimes at farm sales, country auctions. I like to go myself when I can get the time off, you can pick up all kinds of useful bits and pieces. Hilda's very sharp about what she buys. I did offer to give her a hand once or twice in the beginning, help her to load stuff she'd bought onto her wagon. She was polite enough but she didn't feel the need of any help, she made that clear.'

He finished his soup and laid down his spoon. 'I've seen her up on the roof, fixing tiles and guttering. I've seen her chopping wood, felling a dead tree. She even knocked up a carport a month or two back. When they moved into Greenfield there was quite a bit of work wanted doing on the place; it was advertised like that; it had stood empty some time. But she never got anyone in to it, she did it all herself.' He chuckled.

'It's not often you come across a woman like that, even in these days.'

Mrs Inskip brought in a pair of roast ducklings and her husband set about carving them – with surprising skill and delicacy for a man with such huge, gnarled hands. 'Where Greenfield stands,' he said as he carved, 'that used to be a meadow. Well over an acre, it was. The chap that had the bungalow built, he was a major come back from the First World War; he wanted peace and quiet after what he'd been through. Then, about twenty years ago, after the major died, the bungalow was bought by a retired businessman; pretty well-to-do, he was.

'His wife was an invalid, some spinal injuries; she'd been thrown from a horse, never able to walk again. He had the place adapted and modernized. Lovely people they were, joined in everything that was going on locally.'

'The wife used to do all the typing for the Women's Institute,' Mrs Inskip put in. 'He used to bring her to all the meetings and call for her again afterwards. Very devoted he was. They had a woman from the village used to go in every day to help in the house. Then the wife died and a year or two later the husband died, and the place stood empty till Miss Jerrom bought it.'

The ducklings were superb, the vegetables fresh from the garden, the gravy and apple sauce beyond reproach.

'The garden had all gone to rack and ruin by the time the Jerroms moved in,' Inskip went on. 'It was beautiful when the businessman and his wife lived there. He was a very keen gardener; it was his hobby after he retired. Two greenhouses he had; he used to grow peaches and grapes, as well as tomatoes. He always sent some round if anyone in the village was ill. They thought the world of him and his missus round here.'

He saw that Lambert's plate was empty. He looked across at his wife. 'You've done these ducklings a treat. I'm sure Mr Lambert could manage another couple of mouthfuls.'

And he was correct in his assumption. Mr Lambert was able with no difficulty at all to manage several more mouthfuls.

CHAPTER 14

The fine weather continued to hold. After another vast and leisurely breakfast Lambert set off next morning for the village of Pennyhill, thirty-odd miles from Bowpatch. He took with him a small overnight bag in case he decided for any reason to stay the night. He didn't mention this to Mrs Inskip; he could always give her a ring.

Pennyhill lay deep in hunting country. As he drew near he began to recognize the terrain: the hills, woods, streams he had glimpsed in the watercolours adorning the walls of Greenfield. He drove slowly round the village, pretty enough, prosperous looking.

On rising ground on the outskirts of the village a church tower rose above the trees. He knew that square tower from Blanche Kinnaird's paintings. Nor did it take him long to find the large Victorian house he had seen in the picture in the Greenfield sitting room. Today no children played on the lawn, no ladies took tea on the terrace, but the massive cedar of Lebanon still dominated the garden with the horizontal planes of its dark branches.

He halted briefly near the house and walked across to the entrance gates. An elegantly lettered board informed him that he was looking at the Old Vicarage Flats.

He got back into his car and drove up to the church; he parked the car and walked round to the churchyard. From here he was able to look down over the village and surrounding countryside, an age-old patterning of fields and spinneys, hedging and walling, wheatfields and pastureland, brooks and ponds, inns and farmhouses, barns and cottages: the stuff of Blanche Kinnaird's work.

In the churchyard a pleasant breeze stirred the long grasses glittering between the tombs. Ancient trees still stood sentinel, angels in stone and marble still stood poised with open wings and folded hands. But everywhere there were signs of neglect and decay. Rotting graveboards, their painted inscriptions no longer decipherable; greening, mossy headstones leaning at an angle; flaking cherubs, eroded scrolls, lichen-encrusted slabs.

In an area reasonably well kept he came upon the Kinnaird graves: Edmund, rector of this parish; Blanche, wife of the above. He saw that Blanche had survived her husband by twenty-five years.

In the wildest part of the churchyard a young woman in T-shirt and jeans was attacking the grass with a billhook. She straightened up and looked across at him. After a moment she came over.

She gave him a friendly smile. She wore steel-framed spectacles; her face was scrubbed clean, her hair scraped back into a single plait, like an old-time seafarer. She asked if she could help, if he was looking for any particular tomb.

He told her he was interested in the life and work of the painter, Blanche Kinnaird. He was on holiday in the area; he had come to take a look at the village where she had lived all her life.

Yes, the young woman knew the name Kinnaird. She was Pennyhill born and bred, a student at the neighbouring university. The Kinnairds were still remembered in the village. 'But there are none of them left round here now,' she added. 'We don't have a vicar living in the parish any more.' Pennyhill had been amalgamated years ago with neighbouring parishes. 'I hate to see the way the churchyard has got so neglected,' she confessed with a grimace. 'I come along in the vacations whenever I can. I do my best.'

She offered to show him where other members of the Kinnaird family were buried and he followed her to a group of graves under a willow.

'Blanche Kinnaird had two daughters,' she told him. 'Phoebe and Louise. They're both buried here, with their husbands.' All the graves were neatly kept, with fresh posies of flowers. The student indicated the grave of the elder daughter, Phoebe, and her husband, Alfred Raybould. 'They didn't have any children – Phoebe didn't marry till she was well into middle age.' Lambert saw from the inscriptions that Phoebe had been eight years older than her husband and had died three years before him.

The student moved on a couple of yards. 'This is the grave

of the younger daughter, Louise. She married her father's curate, Nicholas Jerrom. When her father died, the living passed to Nicholas. Pairs of girls seem to run in the family – Louise and Nicholas had two daughters, Cicely and Hilda. As far as I know, they're both still alive, but I've no idea where they are now. They left Pennyhill years ago. I remember Cicely from when I was a child; I used to see her at church.'

She looked up at Lambert. 'She wasn't very bright. She always looked so downcast and miserable when I saw her in church; she never joined in the singing. I used to feel sorry for her; she looked like a lost soul. The other sister, Hilda, I don't remember her at all; she'd left Pennyhill and gone off to Australia. She came back when Alfred Raybould died – Alfred was the man who'd married Hilda's Aunt Phoebe. I never actually saw Hilda but I remember hearing she'd come back. That would be about ten years ago now. Hilda and Cicely left the village not long afterwards. I don't think either of them has been back since.'

Lambert asked which of the two sisters was the older. 'Cicely,' she answered without hesitation. She asked if he was staying in the village and he made up his mind on the spot. 'Yes, I am,' he told her. 'Just for the night.' She asked if he had found anywhere to stay. He shook his head. 'In that case,' she advised him, 'I suggest you go along and see if Mrs Osgood will take you in. She worked for the Kinnaird family for donkey's years; there isn't much she doesn't know about any of them.' She smiled. 'Once she gets going on the Kinnairds you'll find it hard to stop her. It's Mrs Osgood that looks after the Kinnaird graves, along with the graves of her own family.'

She walked with him to the road and gave him directions. 'Tell Mrs Osgood I sent you and I'm sure she'll find you a bed. She doesn't make a proper business of the visitor trade these days but she still does a bit now and then, if she feels like it.'

The church clock struck noon as he got into his car and drove down again into the village. Mrs Osgood's cottage stood behind a white picket fence near the village green. A sizable dwelling, many-gabled and lattice-windowed, of mellow, rosy brick. A glorious display of delphiniums filled the front garden: white, violet, heliotrope, shocking pink and raspberry, every shade of blue from palest sky to darkest gentian. Lambert pushed open the gate and walked up the path to the door, wreathed in perfumed clusters of blush-pink climbing roses.

93

Mrs Osgood opened the door to his ring. She stood gazing out at him in silence, with majestic composure, the mildest of questions in her heavy-lidded, china-blue eyes.

A lady of Junoesque proportions, large-boned and broad-faced, with a creamy, waxy skin and unlined brow, hair of grizzled chestnut wound round her head in thick, shining coils. She wore a voluminous apron, spotlessly clean, with a bib pinned over the capacious bosom of her crisp print dress.

She listened in regal calm as Lambert explained his reason for arriving on her doorstep. At his reference to the student she permitted herself the merest suggestion of a nod, but as soon as he mentioned the Kinnaird family, his interest in the work of Blanche Kinnaird, her air of unruffled serenity vanished abruptly. She held up a large, pale hand. 'If you're one of those art dealers, you're wasting your time.' Blue fire flashed from her eyes. 'I've nothing to say to you about Mrs Kinnaird and I most certainly have none of her pictures to sell.' She stepped back and made to close the door against him.

'One moment.' Lambert in turn held up a hand. 'I'm no art dealer, I give you my word.' The door paused in its track. 'I'm very interested in Blanche Kinnaird, in her work and her life. I'd be glad to hear anything you might care to tell me about her or her family. But I most definitely have no interest at all in buying any of her paintings.' He grinned. 'For one thing, I couldn't possibly afford it. All I'm asking for is a bed for the night, supper if you care to provide it. And a chat about the family if you feel so inclined.'

She regarded him with an unwinking, assessing gaze. 'Very well,' she announced at last, Boadicea conferring a favour. She gave a warning inclination of her head. 'But if it does turn out you're a dealer, out you go, on the spot, bag and baggage. Understood?'

'Understood,' he acknowledged, smiling. 'I really am not a dealer.'

She glanced down at his feet. A faint gleam of a smile touched her features. 'If you are a dealer, you'll be the first I've ever seen in training shoes. I'll take your word for it.'

She held the door wide. 'You'd better come inside while we talk terms.'

Mingled scents of roses and lavender greeted him as he stepped over the threshold. She took him into a sitting room, immaculately clean. Oak beams, a bowl of sweet peas on dark, polished wood, old country-made furniture; an open hearth with an inglenook, screened now by an arrangement of summer flowers.

'This is the sitting room my visitors use,' Mrs Osgood informed him. 'I keep another for myself.' She adjusted a fold in the chintz curtains. 'Now, if you'd like to see your room.' She preceded him with an unhurried step up the stairs and along a landing.

Dappled green sunlight filled the bedroom. A chintz-covered, cushioned window seat, a snowy coverlet on the bed. 'I can find you a bit of supper,' she pronounced. 'I never do lunches but there are two or three places in the village where you can get a meal.' She gave a little snort. 'I should say the Bluebird Café is the least likely to give you food poisoning.' She told him her terms which he accepted happily.

They processed down the stairs again. Lambert brought in his bag and took it up to his room. 'Seven o'clock, supper,' Mrs Osgood announced. 'Don't be late.'

He lost no time in finding a phone box and ringing Mrs Inskip; he would be back tomorrow, Sunday, in time for lunch. He strolled round the village and ate his lunch, as directed, at the Bluebird Café.

He spent an agreeable afternoon driving about the neighbouring countryside, halting now and then for a ramble through woodland, past orchards and hopyards, fields of ripening barley, pastures dotted with newly shorn sheep. At a wayside cottage he treated himself to a mouth-watering cream tea: featherlight scones, thick yellow cream, homemade strawberry jam.

He got back to Mrs Osgood's in plenty of time to smarten himself up before supper. He ate in solitary state in the dining room. Cold roast beef, pink and tender, raspberry tart, meltingly ambrosial. On the wall facing him hung a pair of what he immediately recognized as Blanche Kinnaird pictures. A view of the vicarage and its gardens; a lovingly detailed painting of the church and churchyard.

Mrs Osgood came in with a pot of coffee and a jug of hot milk. He complimented her on the meal and she received his praises graciously. Somewhat emboldened he went on to say he'd been admiring the pictures.

She made an acknowledging movement of her head. 'I wouldn't part with them for anything. Mrs Kinnaird gave me those two as a wedding present. I'd worked at the vicarage since I left school. That's where I learned to cook – I started as a kitchenmaid. I married the vicarage gardener just after the war broke out. We knew he'd be one of the first to go. I was nineteen years old.'

She sighed. 'He was called up soon afterwards; he was killed at Dunkirk. Just turned twenty-five, he was. I thought the world had come to an end.'

Lambert ventured to suggest she might care to join him in a cup of coffee.

Yes, she would. She would fetch another cup. When she returned she didn't sit down. 'I've half a dozen more of Mrs Kinnaird's paintings in my own sitting room,' she informed him. 'Would you like to see them?'

'Indeed I would,' he answered with alacrity.

She gave a magisterial nod. 'Then if you'll be good enough to bring the tray through, we'll have our coffee in there.'

In the sitting room Mrs Osgood showed him her pictures, all given to her at one time or another by various members of the family. 'I've no need to think about selling any of them,' she told him. 'I don't need the money, I've more than enough to see me out in comfort. My husband was an only child. This cottage belonged to his parents and it came to me when they died.'

When she had given him his coffee and indicated which chair he might occupy she crossed to the bureau and opened a drawer. 'I've some photographs here of the Kinnaird family, if you'd like to see them.' She took out a leather album and an old chocolate box. She carried them over to a table and settled herself comfortably into a vast wing chair. She smiled as she glanced into the box. 'All sorts of stuff in here: birthday cards, Christmas cards, wedding invitations, dried flowers, newspaper cuttings.'

She turned the pages of the album. Herself as a girl, as a young woman. Members of her own family, her husband's family. Blanche and Edmund Kinnaird in a formal studio portrait. Their two daughters, Phoebe and Louise, as young women, Louise pretty enough, with fair, curling hair, Phoebe with a plain, gentle face.

She turned another page. 'Louise's two daughters, Cicely and Hilda; there's the best part of four years between them.' The photograph showed Cicely at nine or ten years old, short and slight, with a pretty, doll-like face, a halo of blonde curls. Hilda, almost as tall, in spite of the age gap; dark and skinny, her expression a good deal sharper and brighter than her sister's.

Mrs Osgood tapped her forehead. 'Cicely never had very much up here. They always said it was on account of a couple of bad illnesses, measles and whooping cough, that she had when she was very small; she had them one after the other.

But I never believed that was the reason, though I dare say it didn't help.' She leaned forward confidentially. 'It's my opinion it was something in the blood. I know for a fact Mr Kinnaird had an aunt who was a ha'penny short of a shilling all her life. The Kinnairds were an old family, by way of being gentlefolk. When you get to the tail end of these old families there's often some unhealthy strain seems to show itself. Anyway, whatever the truth of it was, after Cicely was better from these illnesses, they always coddled her. I believe that was a big mistake, she should have been treated exactly the same as Hilda. I was always sure Cicely could have been taught a lot if they'd set about it in the right way. She was a lovely-natured little girl, cheerful and biddable, always smiling and happy, chattering away, singing little bits of songs and nursery rhymes around the house. She could even pick out simple little tunes on the piano. You can't tell me there wasn't some intelligence there. It could surely have been brought out.'

Lambert asked if either Phoebe or Louise had inherited their mother's talent for painting.

She shook her head. 'Though Louise was always very interested in flowers and plants – herbs and wild flowers, mostly. I suppose you could say that came to her from her mother. Louise married her father's curate. They'd only been married a couple of years when her father died – he'd been ailing for some time. The living went to Louise's husband and of course Mrs Kinnaird and Phoebe had to move out of the vicarage. Mrs Kinnaird wasn't short of money; she'd inherited everything when her parents passed on. She bought a very nice house in the village for herself and Phoebe. She wasn't painting seriously any more by then; she'd stopped when her husband first got ill.

'Phoebe wasn't far off thirty when her father died and anyone looking at her would take it for granted she'd end up an old maid. We none of us dreamed for one moment we'd be standing up at her wedding more than twenty years later.

'I stayed on at the vicarage, to work for Louise and her husband. It wasn't long after my husband had been killed. Louise turned part of the vicarage garden into what she called a wilderness. It was a pleasure to walk round there on a summer day; clouds of butterflies there'd be.

'There wasn't much Louise didn't know about plants and herbs. I still use her elderflower recipe for face cream.' She reached over with calm dignity and took Lambert's hand. She passed his fingers across her cheek. He felt himself almost hypnotized. 'Feel that!' she commanded with regal detachment. 'Soft as a new-born baby's skin.' And indeed it was.

She gave him back his hand. 'Louise had a very strong character but that didn't mean she wasn't softhearted too. She could never bear to see an animal suffer. If one of the vicarage dogs or cats got very old or ill she had a recipe she always used. She made it up from foxgloves mainly, with some other plants – henbane and deadly nightshade, plants like that. She covered up the taste with other herbs so they'd lap it up. Very peaceful, very merciful.'

She rose to her feet. 'We'll take a glass of my damson wine.' She went to a corner cupboard and took out a bottle and glasses. She poured two glassfuls and handed one to Lambert. 'I should value your opinion of this. It's generally well liked.'

Lambert wasn't surprised, the bouquet and taste were superb. He told her as much as she settled back into her chair again with the album. 'Nicholas Jerrom had a bit of money,' she said. 'Not a fortune, but it meant he and Louise had enough to live comfortably at the vicarage. He was killed out hunting, twenty years after he became vicar. The living went to a stranger and of course Louise and the two girls had to leave the vicarage. Cicely would be about nineteen by then and Hilda fifteen. Louise had been left fairly well off and she bought a cottage in the village – nowhere near such a good house as her mother had bought, but it served well enough.'

She drained her glass and looked across at Lambert. 'Time for a refill,' she announced with increasing affability. 'If you wouldn't mind doing the honours.'

The damson wine began to slip down sweetly again. 'I still went on working for Louise,' Mrs Osgood continued, 'but I didn't live in at the cottage, there wasn't the room. And my husband's parents were getting on, so I decided to move in here with them.

'Then, all at once, Mrs Kinnaird started to fail. I could see she wasn't going to live much longer.' She gave Lambert a glance full of significance. 'And so, it seemed, could someone else. Alfred Raybould started courting Phoebe. I'd known Alfred Raybould all my life, and I'd never been much taken with what I knew. We'd been at the village school together. He always

99

fancied himself, even then. He was forever combing his hair, looking at himself in any mirror that was about. He was only an ordinary village boy; he lived with his mother in a rented cottage. She was a widow; she took in dressmaking after her husband died – he'd been a labourer for the council. But Alfred fancied he'd risen above all that. He was a clerk with the Gas Board, no less. He used to cycle into work every morning. After his mother died he went on living in the cottage on his own. He never had any other relatives, leastways none that I ever heard of. He never got married; none of the local girls was good enough for him.

'He always had ambitions to be a gentleman and marrying Phoebe Kinnaird would be the nearest he was ever likely to get to that. He was well spoken, always had good manners. I suppose some would have called him charming. I thought he had the cheek of the devil to go setting his cap at Phoebe. Anyone with half an eye could see what he was after. Mrs Kinnaird's house would be sure to go to Phoebe and very likely a nice sum of money, too, along with the furniture and pictures and all the rest of it.

'Anyway, Alfred starting making sheep's eyes at Phoebe and I soon saw she was quite taken with him.' She took a drink of her wine. 'Give the devil his due, I suppose he wasn't bad looking, if you like that smarmy type. He had a little moustache; he always put me in mind of what Douglas Fairbanks Junior might have looked like if he'd been reared in a two-up-and-two-down and got himself a job with the Gas Board.'

She took a longer drink. 'Sure enough, when Mrs Kinnaird died a couple of years later, Phoebe married Alfred Raybould as soon as it was decent. Mrs Kinnaird had more or less split what she left down the middle. Phoebe got the house and most of what was in it, and a certain amount of money, stocks and shares, that sort of thing. The bulk of the money went to Louise. Alfred moved out of his rented cottage and into Phoebe's house.' She grimaced. 'And there he lived, like a pig in clover.'

CHAPTER 16

Lambert asked if the marriage had prospered.

She inclined her head. 'I have to admit they did seem happy enough. Phoebe bought Alfred a little car. He got rid of his bike and started driving into work every day like Lord Muck.'

Her glass had emptied itself again. She gestured to Lambert to carry out another refill. 'Louise didn't make old bones; she only lived to be fifty-four.' She pulled down the corners of her mouth. 'Cancer. She had a pretty rough time of it. I knew she wouldn't be sorry when the end came. Except for Cicely – she worried about what would happen to Cicely after she'd gone.

'Cicely never had anything you could really call an education. She did go to the village school for a while but the children teased her and she was in tears most of the day. In the end Louise decided to keep her at home. She did her best to teach her herself, but it isn't the same. And not mixing with the other children, that kept Cicely more babyish than ever.

'Hilda was a different kettle of fish altogether, always a tomboy, always wanting to be out of doors. And strong, for all she was so skinny. I never knew her ail a day.

'She and Cicely always got on well together. There was nothing Hilda wouldn't do for Cicely – too much so, if you ask me. It stopped Cicely even more from trying to stand on her own feet.

'Hilda went into town every day to a private school. After she left school she would have loved to go abroad, she often told me so. She wanted adventure, to see the world, spread her wings, but she couldn't turn her back on her mother when she was so ill – and there was always Cicely to be looked after.

'When Louise realized she hadn't much time left she went to see her sister Phoebe. Phoebe had been married to Alfred Raybould a few years by that time. Louise asked the two of them if they would be willing to act as joint guardians for Cicely after she was gone. Louise's cottage would be sold after her death and the money from the sale, as well as most of the rest of what she had to leave, would be put in trust for Cicely; Phoebe and Alfred would be joint trustees. All Cicely's living expenses and so forth would come out of the trust fund. Hilda would get just enough to start her out in the world, that was all she wanted. Louise had talked it over with Hilda, in fact it was Hilda who had suggested the idea in the first place. She didn't mind giving up most of her own inheritance if it meant she could be free to do what she chose.'

She looked down into her glass. 'Louise was dead within the year. Cicely went to live with the Rayboulds and Hilda went off to Australia. She was twenty-two years old – that would make Cicely twenty-six, though you'd still have taken her for a little girl.

'Phoebe asked me to go to work for her and that suited me nicely. It didn't take Master Alfred long to get rid of the little car and buy something a good deal more expensive. He was still only a clerk at the Gas Board but with all the extra money coming into the house from the trust fund he started coddling himself with a bottle of good whisky, some old port or brandy, a fine cigar. Phoebe never objected to any of it. Nothing she liked better than to see her beloved Alfred enjoying himself.'

Lambert asked if Cicely had settled down well at the Rayboulds'.

She nodded. 'She was very happy there for a long time. Phoebe was always very kind to her, bought her pretty clothes, brushed her curls till they shone, took her about. I made it my business to teach her easy little household tasks, some simple cooking.'

Lambert asked how Hilda had got on in Australia.

'She moved about a lot,' Mrs Osgood told him. 'She worked on farms and ranches, any kind of work. She saw the country, did all the things she'd always wanted to do, riding, shooting, fishing. She wrote once in a while; Phoebe always showed me any letter from her. And she never forgot Cicely's birthday; she always sent her a pretty card, and the same at Christmas. She'd send a bright picture postcard now and then; it was usually from a different address every time.

'Then, ten years after Hilda went to Australia, Phoebe died. That left Alfred Raybould as Cicely's sole guardian and trustee.'

She threw Lambert a glance charged with significance. 'Phoebe left it in her will that Alfred could live in the house for the rest of his life and she left her own money the same way – Alfred was to have the income from it as long as he lived. After his death the whole lot, the house and Phoebe's own money, would go to the two girls.'

'And the trust fund?' Lambert asked. 'What was to happen to that after Raybould's death?'

'Hilda was to act as guardian and trustee,' Mrs Osgood replied. 'That didn't mean she'd be obliged to come back from Australia to look after Cicely herself if she didn't want to, but it would be her responsibility to see the trust money was properly used, to provide a home and proper care for Cicely. If Cicely died before Hilda, then whatever was left of the trust fund would go to Hilda.'

She sat silent, shaking her head. 'Phoebe was barely cold in her grave when Alfred started making changes. He wasn't far off sixty by then and he took early retirement as soon as he could arrange it. He set himself up right away as a full-time gentleman – or as near to it as he could get. He joined a club in the town, he took up golf.

'But the very first thing he did was to show me the door. He wouldn't even let me serve out my notice, he gave me extra wages in lieu. He told me he would be keeping on the cleaning woman for the rough work and he'd be eating out at his club as often as not. He'd run the household himself, and any other little tasks that wanted doing Cicely could do. He said he'd always agreed with my attitude, that Cicely was a good deal more capable than she was given credit for. A bit of responsibility would be the making of her, she'd improve out of all recognition.

'I didn't look for another job. I was nearly sixty myself by then. I had this cottage, and the holiday trade was going up by leaps and bounds. I decided to do a bit of bed and breakfast, cream teas in the back garden.

'I did my level best to keep an eye on Cicely, mostly through the cleaning woman. I hardly ever saw Cicely out around the village; she'd never been used to going about on her own. I did see her sometimes at church on Sundays but I never once managed to get a word with her alone. Raybould was always there, glued to her side.

103

'If I did happen to catch sight of him in the village – I'd have to be quick, if he saw me coming he'd dodge into a shop – I'd ask him how Cicely was getting on. He always told me exactly the same thing, like a lesson he'd learned off by heart: she was making excellent progress, becoming a good deal more competent all round; she was nowhere near as childish.

'The cleaning woman told me Cicely tried her very best to please Raybould. But she'd got very quiet, never sang or chattered any more. I didn't like the sound of that but I kept hoping it would work out.

'One Sunday at church, about three years after Phoebe died, I particularly noticed how listless and downcast Cicely looked. I thought how dreadfully upset Louise and Phoebe would have been to see her like that. I felt it was up to me to do something. I'd be betraying their trust if I didn't.

'A couple of days later I ran into the cleaning woman and she told me another postcard had come for Cicely from Hilda. I knew on the spot what I was going to do but I'd have to be quick about it in case Hilda moved on again. I asked the cleaning woman to see if she could get a look at the postcard, make a note of Hilda's address. As soon as she brought it to me I wrote off to Hilda by air mail, telling her pretty bluntly what I thought about the situation. I didn't know exactly what I imagined Hilda was going to do about it, all those thousands of miles away, but I got a letter back very quickly, saying Hilda would soon be on her way home by air.

'She turned up on my doorstep a few weeks later, plainer than ever, bony as a kipper and pretty nearly the colour of one. You could see by looking at her it had been a hard, rough old life, but she had no complaints, it had been what she wanted.

'We sat up half the night, talking, and next morning she went round to see Raybould and Cicely. Cicely was delighted to see her, laughing and crying, hugging her, hardly able to believe it. Master Raybould wasn't quite so pleased. He told her he wouldn't be able to put her up as she hadn't let him know she was coming, and in any case he didn't feel up to visitors staying in the house, he was far from well. There was some virus going round the town, he thought he might have caught it at his club, some of the members had gone down with it.

'Hilda paid no attention to that. He'd always mollycoddled himself, always made out he had some heart condition whenever he wanted to get out of doing something. But she was really shocked at the change in Cicely, in spite of everything I'd said to warn her.

'She didn't challenge Raybould about the state Cicely was in. He had full legal authority and she had none. She was sure if there was an outright quarrel she would be banned from the house and wouldn't be able to see Cicely at all.

'She stayed here with me for a day or two while she thought what to do. She decided she'd have to get some kind of temporary job right away. She scarcely had tuppence to her name after buying the plane ticket. I told her to forget about the job, she was welcome to stay on here with me as long as she needed to. But she wouldn't have it, she wouldn't impose on me, and I couldn't make her change her mind. You could never do that with Hilda. Once she'd decided something, she was like iron.

'She got herself a job for a couple of weeks on a small farm some distance from here. The farmer had had to go into hospital and the wife was trying to manage on her own. Hilda and the wife were working all hours and Hilda didn't get over here again till the two weeks were up. When she did come she went round to see Raybould and Cicely again. She discovered that Raybould hadn't been putting it on after all, he really was ill, quite ill. The local doctor knew Hilda of course, he'd known all the family. He's retired now and gone back to Scotland to live. He'd already brought a nurse into the house; he knew Cicely wasn't up to nursing Raybould on her own.

'Hilda moved into the house the same day. The doctor was very pleased, she could share the nursing duties. Raybould was in no condition to protest, even if he'd wanted to, he didn't even really know she was staying in the house. Hilda was very good to him, in spite of everything. She sat up with him every night.

'I never met the nurse but Hilda told me she was very efficient.' She frowned. 'What was she called? I do know, it's on the tip of my tongue. Drummond, Redmond, some such name.' She jerked her head. 'Hammond! That was it!

'It was a very nasty virus, something after the style of gastric flu, only worse. Some people got serious complications. It was mostly older folk that went down with it.

'Raybould seemed to be improving but his heart suddenly gave out.' She made a wry grimace. 'It seems he hadn't been swinging the lead all those years, after all. He really must have had a heart condition.'

She expelled a long breath. 'That wasn't the end of the troubles. Raybould had no sooner died than Cicely went into a very bad state, worse even than before Hilda came back from Australia. Very depressed, staring and crying, not making a sound, just sitting there with the tears running down her face. She wouldn't speak to anyone, not even to Hilda. I'd kept out of the house as long as Raybould was alive but as soon as he'd gone and the nurse had left, I started going up there every day to give Hilda a hand. I couldn't get Cicely even to look at me, let alone say a word.

'The morning after Raybould was buried Hilda went into Cicely's bedroom with a cup of tea. She found Cicely lying there with her eyes closed, couldn't move, couldn't make a sound. The doctor thought it was a stroke.

'After a while Cicely started to improve but she never got back the use of her legs, and she still didn't talk. The doctor arranged for a specialist to see her and he said it definitely wasn't a stroke. It was hysterical paralysis, brought on by all the stress and shock. She might recover completely, or partly, or she might stay the way she was. She needed friendly, sympathetic looking after but no fussing. She must be encouraged in every way to do things for herself.

'Hilda gave up any idea of looking for a job. Caring for Cicely was going to be her job from now on. She thought they could just about manage on the trust money if she was very careful. She was determined they would manage, however much she had to skimp and save. If she was forced to take a job she'd have to put Cicely in a home and that she swore she'd never do.

'I asked her if she'd really thought it out; it would mean giving up the rest of her life to Cicely. She told me she fully realized that but it would never be a burden to her. She felt she owed it to Cicely – and to her mother and her Aunt Phoebe. She would never let them down.

'She decided to sell the house and look for something more suitable for a wheelchair. She was sure it would be better for Cicely to get right away from Pennyhill and the doctor thought so too. She sold Raybould's car and bought a second-hand station wagon that had already been adapted for a wheelchair.

She found a bungalow, about thirty miles from here. There'd been an invalid lady living there at one time; it was quite suitable. And it had a good big piece of ground – I think that was what really decided her. She knew she wouldn't have much freedom any more, not if Cicely didn't get a great deal better, but at least she'd have the bit of land. She could always get outside when she wanted to. And she could grow what fruit and vegetables they needed; it would all help with the living expenses.'

She gestured towards a glass-fronted cabinet. 'That pair of Dresden figurines on the top shelf, Hilda gave me those the day they left, to remember them all by. They'd belonged to her mother, and before that, to her grandmother.'

She fell silent for a moment. 'The way she spoke, the way she looked at me, I knew in my heart I was never going to see or hear from her again. I could understand how she felt.' She looked across at Lambert. 'But I would just have liked to know how it all turned out, if Cicely ever did get better.'

Sunday morning was well advanced by the time Lambert woke from a wonderfully deep and soothing sleep. He found himself, to his astonishment, with clear eyes and no trace of a headache.

And Mrs Osgood was as calm eyed and composed as ever when he came downstairs. She greeted him in a manner markedly more friendly than the one she had employed when she first surveyed him on her doorstep. She wasn't in the least surprised to learn he had slept soundly and woken refreshed, she well knew the virtues of her wine. She was sure his appetite wouldn't have suffered; she had cooked him a substantial breakfast. And she was quite right; he was able to do it full justice.

As soon as she had cleared the breakfast things she set about making herself ready to attend morning service in the next village; a friend was giving her a lift.

When Lambert left she came out of the house with him and locked the door behind her. She halted outside the gate, on the watch for her friend. She looked even more like a royal dowager in her loose summer coat, a flowery hat set squarely on her gleaming coils of hair.

Lambert thanked her for her exceptional hospitality. A smile lit up her broad, tranquil features. 'I haven't enjoyed such a nice long chat since that girl was here, back in May.'

'Girl?' Lambert echoed.

'She came along here one afternoon. She'd been looking round the churchyard and got sent here, the same as you. Nice little thing, she was. Pretty enough, too, for all she had her hair cut like a lad. She wanted to know all about Blanche Kinnaird. Beautiful sunny afternoon; we had tea out in the garden. Afterwards I showed her my scrapbook and album.'

A car turned into the road. She stepped forward and raised a hand. She turned back for a moment to Lambert and gave him a warm smile. 'I hope the weather keeps up for the rest of your holiday. Any time you're this way again, be sure to look me up; I can always find you a bed for the night. Next time you must try my parsnip wine.'

The remainder of Sunday passed in luxurious idleness. But Sunday night passed less restfully; he was seized more than once with a fit of coughing. He woke early, conscious of a return of the ache in his limbs. He could hear no sound from the Inskips.

He switched on his bedside light and got silently out of bed. He found a pen and paper, the envelope Simon Norbury had given him. He got back into bed and propped himself up against the pillows. He spent some time scrutinizing the jottings on the back of the envelope, puzzling over them, interpreting them this way and that. He wrote out several different versions before deciding on his final rendering:

Repairs/extension/phone/garden, etc., say £45–£50,000.
Increase some monthly amounts? Lang, Mgt & H/V? Or Lang, H.J. & H/V?
Or increase all monthly amounts?
Or a one-off extra all round?

Underneath this were two small addition sums, with some of the figures crossed out. He read them as:

Mgt	4	4
Lang	1̶0̶	11
W/Y	9̶	10
H/V	8̶	10
Frs	6	6
H.J.	8̶	9
	—	—
	45	50

Underneath the sums, more scribblings which he made out with equal difficulty:

Why not both? Increase monthly amounts all round, plus a smaller one-off extra all round:

Mgt	4
Lang	8
W/Y	8
H/V	8
Frs	4
H.J.	8
	—
	40

Below that, three words he made out as:

Best do both.

A large blue-ink tick had been dashed down beside the three words. The words and the tick had been heavily ringed in blue. And beneath all that, one remaining scribble that took even longer to make anything of. He finally deciphered it as:

But not just yet!!!!

The four exclamation marks had been jabbed down with force.

His next task was to write out on a fresh sheet of paper a fair copy of his final version of all the jottings. When this was done he folded the paper and slipped it inside the envelope, beside the letter signed H.J.

He felt his eyelids begin to droop. He put the envelope on the bedside table and switched out the light. Within a couple of minutes he was asleep again.

It was broad daylight when next he woke. Sunlight streamed in round the edges of the curtains. He knew the moment he opened his eyes how he was going to spend the morning: in the Yelmerton reference library, searching through phone books, directories, Yellow Pages. He knew precisely how tedious and time-consuming the chore would be, but he was in the mood for it and that was always more than half the battle.

It was not far off ten o'clock by the time he drove into the outskirts of Yelmerton. It was possible that on market days the little town might spring into noisy bustle, but at this time on a Monday morning there were few citizens to be seen.

In the long, wide, main street a central war memorial stood flanked on either side by a bronze statue. A seated Queen Victoria, heavy faced and unsmiling, brooding over the cares of Empire. And a local worthy standing erect and fearless, one hand behind his back, the other pointing forward, presumably to the future; his name and face conveyed nothing to Lambert. He made his way past an ancient market hall, converted into a tourist information bureau, to the public library.

There was no one in the reference room. He settled himself down at a table beside the shelves of phone books and directories. He took out his final version of the envelope jottings and studied it again. Lang, he decided. I'll begin with that. And I'll start with the phone books.

It took him only a few minutes to realize that as far as Lang was concerned he was wasting his time. Apart from the name Lang itself, the first phone book he consulted disclosed two full pages of names starting with Lang – and he had no means of knowing if any of the jottings were indeed abbreviations of surnames, or referred to people at all. Right then. He could forget Lang for the moment.

He considered the other abbreviations. Assuming that H.J. stood for Hilda Jerrom – a totally unwarranted assumption, he reminded himself – then what of the other four?

The first of these suggested the name Margaret – not much to go on. The next abbreviation appeared once only but that once was clearly written; he had never been able to read it any other way than W/Y. The next abbreviation had presented more difficulty. He had earlier decided that it read H/V but it seemed to him now that it might equally be made out as H/U. It's possible, he mused, that these last two abbreviations might stand for hyphenated surnames. That, at any rate, was the assumption he would work on, and it was with this pair that he would start again – for lack of any better inspiration. The remaining abbreviation Frs, suggested nothing at all to him.

He set about his task again. He went systematically through the county phone books, starting with the local book, then widening out in a circle round Yelmerton, further and further afield.

At the end of fifty wearisome minutes he had found only one

name in the W/Y category and none at all in either the H/V or the H/U.

He was beginning to flag, to ask himself what on earth he was doing all this for. He abandoned the phone books and made a half-hearted start on the trade directories. Fifteen minutes later he had come across not a single relevant name.

What was left of his patience and perseverance suddenly evaporated. That's it, he decided abruptly. He couldn't face any more today – and he harboured a shrewd suspicion that he wouldn't be able to force himself back to the chore on any future day, either. It was scarcely a holiday task; it bore far too strong a resemblance to some of the more tedious slog of everyday police work.

At least his endeavours had produced one name, for what it was worth: Mrs F. Wynn-Yeatman, and an address in a smallish town some distance away.

It was almost noon by the time he located Mrs Wynn-Yeatman's house in a high-class residential suburb. A substantial, detached, Edwardian villa, set back from a tree-lined road. An estate agent's board proclaimed that the property was for sale.

He left his car parked outside the entrance gates and walked up the long, well-kept drive. The gardens were carefully tended, with nowhere any sign of neglect. But he knew before he reached the front door that he would find the house empty; there hung about the place the silent, deserted air that soon envelops any unoccupied dwelling.

He rang and knocked at the front door. He went round to the back door, then to a side door, rang and knocked again. All without result. He made his way down the drive again to the gate.

Some distance away, at the other side of the road, he spied a milk float. He set off towards it. The milkman came out of a driveway a few moments after Lambert halted by the vehicle. He flicked an inquiring look at Lambert as he refilled his crate.

'I'm trying to get in touch with Mrs Wynn-Yeatman,' Lambert explained. 'I see the house is up for sale. Do you happen to know where I could find her?'

The milkman ran a shrewd, assessing eye over him. When he seemed satisfied that Lambert wasn't up to any mischief he answered good-naturedly enough.

'She went into a nursing home back in the spring. She's not been well for a year or two; she was very poorly all last winter. I understand she's decided to stop where she is.' No, he didn't know the name of the nursing home. But he could and did tell Lambert where he might find Mrs Venables, the daily woman who had worked at the house for a good many years. 'I'm sure she'll be able to tell you where Mrs Wynn-Yeatman is now,' he added. 'The house was put up for sale a couple of weeks back.' He pursed his lips. 'Best thing, in my opinion. She's knocking on now. Not a good idea, living in that big house, all alone, at her age. The only family she's got left is that grandson and I understand he's out in Canada now – he's had more sense than to try coming back here to live.' He gave a brief laugh. 'Not many local folk would have welcomed that young gentleman living here. He's only a stepgrandson at that – she was the second wife.' He blew out a breath. 'She's much better off in a nursing home. She's never been the same since all the upset over the accident. It's some years ago now, of course, but her husband died not long afterwards. Coming so soon on top of the other trouble, it fairly took it out of her.'

'How long ago would you say it was?' Lambert asked with an air of easy interest.

'I've no trouble remembering that,' the milkman responded with a grin. 'It was when our first child was born. I remember, clear as anything, the first I heard of the accident. It was on the local radio, on the eight o'clock news, when I was driving my wife to the hospital on the Saturday morning. Seven years ago last November 28th, the day my son was born. There was a piece about the accident in the evening paper and a lot more in the local paper the next week.' He grimaced. 'Rotten business. And they never did get to the bottom of it, which made it even worse. There were never any charges brought. A lot of folk round here were positive young Martin – the Wynn-Yeatman lad – was mixed up in it and there'd been a cover-up, the Wynn-Yeatmans being who they were. He'd been a big employer in the town till he sold up when he retired.' He narrowed his eyes. 'There are plenty of local folk think that to this day; it's never been forgotten in these parts. They say a working-class lad would never have got away with it.' He pointed up the road. 'You should hear the newsagent along there on the subject when he gets going.'

'What's your own opinion?' Lambert asked.

He gave another short laugh. 'It never paid me to have an opinion one way or the other, all these years. The Wynn-Yeatmans were always good customers of mine. But that's over now. I can say what I choose.' He moved his shoulders. 'The truth of it is, I don't really have any rock-solid opinion. I don't know the real facts, any more than the rest of the folk round here. I only know what I heard at the time, what I read in the papers.' He slanted an eye at Lambert. 'Mr Wynn-Yeatman was a magistrate for donkey's years, till he took ill with Parkinson's disease after he retired. And his wife did a lot of good work in the town, in her day. They were always at all these posh functions; you were forever seeing their photo in the paper with all these high-ups – top police brass, as well.' He pulled down the corners of his mouth. 'Stands to reason that sort of contact can't do any harm when the chips are down.'

He glanced at his watch. 'I've got to be getting on. You pop along and have a word with Mrs Venables. She'll be able to tell you which nursing home it is. But what sort of state Mrs Wynn-Yeatman is in now, whether they'll let you see her or not, that could be another matter.'

Lambert didn't immediately call on Mrs Venables but drove instead to the town centre in search of the offices of the local newspaper. In a very short time he was poring over the issues for December, seven years ago. The accident the milkman had referred to had been given considerable coverage.

A young man by the name of Abbott, twenty-one years old, an assistant in a sports goods shop in the town, had been cycling home from work that Friday evening; he lived with his widowed mother in a cottage a mile or two outside the town. The evening was dark but dry. As he rounded a bend in the country lane he was struck from the rear by some vehicle which failed to stop; there were no witnesses. The time of the accident was clearly established from Abbott's wristwatch which stopped when he hit the ground; it showed 6.22.

Another motorist arriving on the scene a few minutes later had summoned help. Abbott was taken to hospital unconscious; he had suffered several fractures and lacerations.

Later that same evening, at around 10.45, a man walking his dog a couple of miles away came upon the newly burned-out

114

wreck of a car in an area of scrubland; he immediately contacted the police. Tests the following day showed the car to be one stolen the previous evening from a driveway in a residential suburb of the town. The owner had become aware of the theft at around ten o'clock and had at once reported it to the police but the theft could have taken place at any time in the previous four hours. Over the next day or two, further tests on the slivers of paint and fragments of headlamp glass recovered from the scene of the accident indicated that the car involved was of the same make and year as the stolen car but could not show – or be expected to show – that it was the identical vehicle.

Two days after the accident Abbott regained consciousness but had no recollection at all of what had happened.

Police later disclosed that a youth had been interviewed in connection with both the theft and the accident but no charges had been made against him.

It was almost one o'clock when Lambert left the newspaper offices. He decided to give Mrs Venables time to eat her lunch before turning up on her doorstep; it might gain him a better reception. In the meantime he could try for a word with the newsagent the milkman had mentioned; his shop might stay open during the lunch hour.

And he did find the shop open, with a solitary customer inside, being served by a female assistant. When the customer had departed Lambert asked the assistant if he might speak to the newsagent. The assistant went through to the rear quarters and returned with the owner, a sharp-looking man in his fifties. Lambert apologized for disturbing him. He disclosed his identity and returned to the events of that Friday night over seven years ago, indicating that they might have some bearing on a case he was currently dealing with. He would greatly appreciate the opportunity to hear the newsagent's recollection of the affair.

The newsagent was very ready to oblige. 'Come through to the back,' he invited. He took Lambert into a small office opening off a stockroom. He sat the sergeant down and made coffee as they talked.

His memory of the matter was very clear and it was plain that it was still a sore point with him. He didn't ask in what way those distant events might relate to the case now engaging Lambert nor did he inquire what had brought Lambert into his shop. He seemed only too eager to unburden himself of a long-nursed sense of dissatisfaction with the outcome – or lack of outcome – of the whole unfortunate business.

He didn't live over the shop but in a residential area a few minutes' drive away. A regular customer who lived in the next avenue to him had come into his shop as usual that Saturday morning for his newspaper and cigarettes. He had mentioned with a good deal of annoyance that a car had been taken from his driveway the previous evening. It wasn't his own car but belonged to a colleague, recently appointed, new to the area, whom he'd invited home for supper and to spend the evening. The colleague had parked his car in the drive at around six. When he said goodnight some four hours later he found the car had gone.

The moment the newsagent heard the customer's story he recalled an incident that had occurred the previous evening outside his own house. He had left the shop shortly after 5.30 to visit a friend in hospital. He had called in at his home on the way. He hadn't bothered to garage his car as he intended stopping only long enough to wash and shave; he left the car standing in the road, by the gate.

As he was about to leave his bedroom on his way downstairs again, he chanced to glance out and caught sight of a lad by the car, tinkering with the lock of the driver's door. He at once flung open the bedroom window and called out. He ran swiftly downstairs but by the time he had thrown open the front door and reached the car the youngster had vanished.

'I was pretty certain I'd recognized him,' he maintained. 'It was Martin Wynn-Yeatman. His grandparents were customers of mine. He was home from his boarding school for the week-end; he'd be rising fourteen at the time. He often came into the shop when he was home on holiday. I made a point of keeping an eye on him; he always struck me as a boy that needed watching, though I never actually caught him out in any thieving.

'As soon as I heard about the theft of the car I got on to the police and told them about the lad I'd seen monkeying with my own car. I didn't know anything about young Abbott's accident or the car that had been set on fire. The police told me about them when they came round – which they did right away. By that time they'd got the chassis number of the burned-out car; they knew it was the car stolen from the driveway. They wanted to know why I was so sure it was Martin Wynn-Yeatman I'd seen when I'd only caught a glimpse of the youngster, and it was a dark evening. Was there something distinctive about his appearance?' He pulled down the corners of his mouth. 'I had to admit, there wasn't but the lad had looked up at me when I called out; I'd got a good squint at him under the streetlights. I described the jacket he was wearing – the jacket I'd seen him wearing earlier that day. But they didn't think much of that; they said every second teenager in the town had a jacket of that sort. Had I seen which way the lad had run off? No, I hadn't. So he could have run straight home – wherever that might be – for all I knew. There wasn't a shred of evidence that the lad tinkering with my car was the person who had stolen the other car.

'They did go round to the Wynn-Yeatmans'. They didn't speak to the old man, of course, he was in a bad way by then; he died not long afterwards. They spoke to Mrs Wynn-Yeatman and Martin, and to a nurse that was living in the house at the time, looking after the old man. All three of them told the same tale: Martin was in the house the whole of Friday evening. The three of them had had supper together at half past six. Martin had helped prepare the meal and wash up afterwards; they'd all watched TV.' He grimaced. 'So that was that. There wasn't a scrap of evidence against Martin. He went back to his boarding school on the Sunday evening.' He jerked his head. 'I'd have given a lot to have a go at him myself. I was sure I could have got the truth out of him but I never got the chance. He never set foot in the shop after that; I never laid eyes on him again. The Wynn-Yeatmans cancelled their order with me and took their custom elsewhere.'

'What happened to young Abbott?' Lambert asked.

'He made a pretty good recovery and got on with his life.' He shook his head slowly. 'I never changed my opinion. I believe to this day that the lad I saw was Martin. I believe he stole the car. I believe he ran young Abbott down, going too fast in a car he couldn't handle. I can understand Mrs Wynn-Yeatman being ready to perjure herself for the sake of the family and of course it was no more than you'd expect for the lad to lie his head off, but the nurse . . .' He shook his head again. 'It was her evidence swung it in the lad's favour, the police couldn't go against that.' He moved his shoulders. 'She'd been staying in the house some time; I dare say she'd got pally with them all. And who knows?' He rubbed his fingers together in a significant gesture. 'Could be some money changed hands. The Wynn-Yeatmans were pretty well heeled; Mrs Wynn-Yeatman could afford to square the nurse handsomely.' He slanted a shrewd look at Lambert. 'I'll wager Mrs Wynn-Yeatman's chequebook could tell a tale if it could talk.'

After a snack lunch eaten in a lay-by Lambert set off to locate the address the milkman had given him for Mrs Venables. It took him to a neat terrace house in immaculate order. He had timed his call well; Mrs Venables had just finished clearing her lunch things and was about to sit down with her knitting in front of the TV.

Lambert apologized for disturbing her and explained that he was anxious to contact Mrs Wynn-Yeatman. He had been round to the house and had learned from the milkman he had encountered nearby that the good lady was now in a nursing home.

'That's right,' Mrs Venables confirmed. She was a motherly-looking woman, sixty or so, with a friendly smile. She mentioned the address of the nursing home. 'But you won't find her there just now,' she added. She was at the seaside, in another home belonging to the same group, used for convalescence and holidays by all the homes in the group. 'I expect you saw the house is up for sale,' she went on. 'I go along there every morning to open the windows and dust round, keep an eye on the place. The gardener sees the grass is cut and the beds and borders are tidy. We're both being kept on till the house is sold.' She sighed. 'It'll seem strange not working there any more. I've worked there ever since I was widowed – twenty-five years it is now. Mrs Wynn-Yeatman's always been very good to me. I'd never hear a word said against her, no matter what some folk –' She broke off abruptly.

'You mean that business over the accident to young Abbott a few years back?' Lambert said.

She gave him a quick glance. 'You know about that?' He nodded.

Her tone grew confidential. 'It was really awful at the time, very distressing. Mrs Wynn-Yeatman was terribly upset, especially with her poor husband being so ill.' She paused and gave him an interrogative look. 'If you're not in a hurry, could I offer you a cup of tea?'

'That's very kind of you,' he responded heartily. 'I'd be very glad of one.'

She took him into the spotless kitchen and sat him down. 'It's wicked the way gossip and rumour can affect innocent lives,' she said as she set about making the tea. 'Martin wasn't exactly an angel, he'd been in quite a few scrapes in his time, but he'd never get up to anything really criminal like stealing a car, knocking a cyclist down and then clearing off and setting the car on fire. I admit the Wynn-Yeatmans had rather spoiled him but it was natural enough in the circumstances. His parents were killed in an avalanche when they were skiing in Switzerland. Martin was only ten at the time. He accompanied them on holiday but he wasn't out skiing with them, he was too young. He was with the other youngsters from the hotel, having a skiing lesson.' She poured the tea. 'It was a dreadful blow for the Wynn-Yeatmans, Martin's father was the only child. Mr Wynn-Yeatman was retired by then. He'd already got this Parkinson's disease but it was still in the early stages.

'They sent Martin to a boarding school quite near here, an easy-going, understanding sort of place; they didn't want anything too strict – things were hard enough for him, losing his parents like that. He was pretty disturbed for some time; he could be very difficult.' She pulled herself up sharply. 'Not that he'd ever do anything really wrong. Mrs Wynn-Yeatman was always very good to him, very kind. She was terribly upset when the police came about the car accident. She was never one to cry, she was always a strong woman, but she looked dreadful, not eating anything, and I was sure she wasn't sleeping.

'The police came back again, a few days later. They spent quite a time talking to Mrs Wynn-Yeatman and Nurse Hammond. They wanted to go over to the school to talk to Martin again but Mrs Wynn-Yeatman wouldn't have that. She rang the school and had Martin come over here. The police talked to him with her in the room. Of course it never came to anything – how could it? Martin hadn't done anything. In the end of course they had to drop it, but not before it worried the life out of Mrs Wynn-Yeatman. She went to skin and bone over it.'

'How did Martin get on afterwards?' Lambert asked.

'Very well,' she told him with a smile. 'He was due to move on to another school so Mrs Wynn-Yeatman decided to send him to one up in the Lake District, one that went in for the outdoor life, climbing, sailing, all that sort of thing. It was a lot stricter than the other school and it suited him very well. She used to go up there to see him. He didn't come here any more – she thought that best, with there being some feeling locally. Very unfair, but there it was. I always asked her about him and she always told me how he was getting on, and she used to show me photographs. He went to camps and on trips abroad in the holidays, he enjoyed that. When he left school he went out to Canada, to some cousins of Mr Wynn-Yeatman; he went to college there. He's just about finishing at college now. I believe he's going into some family business out there. They're all very pleased with him.'

She sighed. 'The worst thing about that car business was it happened when Mr Wynn-Yeatman was pretty near the end of his life. Mrs Wynn-Yeatman was that devoted to him, she'd do anything not to make his last days any worse than they had to be. Of course she had Nurse Hammond here, she was a godsend. She stayed on till after the funeral.' She poured more tea. 'It brought it all back to me when a young lady called here, a couple of months back, asking for Nurse Hammond.'

'Oh?' Lambert encouraged her.

She nodded. 'Yes, it was quite a surprise. I'd never had anyone calling before, asking for Nurse Hammond, not in seven years. She said she'd known Nurse Hammond years ago, she was a friend of the family, and she needed to get in touch with her again over some family business that had come up. She knew she'd worked for Mrs Wynn-Yeatman for some months at one time. It was a bit of a long shot but she thought she might have kept in touch. I had to tell her I was sorry, I couldn't help her, I'd no idea where Nurse Hammond was now. I'd never had any contact with her after she left.' She smiled. 'She was a very pleasant young woman. She came in and sat down; I made her a cup of tea. We had a nice long chat.'

'And this was quite recently?' Lambert asked casually.

'I can tell you exactly when it was,' she responded with energy. 'I'd just come in when she rang the bell. I'd been up to the churchyard, taking flowers to put on my mother's grave. May 22nd, it was, my mother's birthday.'

She came to the door with Lambert when he left. 'You can try at the nursing home for Mrs Wynn-Yeatman in another week or two,' she said. 'She should be back by then. I should think she'll be feeling a lot better, she's had a good long spell by the sea; she's been there since the end of April.'

Lambert decided to spend the rest of the afternoon relaxing; there was a stately home over this way he'd never got around to visiting. He still hadn't bought his holiday presents and he should be able to find something suitable over there; there was sure to be a souvenir shop.

He set off in a determined holiday mood. When he arrived at the stately home he tacked himself onto a guided tour of the house. He took tea in the orangery, strolled beside the lake. He had no difficulty in finding an offering for his Cannonbridge landlady and another for Mrs Inskip, to be handed over at the end of his stay, as a mark of appreciation.

All in all, he concluded as he got back into his car again, it had been an agreeable afternoon, even though the wandering aches and pains had returned intermittently to plague him. As he put the gifts away in the glove compartment it occurred to him that he had forgotten all about the jigsaw puzzle he'd meant to drop in at Greenfield this morning. He made a mental note not to forget it again tomorrow morning.

Before he went to bed he took a long hot bath, to dispel his aches and pains. He lay immersed in the steaming water, letting his mind range idly about. At some point a memory of Iris, the Calcott House waitress, floated up before him: Iris, with her frizzed hair and vermilion lips, patting the sofa beside her. Olive Hammond was born on a council estate, Iris had said. By dint of concentrating his mind he succeeded a few moments later in dredging up the name of the town.

He might do worse than pop over there tomorrow morning, see if he could come up with anything. And tomorrow was the first day of an agricultural show being held in that area; he could spend the afternoon there. It was years since he'd been to an agricultural show, he'd always enjoyed them as a lad.

121

Tuesday dawned markedly cooler. The radio spoke of showers and sunny intervals. As Lambert shaved he was seized by a sharp fit of sneezing. He felt the treacherous ache start up again in his bones. He took an extra supply of handkerchiefs with him when he set out after breakfast. And he remembered also to take the jigsaw puzzle.

He had been driving for no more than a couple of minutes when he was again convulsed by an attack of sneezing. He was forced to pull up and let the paroxysm take its course. At last he was able to blow his nose, mop his streaming eyes and set off again.

Today there was no sign of Cicely on the Greenfield verandah but Hilda was busy in the front garden. She was stooping, trowel in hand, over a bed of giant pansies in brilliant colours. She straightened up at the approach of the car and stood watching, her bony features calm and impassive, as Lambert pulled up onto the grass verge and got out.

He reached back into the car for the jigsaw puzzle in its bright wrapping. Hilda's eyes came to rest on the parcel; her expression remained inscrutable.

Lambert pushed open the gate and walked up the path. He stopped by the bed of pansies. Hilda spoke not a word but continued to regard him.

'I just stopped by for a moment,' he began with some hesitation, seeing her marked lack of welcome. 'I hope you won't think it a liberty on my part but I brought this for your sister.' He held out the parcel. She made no move to take it. 'I saw it in a craft shop the other day,' he went on awkwardly. 'I thought your sister might like it.' She made no response. 'It's a jigsaw puzzle, the pieces are big. It would be much easier for her than the one she was trying to do the other day.' Still she said nothing.

All at once what had seemed to him until this moment a perfectly straightforward, innocuous action appeared now in a totally different light: patronizing, condescending. 'I meant no offence,' he concluded lamely. 'I hoped it might give your sister some pleasure.' He kept the parcel extended.

Hilda's face suddenly broke into a smile. 'No offence taken,' she assured him warmly. She stooped and set down her trowel, rubbed her hands clean against the stuff of her jeans.

She reached out for the parcel. 'It's so beautifully wrapped.' She peered down at the nursery-rhyme characters. 'Such pretty paper, full of interest. Cicely will spend hours just looking at the paper; it'll be one of her great treasures. And the lovely pink bow.' She looked up at him. 'It was very kind of you to think of her.'

He felt immensely relieved. 'I do hope she likes it,' he said as he turned back towards the gate.

'You're not going?' Hilda cried out after him. He halted. 'Do come in and give it to her yourself,' she urged. 'She'll be dreadfully disappointed if you don't. She'll never forgive me if I let you go.'

He hesitated. 'I wouldn't want to intrude, to take up your time. I know you must have a great deal to do.'

She brushed aside his scruples with an impatient gesture. 'Do come along inside. Cicely's in the sitting room; she's trying to knit.' She moved her shoulders. 'Poor darling, she does her best. She tries to knit those diamond shapes for charity – you sew them together to make into blankets for Third World countries.'

She began to walk towards the house and he fell in beside her. 'I usually have to pull the wool back and knit them up all over again,' she said lightly. 'Without her knowing, of course, she'd be terribly upset if she had any idea. We pick up a box of wool oddments at the Oxfam shop in Yelmerton – people hand them in there, for knitting up. We take the blanket back there when it's finished.' She laughed. 'It takes us a long time to finish one but we get there in the end. I like to think it gives Cicely some sense of purpose, some notion of a wider world away from Bowpatch.'

They went up the verandah steps and in through the front door. She handed Lambert back his parcel as they came into the hall. She crossed to the sitting-room door which stood open and put her head round it.

123

'You'll never guess who's here,' she called out in a voice of tender affection. 'A visitor to see you. Bringing a present, too.' She stood back, smiling at Lambert, gesturing him inside.

The sitting room was bright and spacious. Cicely was seated in her wheelchair beside a table spread with her things. On a tea trolley nearby other possessions were ranged: a pottery mug holding coloured pencils, a drawing book, a box of crayons, children's books and puzzles, an old Victorian jewel box. She was struggling with a pair of thick knitting pins from which depended a few inches of uneven, lumpy work.

Lambert went towards her, holding out the parcel. 'I brought you this. I saw it in a shop the other day; I thought you might like it.'

Her eyes sparkled with excitement. She put down her knitting and took the parcel. She made no attempt to open it but began to peer closely at the paper with its nursery drawings. She ran her finger caressingly over the pink satin bow.

Hilda advanced a little way into the room and stood smiling at the scene with shared enjoyment. Still Cicely showed no inclination to unwrap the parcel. 'Don't you want to know what's inside?' Hilda moved forward. 'Would you like me to help you open it? We'll be very careful with the paper, we won't cut or tear it, then you can keep it and look at it whenever you want.'

Cicely relinquished the parcel and Hilda began to undo the bow. She rolled up the satin ribbon and set it down on the trolley. When the jigsaw puzzle finally came into view she exclaimed with pleasure 'How lovely!' She looked up at Lambert. 'This is no ordinary puzzle, it's a work of art.'

Cicely clasped her hands in delight and drew a long quavering breath. She didn't try to take the puzzle to pieces but sat stroking the silky surface of the wood with feathery touches, the head, the body, the bushy tail, lingering over the tiny nut held between the paws.

'The work is so very fine,' Hilda said with deep appreciation. 'Cicely does love small things that are beautifully made.'

'She should be able to take it apart and put it together again on her own,' Lambert said.

Hilda turned towards the door. 'I'm going to make a hot drink,' she told Lambert. 'I'm sure you'd like one. It's not all that warm today.'

124

Lambert raised a protesting hand. 'Please don't bother on my account. I'm on my way. I've taken up enough of your time.'

Cicely stared up at him with disappointment written large on her features; she looked as if she might burst into tears.

'Do stay, just for a few minutes,' Hilda pressed him.

He could scarcely refuse. 'Very well,' he agreed. 'I would like to, thank you.'

As Hilda moved off again Lambert was abruptly seized by another violent fit of sneezing. He whipped a folded handkerchief from his trouser pocket and shook it out. He saw a small coin, a bright new penny piece, caught up in the folds of the handkerchief, describe an arc through the air, glinting like gold. It landed on the carpet close by Cicely's chair.

In an instant she had reached down, the coin had vanished into her fingers. Her face wore a look of joyous childish mischief. With equal speed she raised the lid of the Victorian jewel box. A moment later she was sitting upright again, both hands displayed palm upwards, fingers artlessly open, her expression one of guileless innocence.

Hilda halted on her path to the door. She had seen nothing of the little incident. She turned and watched as Lambert continued to explode into his handkerchief. 'Have you caught a cold?' she asked with concern when the outburst had at last subsided.

Lambert apologized, dabbing at his eyes. 'It's not a cold,' he told her. 'I would never have come inside the house with a cold; I wouldn't have risked giving it to either of you.' He explained about the virus of a couple of months back, the sneaky fashion in which it had appeared to accept defeat but had merely lain doggo for a while, rearing its head again at unpredictable intervals.

'I know the very thing to deal with that,' Hilda assured him with conviction. 'Another of my mother's recipes; it never fails. I'll make you some now; it won't take a moment.' She went swiftly off towards the kitchen. Lambert stood looking down at Cicely who had by now taken the squirrel apart and was busy putting it together again, happy and absorbed.

Hilda came back with a tray holding steaming mugs. 'I thought we might as well all have some, while we're about it,' she said lightly. 'I've made yours stronger than ours. Drink it down while it's hot, it does more good that way.'

125

Lambert raised the mug to his lips. It had an agreeable herbal aroma with an overlay of lemon. It tasted like nectar. 'I wish all medicines were like this,' he said.

Hilda looked pleased. 'All the herbs are home-grown, of course; we try to be as self-sufficient as possible. Hyssop, elderflower, coltsfoot, yarrow, horehound. And honey and lemon. If it doesn't cure you, at least it won't do you any harm. But I think you'll find it will do the trick. I'll put some up in a packet for you, enough for tonight and another two days.' She gave him directions for making the potion. A good job the Chief's not here, Lambert thought. He'd be begging her for the rest of her mother's remedies, scribbling them down as fast as he could.

The place where Olive Hammond had spent her youth was an unprepossessing, workaday town of no great size. It appeared prosperous enough; citizens made their way about the streets with an air of purpose. Few signs of vandalism, scarcely any litter.

Lambert stopped at the first newsagent's and bought a paper. A brief conversation with the owner supplied him with the location of the council estate answering the description Iris had given him; another few minutes took him to the estate, on the outskirts of town.

The sun was breaking through as Lambert parked his car. He got out and looked around. The greater part of the estate was clearly now in private hands. Wherever there was space, garages and extensions had been built, porches added, conservatories tacked on, patios laid out, roof spaces turned into attic bedrooms. Scarcely a single original window remained, almost every dwelling sported its bows and bays, its bull's-eye panes. Trellises and rustic arches, awnings and canopies, reproduction front doors of every architectural period.

After some minutes of feasting his eyes on these remarkable transformations Lambert set about finding the house where Olive Hammond had lived as a girl. He spotted an old, hump-backed woman, still brisk of step and bright of eye, returning from the shops with a bulging carrier bag.

Yes, she did know of a Hammond family. There were none of them left on the estate now and the house where they had lived was currently standing empty. A postman by the name of

Cutler lived in the house next door; he had lived there all his life. 'He'll be able to tell you anything you want to know about the Hammonds,' she declared with certainty. 'Or about anyone else round here, for that matter.'

Lambert found the house without difficulty. Cutler was at work in his back garden but he broke off readily enough. He was a vigorous-looking man with a cheerful, friendly face; he listened to what Lambert had to say with good-natured interest. 'I don't know about you,' he said amiably when Lambert had finished, 'but I could do with a cup of tea. You'd better come indoors while we talk.' He explained as they walked to the back door that he was currently taking some of his annual leave to do the garden and decorate a bedroom. He was a widower, living alone.

He settled Lambert down in the sitting room and went along to the kitchen to put the kettle on. 'You're not the first person to come looking for Olive Hammond recently,' he told Lambert when he returned with a tray. 'There was a girl called here one Sunday a couple of months back.' He poured the tea. 'Pretty-looking girl, hair cut like a lad. Very interested in life round here, all the changes there've been. She asked me no end of questions.'

He handed Lambert his tea and took his seat opposite him. 'Well now, you want to know about the Hammonds and where Olive might be these days. I can tell you right off what I told the young lady: I don't know where Olive is, but I'll tell you what I do know. It may give you a few pointers, show you where you might start looking.' He didn't ask why Lambert wanted to find Olive and Lambert volunteered no explanation.

'Olive used to be the district nurse here, years ago,' Cutler said. 'She left here around twenty-five years ago, to go into agency nursing. She came back sometimes, to see her parents.' He didn't know of any other relatives; Olive had been an only child. He'd last seen her at her mother's funeral, nine or ten years ago; her father had died some time before that. He'd had a word with her after the funeral. 'She told me she'd taken up private nursing; she liked it better than agency work.' He looked reflective. 'There's been a lot of changes here since she was the district nurse. It used to be all fields and open country past here at one time. That was before all the development, before old Langstaff died.'

Lambert had his cup at his lips; he was about to take a sip. A bell rang sharply in his brain. He set down his cup. 'Langstaff?' he echoed. Among the scribbled envelope jottings the abbreviation he had made out as Lang rose up before him.

CHAPTER 19

'Old Bert Langstaff,' Cutler enlarged. 'If you know this part of the county you've more than likely seen the name: Langstaff's Stores – they're grocers, in every town round here. It's old Bert's nephew owns the stores, Arthur Langstaff. Old Bert died twenty-five years ago and his cottage – and the land that went with it – was sold to the sand and gravel company. That was the start of all the changes round here, the start of Arthur Langstaff's fortune, too.'

He drank his tea. 'It was Olive Hammond nursed old Bert at the end. It was soon after Bert died that Olive left here and went into agency nursing.'

He smiled. 'Real character, old Bert. He had a horse and cart. He did a greengrocery round, went out to all the villages. I used to help him on the round when I was a lad. He lived a couple of miles from here, a tiny little hamlet it was then. Now it's all built over, developed; the hamlet's swallowed up.

'Bert's cottage isn't there any more. The sand and gravel company pulled it down when they bought the place; it was the land they were after. It was a fair-sized piece of ground; it stood in between two halves of their workings. They'd been trying to get hold of it for years. They kept upping the price but old Bert would never sell, whatever they offered.

'Bert had a brother, a lot younger. They'd never got on. The brother lived here, on the estate. He was married with a son, Arthur. The brother was killed in the war. His widow married again after Arthur was grown up; she went away to live with her husband, somewhere down south. Arthur moved into digs here on the estate. He worked as a counterhand in a high-class grocer's in the town. Quiet chap, well spoken, always smartly dressed, very good manners, always gave me good day if I met him in the street.

'He was old Bert's only living blood relative but Bert had

never had anything to do with him. Bert had been married himself at one time. He never had any children. His wife died when she was middle-aged. She had a younger sister; the sister's husband was a gardener in the local park. I never liked either of them, a very grabby couple. Far too fond of the drink, both of them. Any spare cash they had they'd be down at the pub or in a club, boozing.

'They had an eye on Bert's property and they started making up to him, inviting him over for Sunday dinner, remembering his birthday, making a fuss of him, all sorts of soft soap.

'Bert usually kept fit enough but when he was turned sixty he had a nasty go of bronchitis two winters running; it really pulled him down. Then his horse went and died. He was that fond of the animal, it just about put the tin lid on it. He wouldn't get another horse, so of course that meant giving up the round; his heart had gone right out of it. He just stayed at the cottage all day, pottering about. I always made a point of stopping by for a word, for old times' sake. I could see him going downhill.

'The New Year's Eve before Bert died I was up at the Legion. Bert's sister-in-law and her husband were there, knocking back the drinks. They started talking to me about old Bert, how he'd told them he was leaving them the property, he was so grateful for all they were doing for him. I paid no heed. Just the drink talking, I thought.

'A few months later I stopped by Bert's cottage as usual one morning but I couldn't see him anywhere about. I couldn't make him hear though I could hear his dog barking inside – fairly going mad, the dog was, knowing I was outside. I looked in through the window and there was Bert, lying on the kitchen floor, with the dog standing over him, barking his head off.

'I got the doctor and Bert was taken to hospital. It was a stroke. And a bad one, too, they told me when I called in at the hospital that afternoon. He wasn't likely to live long.

'I got to thinking about what the in-laws had said on New Year's Eve; I thought maybe there might be something in it, after all. So I made it my business to go round to see Arthur right away, tell him what had happened to his uncle – and what might happen to his uncle's property. Arthur didn't need telling twice. He got leave from work and took old Bert back home to his cottage. He moved in there himself. He looked after Bert till he died three weeks later. Olive Hammond went in two or three times every day. Towards the end she slept in the house. She knew Arthur well, of course. They're the same age. They grew up together here on the estate and went to the same school.

'There was no will found, so of course everything went to Arthur.' Cutler chuckled. 'The in-laws were hopping mad; it was a pleasure to see them. They tried to make a case of it. They went haring off to a solicitor but he told them they didn't have a hope in hell.

'Arthur left his job. He sold the property to the sand and gravel company; he got a wonderful price for the place. He used some of the money to buy a run-down grocer's shop in the town; he worked every hour God sent to make a success of it – that was the start of his business.

'He got married after a year or two; he's got a lovely family. They live out in the country now, big posh place, but Arthur's never forgotten where he came from. He and his wife do a lot of good work for local charities. And they've done a lot for this neighbourhood, built a fine community hall here on the estate.

'Arthur's got the name of being a first-class employer. They think no end of him in the town, and in the rest of the county, too; he's created a lot of work, brought a lot of prosperity. Very go-ahead, he is.' He picked up a copy of the local paper from a side table. 'There's a piece about him here, in this week's paper; there's often something about him.' He opened the paper. 'There's a picture, too – him and his wife.' He passed the paper to Lambert who ran his eye over it. Arthur Langstaff looked every inch the successful businessman: alert, energetic, jovial. His wife, at his side, appeared relaxed and smiling, casually elegant. It seemed they had left a few days earlier on a tour of the United States, combining a holiday with a search for fresh ideas, new methods in business; they would be away for the next six weeks.

As he walked with Lambert to the door, Cutler suddenly said with a sideways glance at Lambert, 'Maybe the in-laws had managed to talk old Bert into signing some sort of will, leaving them the property.' He moved his head. 'And maybe Arthur had a root round after he moved into the cottage. Maybe he found the will and chucked it on the fire. What of it? The property was Arthur's by right. And if Olive Hammond did chance to find out what Arthur had been up to, I'm sure Arthur would have been able to persuade her to keep quiet about it; I dare say he may have made it worth her while. Money was always pretty tight with the Hammonds; nothing Olive would like better than the chance of a bit of easy money. And if I know Olive Hammond, I dare say she'd see to it that Arthur went on handing over a bob or two for a good long time afterwards. It was very soon after Bert's death that she gave up the district nursing and went into agency work.'

He moved his shoulders. 'If I'm right about all that, I can't honestly see what harm any of it did. Arthur's made very good use of the money. The in-laws would have run through the lot inside a few years, with nothing to show for it.'

Before Lambert went to bed he assembled in the kitchen the materials for his herbal potion: Hilda's packet of herbs, the bag of lemons he'd bought at a greengrocer's, a jar of honey from the agricultural show where he'd spent the afternoon. He put the kettle on to boil and looked out a capacious beaker. The dose Hilda had given him had certainly done him no harm; he hadn't coughed or sneezed once since he'd downed it.

And the potion worked like a charm once again. He enjoyed a night free from coughing, a long, sound sleep.

When he woke the sun was stealing into the room. He had been dreaming of Calcott House: himself and Julie strolling in the April gardens, Olive Hammond gazing down with admiration at her own short, broad feet in their serviceable, laced, oxblood leather shoes. And another, older woman, in a pretty, floating gown, coming along a path with a small black-and-tan dog trotting by her side.

He linked his hands behind his head and cast about for the woman's name. After a moment or two the computer in his brain obediently sent up the information: Mrs Passmore. Something else came back to him too: Olive Hammond on her way out of the dining room, walking across to Mrs Passmore's table, inviting her to the cottage. 'I'm playing bridge,' Mrs Passmore had told her. 'Some other time, perhaps.'

He sat up in bed. Mrs Passmore – why hadn't he thought of her before? She must have known Olive Hammond for quite some time at Calcott House; she was sure to have gone over to the cottage after Olive moved in; she might very well know where Olive was at this moment. He flung aside the bedclothes and sprang out. How to get hold of Mrs Passmore? She was off to join some widowed friend, Iris had said; they were going to share a house together.

He didn't in the least fancy going back to Calcott House to

ask for Mrs Passmore's address; he hadn't the slightest wish to speak to either of the Marchants again. And it was far from certain that he would be given the present address of a former resident without some very good grounds for asking. He was currently operating in a tricky unofficial capacity; he was in no position to press them if they refused. Another thought struck him, rather more unpleasant: suppose one of them asked him for the name of his superior officer and then picked up the phone and rang Cannonbridge, demanding to know if they could be compelled to disclose confidential information about a former resident without that resident's knowledge or permission. He shuddered at the vision of the hornets' nest that would stir up.

Iris! Of course! She might very well know Mrs Passmore's address – or might be able to find out for him if she didn't know. And she wasn't likely to make difficulties about passing the information on to him.

As soon as he had finished his breakfast he rang Iris at home. 'You're lucky to catch me,' she told him cheerfully. 'I've usually left for work by now.' She'd got the day off; she'd filled in on Sunday for another waitress. 'I'm going to give the kids' rooms a really good turnout,' she declared with relish.

Yes, she did know Mrs Passmore's address. She showed no reluctance about passing it on after he explained why he wanted it. 'It's an easy address to remember,' she said. 'That's how it happened to stick in my mind.' It was a very short address: The Old Forge, and the name of the village. 'And don't forget,' Iris reminded him, 'you're welcome to call in here any time you're over this way. You know my usual hours.'

Forty-five minutes later Lambert drew up before The Old Forge, a modernized, altered, extended, improved dwelling that bore no resemblance now to any forge Lambert had ever clapped eyes on. He pressed the doorbell long and hard, remembering Iris telling him Mrs Passmore was pretty deaf. He was about to press the bell again, still more loudly, when he heard movement inside.

The door opened to reveal a woman he couldn't for a split second recognize as Mrs Passmore. The same generous proportions, a flowing gown, a waft of French perfume, elegant walking stick – but her hair was now a gleaming chestnut.

134

Her little spaniel suddenly appeared at her side, gazing alertly up at the visitor.

Before Lambert could speak, Mrs Passmore's face broke into a lively smile of welcome. She held up a hand.

'Don't tell me. I know you. I've seen you before.' She tilted her head back, half closed her eyes. 'Two or three months back. I never forget a face.' Her eyes jerked open in triumph. 'Calcott House, in the spring. You came to lunch with that pretty girl with the lovely hair.' Lambert acknowledged she was right.

'I can't remember the girl's name,' she added.

'Julie Dawson,' he told her.

'Yes, that's it. I remember Julie telling me you were in the police, the CID. A detective sergeant.'

'That's right.'

She laughed. 'I could see you didn't recognize me for a moment.' She primped her shining hair. 'My new wig,' she explained without a trace of self-consciousness. 'I decided to go for something brighter this time.' She glanced down at the dog. 'It picks up one of the colours of his coat, in a lighter shade. Rather a striking effect, don't you think?' She turned her head for him to admire and he saw she was wearing a hearing aid.

She spotted instantly that he had seen it. 'My friend – the one I'm living with here – she made me get the aid. I can't think now why I was so silly about it for so long. I must have missed a great deal.'

She suddenly directed at Lambert a shrewd, serious glance. 'I don't imagine you've called to admire my new wig or my hearing aid. I hope nothing's wrong?'

He moved a hand. 'I can't give you a straight yes or no to that. There may be something wrong, or there may not. You mentioned Miss Dawson just now. It's in connection with Miss Dawson that I'm here. Her relatives are worried about her; she seems to have vanished. So far we haven't been able to trace her.'

'You'd better come inside.' She stood back for him to enter. 'How do you think I might be able to help?' she asked as she closed the door behind him. 'I chatted to Julie while she was at the hotel that weekend, and she phoned me here one day a couple of months ago. I haven't come across her since.'

She led the way into the sitting room. 'I took quite a liking to Julie. I do hope nothing's happened to her.' She asked Lam-

135

bert to sit down. 'My friend's gone into town,' she explained. 'There's just the daily woman here. I'll pop along and have a word with her, then we won't be disturbed.' She turned in the doorway. 'Coffee? Or tea?' Lambert settled for coffee. The spaniel followed her from the room.

She came back a minute or two later, without the dog. 'The coffee won't be long,' she told Lambert. Until it arrived she made casual conversation but as soon as the daily woman had brought in the tray and departed again her manner became briskly businesslike. 'You can fire away now,' she invited as she poured the coffee.

Lambert told her how he had traced Julie to the caravan at the end of her holiday at Calcott House in May, but he hadn't been able to discover where she had gone from the caravan. 'I thought she might have visited Miss Hammond at the cottage and Miss Hammond might know where she went. I went over to the cottage but Miss Hammond seems to be away. I thought you might know where I could get in touch with her.'

She shook her head with regret. 'I'm afraid I've no idea. I never did go over to the cottage though I promised I would. I didn't give Olive more than a passing thought after I moved here. She hasn't been in touch with me since I left Calcott House.'

'You say Julie phoned you here one day a couple of months ago?' Lambert said.

She sipped her coffee. 'Yes, she rang me from a call box. She said she'd been staying at Calcott House and she was now renting a caravan in the area; she'd been there a few days. She was making various trips and she'd probably be over this way. Would it be all right if she called in?

'I said yes, of course, I'd be delighted to see her any day, she should just give me a ring first, to make sure I'd be in. I could give her a meal, show her round the village, if she'd like that – it's very pretty, there are some interesting houses and a fine old church. She said she'd love to come over. She thanked me. She said she'd ring again in a couple of days but I didn't hear from her again.' She moved her hand. 'I was sorry, I'd quite looked forward to her coming over.'

Lambert asked if Julie had mentioned Olive Hammond at all in the course of that phone call but Mrs Passmore was certain she had not. Nor had she spoken of any other plans she might have had for the rest of her holiday. She hadn't raised any other topic.

She couldn't tell Lambert of any close friend Olive Hammond might have had. 'I don't know that she had any,' she added. 'I never saw any sign of one.'

The only relative she knew of was the old man Lambert had already heard about, the cousin in Hampshire, but she didn't know his address. 'Olive and I were never close,' she observed. 'If we hadn't happened to be living in the same hotel I doubt if we'd ever have exchanged a word, she's not exactly my type.' She made a little grimace. 'She's all right in her way. I'm sure she was an excellent nurse.'

'She seems to have retired rather early,' Lambert commented.

'Nursing's pretty heavy work,' Mrs Passmore pointed out. 'Particularly when you're single-handed in private houses. She probably retired as soon as she felt she had enough put by for her old age. You can save a good deal if you take well-paid, live-in jobs. And I dare say she had her share of grateful patients who left her something in their wills.'

She moved her head. 'I expect she bought herself annuities, made investments. She struck me as a shrewd businesswoman. She always looked at the financial pages and listened to the market reports on the radio.'

She narrowed her eyes at him. 'I believe she had some sort of private income from some other quarter as well. She always hung about, waiting for the mail to be put out, round about the start of every month. She'd always snatch up any letters that came for her then. She hardly ever got any mail except around the beginning of the month. When it came she always went into town right afterwards. Sometimes I'd be in town myself, that day; I'd see her going into her bank or coming out of it.' She gave him a deprecating smile. 'You must think me a nosy old woman but you can't help noticing things like that when you live that kind of hotel life.'

She leaned forward. 'I always assumed she got special rates at Calcott House – or even paid nothing at all.'

She saw Lambert's look of surprise. 'It was just an impression I got,' she enlarged. 'It stuck in my mind. It was one time when they put the prices up at Calcott House. I was in the office, making out my cheque and I said to Evan Marchant, knowing how sharp Olive always was where money was concerned,

137

"You'll have Miss Hammond protesting about this," and Evan gave me such an odd sort of look, as if to say: That's all you know. It just made me think: maybe she doesn't pay anything at all. So a little later I said something to Olive about the new charges and she wasn't in the least interested. That made me think I could be right – she was always so interested in money, not stingy exactly, but you got the feeling money meant a lot to her, the way it does to people who never had much when they were young.'

'Why would the hotel let Miss Hammond stay there for nothing?' Lambert asked.

'Because she nursed the old lady,' Mrs Passmore responded at once. She smiled slightly. 'Though now I say it, it does seem rather excessive gratitude, letting her stay free of charge for so long.'

'Which old lady was it that she nursed?' Lambert inquired.

'The owner of the hotel, Mrs Marchant's mother, Evan's mother-in-law. Olive nursed her in her last illness. I gather she was very good to her, very devoted. Mrs Marchant helped with the nursing. She was very upset about losing her mother. The old lady died one night when Mrs Marchant was sitting up with her.'

'When was this?'

She cast her mind back. 'About five years ago. It was in the winter. I was away at the time, staying with friends who'd taken a villa in the south of France. I didn't get back to Calcott House till the spring. The other residents told me all about it then. The old lady wasn't very well when I left. She died of pneumonia, I understand. She'd held the reins right up until then, held them pretty tight, too. She ruled everyone with a rod of iron. Everything run very strictly, very traditional. She wouldn't have change, didn't hold with it. She'd be speechless if she could see the hotel now. She'd never take in any casuals, any bed-and-breakfasters, any tourists or holiday-makers – and as for foreigners, utterly unheard of. Only long-stay residents.

'After her death the hotel went to Mrs Marchant, of course – she was the only child. She and Evan had been married a couple of years by then. He'd come to the hotel one summer, the old lady took him on as a temporary worker, but the next thing was, he'd married the daughter. The pair of them made a lot of changes very quickly after the old lady died – all changes for the better, in my opinion, and long overdue.'

She pulled a little face. 'Not a gentleman I ever took to, Evan Marchant, but give him his due, he does know how to run a hotel. I understand that's what he'd been doing before he came to Calcott House, moving round, working at different hotels, here and abroad, learning the trade.

'He's a man who likes his own way. He's certainly the kingpin in the hotel now, though I must say he and his wife always seem to get on very well together. And the brother, too, Luke Marchant, they all three pull together. Evan dominates the other two but neither of them ever seems to resent it.'

She drank her coffee. 'I'm sure you saw what a magnificent job Luke Marchant made of the hotel gardens; they're a great feature of the place now. All the ideas for the garden came from Evan but it was Luke who carried out all the work.

'Luke came to the hotel soon after the old lady died. I was away in France when he arrived but they told me he appeared out of the blue, no word of him beforehand. He's an odd sort of fish, never has a word to say, never has anything to do with any of the guests – or any of the staff, for that matter. Someone said once he used to work at a hospital, as a gardener.'

She gave Lambert a look charged with significance. 'I did wonder sometimes what sort of hospital it might have been – a prison hospital, maybe, or a psychiatric hospital. I wondered if he'd been an inmate or a patient, rather than an outside employee.' She shook her head. 'Such a moody man, still waters. You get the impression there's a hostile, aggressive streak there that might suddenly burst out.

'He thinks the world of his brother. I'm sure if Evan told Luke to jump off a cliff he'd do it without a moment's hesitation.' She smiled. 'Maybe Evan rescued him from some dire situation,' she conjectured airily. 'Or got him off some nasty hook.'

She moved her head. 'Whatever reason Evan may have had for taking Luke in when he did, he certainly got himself a first-class, all-round henchman. Luke's a very handy chap indeed. He does all the maintenance jobs on the building, looks after the greenhouses, the boilerhouse, all the sheds and outhouses. He's as strong as a horse.'

139

She laughed. 'I suppose it's a bit much to expect social graces thrown in as well.'

Lambert got to his feet. 'I won't take up any more of your time,' he told her. 'You've been very kind.'

She smiled up at him. 'Not at all. I only wish I could have been more helpful.' A thought occurred to her. 'You could try asking at Calcott House for the address of Olive's cousin, the old man in Hampshire. Olive might have left his address with the office when she went to visit him.' She glanced about for her stick.

He stooped to pick it up. 'Don't disturb yourself,' he said. 'I can let myself out.'

She waved a dismissive hand. 'I shall walk with you to the door. I shall give myself that pleasure.' She took the stick, put a hand on his arm and stood up. 'A touch of arthritis, I fear.' They moved to the door. 'You wouldn't think it now but I had beautiful legs once.' She sighed. 'It all goes, bit by bit, inch by inch. But we keep soldiering on. Put a good face on it, that's my motto.' They reached the front door. She paused and looked up at him. 'Enjoy them while you have them – health and strength and youth. You think they'll last forever. But they won't.'

On a sudden impulse, surprising even to himself, Lambert bent and brushed her cheek with his lips.

'My word!' she said. 'That's something I didn't expect when I got out of bed this morning. Kissed by a young man who actually looks like a man. Not like these skinny lads you see about these days, half of them you can't tell from girls. We'd have made mincemeat of them in my day.' She gave a little snort of contempt. 'And the other sort, lounge lizards we used to call them, never a hair out of place, dressed like a tailor's dummy – like His Nibs.'

Lambert felt the hair rise along the back of his scalp. He had a sudden flash of memory: Olive Hammond standing in front of his car in the Calcott House car park, barring access. 'I'm going to cadge some plants from Luke Marchant,' she had said. 'No need for His Nibs to know anything about it.'

The jottings on the back of the envelope – might it be H/N? Not H/V or H/U?

'His Nibs?' he queried.

Mrs Passmore laughed. 'Evan Marchant. Olive Hammond

140

always called him His Nibs. Behind his back, of course, not to his face or to the staff, that would never do. I picked up the habit from her – just when we were chatting together. Suits him, don't you think? He does have a high opinion of himself.'

As soon as he was clear of the village Lambert pulled up and took from his pocket the envelope Simon Norbury had given him. He closely scrutinized the initials. Yes, he concluded at last, they could be made to read H/N. Just about.

He sat pondering. If only he could get a squint at Olive Hammond's bank account. But there could be no question of that in his present situation. And no question of any access to police records, to see if there had been anything of interest in Luke Marchant's past.

He returned the envelope to his pocket. Time for another call on Iris, he decided. Take her up on that open invitation.

And she greeted him with a delighted smile when he rang her doorbell. She was dressed in T-shirt and jeans, her hair tied up in a brightly coloured scarf. She brushed aside his attempt to apologize for interrupting her cleaning session. She urged him into the sitting room and vanished towards the kitchen. She made tea in a trice, produced cake and biscuits.

He got down to brass tacks without delay. 'You told me that when Julie Dawson called here she asked you about the history of Calcott House, the different owners and residents.'

'That's right,' Iris confirmed.

'Do you remember if she asked you about the last owner, Mrs Marchant's mother?'

'Yes, she did,' Iris replied at once. 'She was very interested in the old lady. She was particularly interested that it was Miss Hammond who nursed her before she died.' She crossed the room to a bureau and opened a drawer. 'I showed her my photographs. They go back quite a way, to when I first started work at Calcott House.' She took out an album and carried it over to Lambert. She pulled up a chair and sat down beside him. She opened the album, turned the pages. 'That's the old lady. I snapped her one day as I was on my way home. I'd been taking photos of the staff and I was able to catch the old lady in the garden – she was standing talking to one of the residents.' She laughed. 'She knew nothing about it, of course. She wasn't the sort of old lady you could ask if you could take her photo, she was a bit of a dragon – but I liked her all the same. You had to admire her, she had a will of iron.'

She went on turning the pages, reminiscing, explaining, giving thumbnail sketches. She paused at a group photograph showing some of the staff relaxing over coffee, during a morning break. 'Julie was very interested in her.' She jabbed a finger down at a girl, seventeen or eighteen, maybe. Stockily built, straight, sandy hair, sandy brows and lashes, pale skin; she looked out at the camera with an unsmiling look, a closed, stoical expression. 'Eva Simcox,' Iris said. She gazed down with a critical air. 'A bit of eyebrow pencil, mascara and lipstick would have made a world of difference to her looks – her features weren't at all bad. But she wasn't the sort of girl you could say that to. She was always very quiet, kept herself to herself. I believe she came from some children's home. She was a first-class worker, I'll give her that. She'd work all the hours God sent, never complained. I was really surprised when the Marchants got rid of her – it was just after the old lady died. I was sure they'd never get anyone else to do the work Eva did for what she was paid.'

'Do you know why they got rid of her?' Lambert asked.

She made a face. 'I don't know for sure. It was said she'd been stealing from the residents.'

'Do you know where she is now?'

'I had a card from her the Christmas after she left – she left in the January. I was surprised to get the card. I'd never had much to do with her, her being so much younger and so quiet. I did ask her the day she was leaving – it was the day after the old lady died and we were all in a bit of a state; I saw Eva going out by the back door with her suitcase – if she had anywhere to go, if she had any money. I'd heard she'd been booted out. She said she'd make out all right. She'd saved most of her wages and she'd been given a week's pay in lieu of notice. I asked if she'd been given a reference and she said she had; she thought she'd soon find another job. When I heard afterwards that she'd been sacked for thieving I thought the Marchants had let her off lightly. They'd treated her better than a lot of employers would; they hadn't brought the police into it. I wished her luck and said I hoped things worked out. The Christmas card she sent just said she had a job she liked, she was doing fine.'

'Did she give an address? Or say where the job was?'

'She said she was working as a chambermaid at the Crown Hotel.' She mentioned a town ten miles away. 'She said it was a live-in job. I thought, well, at least it was a lot lighter work than she'd done at Calcott House. She'd been a general dogsbody there; she had all the rough jobs, all the dirty jobs. I did mean to drop her a line but I never got round to it and then I'm afraid I forgot all about her. I didn't hear from her again.'

Lambert had another query: 'Do you happen to know if Miss Hammond got favourable terms at Calcott House?'

She shot him a sharp look. 'Yes, I do happen to know. I'm pretty sure she didn't pay anything at all. It was two or three years ago, she was complaining about her room one day, said it was too small, didn't have a good view. The clerk in the office said to me: "She's got a nerve, asking for a better room." I said: "Why's that? Does she get cheap rates?" I thought maybe she got a discount, having nursed the old lady in her last illness. The clerk said: "I'll say she gets cheap rates, couldn't be much cheaper; she doesn't pay a brass farthing, never has done."' Iris made a face. 'It just goes to show you shouldn't take folk at face value. I never had the Marchants down as sentimental. I never thought they were all that fond of the old lady. I'd have thought they'd have been glad to see her go. But there you are – they must be a pair of old softies at heart.' She grinned. 'Though I must say you'd never think it, certainly not where it touched their pockets.'

'And did Miss Hammond get a better room?' Lambert wanted to know.

She nodded. 'Yes, she did, and pretty pronto, at the very next opportunity.' She drank her tea. 'Of course now she's moved out, they can let her room for the full price again. I don't imagine that will grieve them too much.'

The phone rang in the hall and she went off to answer it. She was gone some little time and when she came back Lambert got to his feet. He thanked her for her time. 'I'll be off out of your way and let you get on,' he said.

She walked with him to the front door. 'Oh, by the way,' she said as she laid her hand on the doorknob, 'the last time you were here you wanted to know if Miss Hammond had been back to Calcott House since she left and I told you she hadn't, not as far as I knew – well, I'm not so sure now.'

'How's that?' Lambert asked.

'I was talking to one of the kitchen staff the other day,' she told him, 'and she mentioned Miss Hammond. She asked me if I'd been over to the cottage, if I knew how she was getting on, if she liked it out there. I said I hadn't been over there, I'd no idea if she'd settled in. She said she'd seen her in the hotel garden once after she'd left. She was talking to Luke Marchant, so she must be getting on with her garden; she'd very likely been cadging cuttings from Luke. I asked her when that was and she said it wasn't long after Miss Hammond left Calcott House, a few days, maybe, or a week. Later on that day I made it my business as I was going home in the afternoon to have a word with Luke. I managed to track him down by the boiler-house. I said I understood Miss Hammond had come back and he'd seen her. I asked him how she was settling in at the cottage. He said right away he'd never seen her. As far as he knew she'd never been back; he'd certainly not clapped eyes on her. I said one of the staff had seen her talking to him. He said it must have been some bed-and-breakfaster who looked like Miss Hammond. He got quite shirty about it. He said, "I'm not having you putting it about she's been here, trying to get plants off me." I told him to keep his hair on and I left it at that.'

She opened the door. 'And speaking of Luke Marchant,' she added on another recollection, 'we had a driver delivering wine at Calcott House the day before yesterday. He wasn't the usual man, he was a relief driver. I gave him a cup of tea in the kitchen and we got chatting. He said, "I've just seen a guy working in the garden here – is his name Luke Marchant, by any chance?" I said it was, did he know him? He said he didn't exactly know him.' She mentioned a town some forty miles away. 'He said he used to drive for a coach and minibus hire firm over there; he often drove a minibus on a booking from a mental hospital there – one of those big, old places; it closed down a couple of years ago. He said a local girl, fifteen or sixteen, had been attacked and indecently assaulted, not far from the hospital; she'd managed to get away before anything worse happened.

'The police questioned the inmates and staff and there were

some identity parades for the ones that seemed to fit, more or less, the description the girl gave. Luke was one of those they put in the line-ups. He worked in the hospital garden; he was an outside employee. The girl couldn't actually pick anyone out but she stopped quite a long time in front of Luke. They took him in again for questioning but nothing ever came of it. They never brought any charges against him – or against anyone else. There was a lot of whispering afterwards and in the end Luke gave in his notice and left. That was five years ago – that was when Luke turned up at Calcott House.'

A twenty-minute drive took Lambert to the town where Eva Simcox had gone after leaving Calcott House. He had no difficulty in finding the Crown Hotel, an imposing building near the main business area. He asked to speak to the manager, disclosed his identity and inquired for Eva, adding that she was in no kind of trouble but might be able to help in a case currently concerning him.

He was told Eva no longer worked at the Crown. Yes, she had been employed there as a chambermaid a few years back and had given excellent service. 'She had an accident when she'd been here about twelve months,' the manager said. 'It was on her day off; she'd gone out shopping. It was in the winter and there was a lot of ice about. She slipped and fell; she broke her wrist and arm.' Treatment had been lengthy and far from straightforward. He had had to take on a replacement immediately. 'Eva was very sensible,' he said. 'She saw at once, without my having to say so, that I'd need her room for her replacement.' She had offered to move out at once if he could find her somewhere to go. He had found her comfortable digs. 'I told her she could have her job back when she was fully fit again.'

He had kept in touch with her during her treatment. She had spent a good deal of time at the local library, reading and studying. When her convalescence was almost over she told him she wouldn't be returning to the Crown. She had decided to continue her education and had discovered she could get a grant. She would take a course of studies at the local college of further education and see where that led.

He couldn't say where she was living or working at present

146

but he gave Lambert the address of the digs she had moved into four years ago.

Lambert had a bite to eat in a snack bar before setting off to look for the digs. The address took him to a tall, narrow terrace house in a quiet side street. The landlady was a good-natured woman, disposed to be helpful. Lambert didn't tell her who he was but asked if she had a Miss Eva Simcox living there.

Yes, she had. Miss Simcox wasn't in, she was out at work. She wouldn't be in until fairly late in the evening, nine or ten; this was one of her college evenings. She usually went straight from work to the college, had something to eat in the canteen before her class, and often stayed on afterwards, chatting, drinking coffee with some of the other students.

Yes, she could tell him where Miss Simcox worked: she was a receptionist at a large medical practice not far from the college; she gave him the address.

There was an afternoon lull at the surgery when Lambert called in. Four women were at work in the reception office. Lambert spoke to the woman in charge, disclosing his identity and asking if he might speak to Miss Simcox; he would keep her no more than a few minutes. Miss Simcox was not in any trouble with the law but might be able to provide some useful information. The woman made no objection and at once approached one of the others and explained matters. The clerk left her seat and approached Lambert.

'Miss Simcox?' he asked.

She nodded. He would never have known her from the photograph in Iris's album. The straight, sandy hair had been permed and was now a becoming shade of auburn. Her face was no longer colourless; cosmetics had been skilfully used. The stocky figure had been fined down. She was now an attractive young woman, trimly dressed.

She looked at him with calm inquiry, self-possessed and unalarmed, waiting for him to speak. He explained that he would like to ask her about the circumstances in which she had left Calcott House; it could have some bearing on a case that currently engaged him.

Her look altered instantly to one of the keenest interest but she showed no degree of surprise. She assured him at once she would be only too happy to help in any way she could. He

147

asked if she could spare him half an hour after work. Yes, she could. She would finish at five and could meet him outside the surgery. He could go along with her to the college where they could talk in the canteen; her class didn't begin till 6.30. She was well spoken; her manner was confident and outgoing.

Before Lambert returned to the surgery to wait for Eva he rang Mrs Inskip to say he wouldn't be back in time for supper; he couldn't in fact say precisely when he would be back. She told him not to worry, she would keep his supper warm for him; it didn't matter what time he got back.

A few minutes after five Eva came out of the building and crossed over to where Lambert stood by his car, watching out for her. As soon as she was sitting beside him in the passenger seat and had given him directions for the college, she began to talk. 'After I left Calcott House I used to wonder sometimes if anyone would ever come asking about the way the old lady died. Someone did come at last, a couple of months back – and now you've turned up.'

'This other person who came asking,' Lambert said, 'was it a young woman?'

'Yes, it was. Julie Dawson, her name was. Do you know her?'

'I've met her,' Lambert said.

'I always believed I hadn't seen the end of it,' she went on. 'I always thought I'd find myself telling someone about it some day. I told Julie everything I knew or suspected.' She had liked Julie; they had struck up an instant rapport. Julie had given her an explanation for her interest, very much along the lines of what she had told Simon Norbury. 'I was sure she'd guessed right about Nurse Hammond being a blackmailer,' Eva said with conviction. 'The moment she said it I realized it could explain the way she'd behaved towards me when I spoke to her after the old lady died.'

They reached the college and parked the car. In the canteen Eva provided herself with a cheese salad and Lambert got himself a cup of tea. It was clear that Eva had made a number of friends among the other students; she returned smiles and greetings as they made their way to a quiet corner where they could talk undisturbed.

'I'd better begin at the beginning,' Eva said when they had sat down. 'I was brought up in care, from the age of three.' She had moved between children's homes and foster parents, never remaining anywhere long enough to put down roots or make lasting frienships. In some places she had been reasonably well treated, in others quite the opposite, with various gradations in between. She had received only the sketchiest education but had thoroughly learned two lessons: stoicism and the wisdom of keeping a low profile and her thoughts to herself.

She had no recollection whatever of her own parents. The most she had been able to glean about them was that her mother had been unmarried and the identity of her father was unknown to the authorities. Her mother had tried to look after her but had had great difficulty in coping. She had asked to have her taken into care on a temporary basis but had maintained no contact, never returned to claim her, and vanished in a manner that defeated half-hearted official attempts to catch up with her.

Eva had left school – and care – at sixteen and had gone to Calcott House as a general domestic. The old lady ruled the roost then; Eva found her strict but fair.

In the course of cleaning and tidying the rooms of the oldest female residents Eva had very soon become aware that they all possessed jewellery and trinkets which they rarely if ever wore, keeping them stashed away in drawers, cupboards, wardrobes. She was fascinated by these treasures; she had never previously seen such things of beauty at close quarters, let alone handled them. She took every opportunity to finger them, examine them. Before long she grew bolder and took to abstracting a piece, taking it to her room where she could feast her eyes in private, hold it up against herself, even try it on. She would keep the piece overnight, replace it without fail next morning. She had never once, not even for an instant, harboured any notion of actually keeping an item. For the best part of a year her little stratagem worked perfectly but the day came when one of the old ladies decided to look through her jewellery and found one piece missing. She at once suspected Eva as having easy access and lost no time in speaking to the Marchants who immediately carried out a search of Eva's bedroom in her presence. The missing piece – together with one or two more, belonging to other residents – was quickly found. All the trinkets were restored to their owners and Eva was made to apologize. 'I fully expected the police to be told,' she said. 'And I fully

149

expected to be sacked.' But a day or two went by – she wasn't sacked; the police were not informed.

The Marchants sent for her and told her they had decided to give her another chance. She would be kept under a strictly watchful eye. Her wages would be reduced as a punishment. If anything of a similar nature ever occurred again she would at once be dismissed without a reference. As far as Eva was aware, Mrs Marchant's mother knew nothing of all this; she certainly never by word or look gave Eva any reason to suppose she had any knowledge of it.

Time went by. Eva took care never to put a foot wrong again. Her wages were never restored to their former level. 'I realize now, of course,' she observed, 'that I was a useful and underpaid dogsbody; they wouldn't have been able to find someone else to do what I did for what they paid me. But I was very young then, petrified of ending up in gaol – all I could see was that I was lucky to be kept on at all.'

The old lady died when Eva had been at Calcott House a little more than two years. 'Nurse Hammond was a private nurse; they got her in to help with the nursing. It was in the winter and it was very cold. There was a lot of flu about, the hospitals were full, the doctors were rushed off their feet. Nurse Hammond usually sat up with the old lady but after a bit Mrs Marchant started helping with the night nursing. Nurse Hammond would look after the old lady till midnight, then Mrs Marchant took over till five o'clock, and then Nurse Hammond took over again.'

She looked at Lambert. 'I don't know if you've been round the back of Calcott House?' No, he hadn't. 'It's built out on both sides, at right angles to the main block,' she explained. 'It makes a sort of courtyard. All the staff rooms are on the top floors of the built-out parts.' Her own little room was at the very top. 'It had been snowing heavily for a day or two. On this particular night there was a very sharp frost. It was never very warm up in my room but that night it was really freezing.' She had got up in the early hours, in search of more covers to put on her bed; she hadn't bothered to switch on the light. She took her dressing gown from the back of the door, her coat from the wardrobe and laid them on her bed.

Before snuggling back in again she went to the window and drew the curtains a little apart to see what the weather was

doing. Her eye was taken by a subdued light from a room opposite, one floor lower than her own. All the other windows she
could see were closed against the cold, their curtains drawn,
the rooms in darkness. But the curtains of this room were taken
right back; the window stood wide open to the freezing air.

She knew which room it was she was looking down into: the
old lady's bedroom, now her sickroom. In the light of the bedside lamp she could see the naked figure of the old lady lying
on the bed, the covers pulled right back. There was no stir of
movement from the old lady, her white head lay motionless on
the pillows. On a chair beside the bed sat Mrs Marchant, gazing
down at the still figure.

'I was mystified,' Eva said. 'I couldn't make out what was
happening. I half thought I must be dreaming.' She had stood
irresolute, staring down. Silence enveloped the hotel. She began
to shake with cold. Still perplexed and troubled, she closed her
curtains and got back into bed. She had worked long and hard
all day; in no time at all she was fast asleep again.

Her alarm clock woke her as usual at 5.30. By the time she
was dressed and ready for the day she had convinced herself
she had indeed been half dreaming.

An hour or two later news of the old lady's death percolated
through the kitchens and basement. It seemed Nurse Hammond
had gone along at five o'clock to resume her duties and had
found Mrs Marchant asleep in her chair by the bed and the
old lady lying tranquil and lifeless under her covers. In Nurse
Hammond's opinion she had slipped peacefully away half an
hour earlier. By dint of a question here and there, Eva managed
to ascertain that the old lady was dressed in her warm nightdress
and a knitted bed jacket.

But her brain refused to leave the matter alone and before
long her feet took her along to Nurse Hammond. With considerable nervousness and hesitation she described what she had
seen. Nurse Hammond told her at once and with energy that
she must undoubtedly have been dreaming. She sent Eva back
about her business with orders to dismiss these imaginings from
her mind and on no account to repeat them to anyone else.

'She must have gone straight off to Mrs Marchant and told
her what I had said,' Eva continued. Shortly afterwards Mrs
Marchant had sent for her, accused her of deliberate, malicious
troublemaking and dismissed her on the spot with a week's

wages in lieu of notice and orders to remove herself and her belongings from the premises without a moment's delay. 'She told me that if I behaved myself and made no further trouble I could give her name as a reference but if there was any repetition of what I had said to Nurse Hammond there would be no reference and furthermore I would be charged with stealing the jewellery some time before.'

She shuddered. 'I was terrified. I packed my bag and left. When I'd been at the Crown a week or two and was beginning to settle in, I thought over what had happened. In my own mind I was certain it had been no dream, but what could I do?' She made a helpless gesture. 'I decided to put the whole thing out of my mind, concentrate on doing my new job well.'

She had arranged to go out with some friends on the evening Julie Dawson called at her digs; she had been able to spend only a limited time talking to her. 'She said she'd be in touch with me again very soon. In the meantime she'd be very grateful if I would write down everything I'd told her, and anything else I could remember that might be useful; she'd pick it up next time she called. I said I would and when I got in that evening after seeing my friends I sat down and wrote it all out while it was still fresh in my memory. I signed and dated it and put it ready to give her.' She shook her head slowly. 'But she never called again. I never heard another word from her. I didn't know what to think.'

'This account you wrote out,' Lambert said. 'Have you still got it?'

She nodded. 'It's back in my digs; I've kept it safe.'

'I'd very much like to have it, if you've no objection.' He glanced up at the clock. 'There's time for me to drive you back to your digs for it. I can have you back here in time for your class.'

She got to her feet at once. 'Right,' she said with decision. 'Let's get going.'

At the digs he waited in the car while she went inside. She was out again inside a minute or two. As she got back into the passenger seat she handed him several handwritten sheets, clipped together. He ran an eye swiftly over them. The last sheet was signed Eva Joan Simcox, and dated Tuesday, May 23rd.

He started up the engine again. 'If anything comes of this,' she said as they moved off, 'if you need me to stand up and speak, tell what I know, I'm ready to do it. I'm not scared of things any more. I'd never let myself be afraid again, the way I always used to be.' She smiled. 'The accident cured me of that. When I slipped on the ice and broke my arm and wrist I thought it was the end of everything for me. But it was the beginning of a better life than I'd ever dreamed I could have.' She smiled again. 'That accident was the best thing that ever happened to me.'

They reached the college and she got out of the car. 'By the way,' Lambert said on a sudden thought, 'when you were talking to Julie, did she say if she'd been over to Miss Hammond's cottage at all, if she'd managed to see her?'

Eva shook her head. 'No, she said nothing about seeing Nurse Hammond recently or going over to the cottage.'

After she had hurried inside he sat for a minute or two, mulling things over. Eva's evidence would carry little weight in a court of law. A girl with her background, by her own admission guilty of purloining – however temporarily – jewellery from the rooms of elderly residents, she would easily stand accused of spite and malice against Mrs Marchant; any halfway competent barrister could dispose of her inside a matter of minutes.

It would be impossible to prove medically that pneumonia had been deliberately induced. The Calcott House books might indeed show reduced charges – or none at all – for Olive Hammond but the Marchants would have a ready answer to that: recognition of Nurse Hammond's devoted services during the old lady's last illness.

He was strongly tempted all the same to call over now at Calcott House, try for a word with all three Marchants; he could start off by asking if they had the address of the cousin in Hampshire.

Right then, that was what he would do. He set off in the direction of the hotel. He reached a T-junction a few miles from Calcott. Turn right for the village – and turn left, it came back to him, for the farm where Julie had rented the caravan. Something else came back to him, too: on his visit to the farm he had spoken only to the wife; the farmer had been out at a sale.

He sat hesitating. He had geared himself up for an encounter with the Marchant trio. The last thing he wanted right now was to be temporarily deflected, to lose momentum, his purpose and concentration slackened off, the entire proceeding dwindling into just another ineffectual bout of routine, skilfully fielded questioning.

Probably nothing at all to be gained from another visit to the farm, a chat with the farmer, probably a total waste of time; little chance he'd have anything to add to what his wife had had to say.

But the unassailable truth rose up at him: you simply never knew for certain. There always remained that slender ghost of an outside chance.

He gave a long, resigned sigh and turned left, towards the farm.

A few minutes later he drew up before the farmhouse. Again it was the wife who answered his ring. Today she was even more harassed looking, her hair sticking out in even more untidy wisps. She was drying her hands on a towel.

'I don't know if you remember me,' Lambert began.

She gave him a closer look. 'Yes, I remember you,' she answered without enthusiasm. 'You're the detective who called here last month, wanting to know about the young lady in the caravan.'

'That's right, Detective Sergeant Lambert. If you remember, I didn't catch your husband last time I was here. Is he about now, by any chance? I'd appreciate a word with him. I won't keep him many minutes.'

She gave a grudging nod. 'He's out the back. I'll go and tell him.' She didn't ask him in. Indeed she closed the door firmly behind her as if to make sure he didn't get a foot over the threshold.

A few minutes later the farmer came clumping round the side of the house in his wellingtons. A thickset, powerfully built man with skin the colour of a cobnut. He didn't appear best pleased at being interrupted in whatever labours were going forward. He didn't speak, merely gave the intruder a far from friendly glance of inquiry as he ground to a halt a few feet away.

Lambert assumed an affable, cheerful manner. He apologized for disturbing the farmer. He would like to ask a couple of questions about the time when Miss Julie Dawson had occupied the caravan, in the latter part of May.

The farmer gave him a deeply irritated stare. 'Surely you've already been into all that with my wife? There's nothing more I can tell you. I can't remember anything about the girl. I'm not at all certain I ever clapped eyes on her.' He half turned to lumber off again.

'Do you know if Miss Dawson had any visitors while she was here?' Lambert continued, undeterred, resolutely cheery. He saw on the instant by the movement of the man's head that he had struck a chord. 'I'd be very grateful if you could cast your mind back,' he added, pressing home his advantage. 'Anything at all you can remember would be very helpful.'

The man wavered, flung him another glance, marginally less ill-humoured. He turned back to face Lambert. 'Someone did come asking for her.' His tone mellowed further. 'How I come to remember, we'd just had a calf born early that morning, we'd been up half the night. A fine bull calf, strong and healthy.' He had by now forgotten his irritation. 'Have you got a moment?' Lambert assured him that he had. 'You can take a look at him yourself,' the farmer suggested. Lambert expressed a fervent wish to view the marvel.

They walked across to some outbuildings, halting in front of a couple of looseboxes. The farmer thrust his head in at the first, beckoning Lambert to follow his example. A powerful, pungent odour greeted his nostrils as he obeyed.

An enormous, pale gold sow with a hugely distended belly lay bedded down on straw. Fast asleep, stretched out on her side, giving vent to a rhythmic succession of bubbling snores. 'She'll farrow down within the week,' the farmer informed Lambert. 'Her fourth litter. Nine or ten reared every time. Can't beat the Large White in my opinion.' Lambert made admiring, assenting noises.

They moved on to the adjacent box. 'Here's my brave young boyo!' the farmer cried as he leaned in. 'Come on, then! Up you get!'

The calf, a sturdy Hereford, climbed up onto its feet and came over to the door. The farmer leaned down, fondling the dense white curls of its broad, bony forehead. 'Who's a fine young lad, then?' The calf butted at his fingers. 'Take a look at that back,' the farmer invited Lambert. 'Beautiful strong back. Another twelve months and he'll be off to market; we'll turn him into money.'

His mood had grown genial and expansive. 'Well now,' he said as they turned from the looseboxes. 'What was that I was going to tell you? Oh yes, you wanted to know if anyone had

155

come asking for the young lady.' He gave an emphatic jerk of his head. 'And I was telling you yes, someone did come, the morning that young feller-me-lad was born.

'That made us late that morning, as you might guess. To cap it all, I had an appointment in town with my solicitor; I couldn't be late for that. So altogether I was in a bit of a rush. I was hosing down the yard and I heard a car down on the road; I heard it stop. Then a woman came up. She spotted me and came straight over. She said she was looking for the caravan. I asked her if she wanted a let. She said no, she knew the young lady who was renting the caravan, she'd called to see her. I told her the caravan was three or four fields away from the house. Her best plan was to get back in the car and drive along another hundred yards or so. She'd see the opening where she could drive right in. She went off and I heard the car start up again.' He had seen nothing more of the woman.

Lambert asked if the woman was alone.

'As far as I know,' he answered without hesitation.

'And the date when she called?'

'No trouble about that,' the farmer assured him heartily. 'I'll show you my stock book; you can see for yourself when the calf was born. And the interview with the solicitor, that's marked up on the calendar on the kitchen wall. Come along inside. The missus'll make us a cup of tea.'

At the back door he eased off his wellingtons on an ancient iron scraper and stuck his stockinged feet into a pair of shapeless old leather shoes with the laces missing.

There was no sign of his wife in the vast, dark, old kitchen. The farmer sent a shout up the stairs, summoning her down to make the tea. She came hurrying into the kitchen a moment later, her habitually distracted, harassed look overlaid with a strong suggestion of the sulks.

She didn't glance at either of them but busied herself with the kettle and mugs, milk and sugar, the tea caddy. Her husband didn't acknowledge her presence by a word or look. He slipslopped his way across to a large colour-printed sheet of paper thumb-tacked on the kitchen wall – a see-at-a-glance calendar given away free with a farming magazine. He ran a finger down the month of May.

'Here we are!' he cried in triumph. 'Thursday, May 18th.' Lambert went over and looked at the calendar. Clearly inked in was a note of the appointment with the solicitor, the name and time. 'I'll fetch the stock book,' the farmer said. 'You can see the date there, as well.'

While he was gone Lambert attempted a few casual remarks to the woman, commenting on the weather, the animals he had just seen. She made no response of any kind; her mouth remained set in a mutinous, obstinate line.

The farmer came shuffling back with the stock book. He showed the entry to Lambert. No doubt about it: the calf had been born at 4.30 on the morning of Thursday, May 18th.

'That reminds me!' the farmer exclaimed suddenly. He went back to the wall calendar and ran his finger down the columns for July. 'I'd forgotten that!' he grumbled to himself. He cast an abstracted glance at Lambert. 'I'll have to look out some papers. Better do it now, before I forget it again.' He went shambling off.

His wife poured the tea and shoved a mug in the direction of Lambert. With another shove she pushed forward the basin of sugar. She didn't invite him to sit down, she said nothing at all. She poured two more mugs, took one herself and went back upstairs with it.

Lambert picked up his mug and began to drink. He didn't go so far as to sit down, that might be pushing his luck. He was agreeably surprised to discover it was a very good mug of tea, very good indeed. As he drank he permitted his eyes to rove about the room, the worn stone floor, old rag rugs, wooden dresser knocked up long ago by some country joiner, its timbers eyed with knotholes.

He had almost finished his tea when the farmer came back into the kitchen, leafing through a sheaf of papers he was carrying. He addressed his wife as he came, issuing a stream of instructions about some forms that should have been sent off, must now be filled in and dispatched without delay.

He looked up and became aware that his wife was not in the kitchen. He glanced about and his eyes fell on Lambert with momentary surprise. 'You still here?' he asked abruptly.

'Your wife's gone upstairs,' Lambert told him by way of reply. 'She poured your tea.' He indicated the cooling mug.

The farmer gave a grunt. He picked up the mug and drank half its contents in a single swallow.

Lambert ventured one last question: 'The woman who called

157

here that morning back in May, could you possibly describe her? Age, height, colouring, anything you can remember.'

The farmer dragged his mind back from his papers. He regarded Lambert in silence for some moments as if considering whether to answer him or kick him out through the door. Then he downed the rest of his tea and set the mug on the table. It seemed after all that the last of his calf-inspired good humour had not totally evaporated.

'Fifty-five or sixty,' he said. 'Nothing to look at. Plain as a boot. Stout little woman – looked healthy enough, as if she could single a row of turnips without having a fit. Hair done up in a bit of a bun.'

'I'm much obliged to you,' Lambert said. 'You've been very helpful. It was good of you to spare me the time. Please thank your wife for the tea, it was the best I've had in a long time.' He turned to the door.

As he reached the threshold the farmer shafted a final recollection at his departing back. 'She had a limp.' Lambert halted, half turned round. 'She limped coming and she limped going. I thought maybe she'd ricked her ankle on the cobbles in the yard, but she said no when I asked her. She said she'd had the limp since she was a child.'

As soon as Lambert judged he was well away from the farmer's land he pulled up in a quiet spot and sat for some time deciding his next move.

Go over to Millbourne to have another word with Audrey Tysoe, the limping lady? But already he could construct without difficulty two or three totally innocent explanations for her visit to the caravan.

Forget Audrey Tysoe, stick to his original plan and go on to Calcott House? But the longer he considered that notion, the less attractive it now appeared. All impetus, as he had foreseen, had drained from that course of action. He could think of very little he might find to say to any of the three Marchants, very little solid ground of any kind on which to stand while he said it.

He stared out at the sunny evening. Today was Wednesday – what was left of it. On Friday he would be returning to Cannonbridge, back to the newly restored glories of his bedroom. Was he going to spend the last little bit of his holiday chasing after moonbeams? Or was he going to pack it in, relax and enjoy himself?

A loud rumble sounded suddenly from his inner workings. On the instant his mind made itself up: he would forget the whole bag of tricks, put it resolutely and finally behind him, get back pronto to Bowpatch and his supper.

He might do worse than spend tomorrow at a safari park not too far away. He smiled as he switched on the engine.

But Lambert's subconscious continued to nurse very different views about the manner in which he should pass the final section of his leave. It roused him next morning with its decisions already reached, brooking no argument.

Millbourne, it pronounced. Honeysuckle Cottage and Audrey Tysoe.

So, Millbourne it was.

He set off shortly after breakfast. At around 11.15 he turned into the lane leading to the cottage. He drove in through the gate and left his car in the parking bay at the side of the drive. He glanced about as he approached the house. No sign of Audrey in the front garden.

He walked round to make a quick survey of the rear garden. The air was heavy with the rich fragrance of honeysuckle in full summer splendour, wreathing walls, fences, arches with its large clusters of purple-red flowers tinged with yellow. No sign of Audrey here, either.

He turned back towards the front door. I hope she's in, he thought as he pressed the bell. I hope I haven't driven over here for nothing. He felt deeply irritated at the notion.

But he needn't have worried. Audrey came limping to the door. Her hair was tied up in a scarf. She wore an overall that bore witness to the fact that whatever chore had been claiming her attention was a dusty one; she was peeling off a pair of work gloves.

'Sergeant Lambert!' She gave him a friendly smile. 'You caught me up a stepladder, cleaning light fittings.' She laughed. 'I get these fits of housewifely energy. Nice to be able to indulge them after you retire. Makes you feel very virtuous when it's all done.'

She interrupted herself with a deprecating gesture. 'You haven't come over here to listen to me rabbiting on.' She stepped back, held the door wide. 'Won't you come in? I'll make some coffee and you can tell me why you've called.' She broke off suddenly and put a hand up to her mouth. A look of consternation flashed across her face. 'Has something terrible happened? Have you found Julie?' Her colour drained away.

'No, no, nothing like that,' he hastened to assure her. 'I haven't brought bad news. In fact I haven't brought any news, good or bad.'

She stood leaning against the side of the door, her eyes closed, her head lowered, breathing deeply. Her colour began to return.

She looked up at him with a wavering smile. 'How very stupid of me, jumping to conclusions like that. You will think me a foolish woman.' He stepped into the hall and she closed the door behind him.

160

'I could certainly do with that coffee now,' she declared with returning cheerfulness. 'You'd better come along into the kitchen – no need to stand on ceremony.'

He followed her along the passage. In the orderly kitchen he gestured her towards a chair. 'If you sit down, I'll make the coffee – I'm quite house-broken. That was a nasty moment you had back there. My fault – I should have guessed what you might think. I should have told you right off I hadn't brought bad news.'

'That's very kind of you.' She settled herself into the chair while Lambert made the coffee under her directions. They chatted casually, about the garden, the weather, the neighbourhood, until they were both sitting down, drinking their coffee. Audrey appeared relaxed now, composed and at ease.

'Please don't feel in any way awkward about this,' Lambert began gently. 'There are a couple of questions I'd like to ask you. Please take time to think before you answer. Don't say something now just because you said it before, and you think it might look odd to say something different this time.' She was half smiling by the time he had finished this preliminary spiel. The look on her face said as clearly as words: I know what you're going to ask me.

He pressed on. 'Did you have any contact with Julie after she left here in May for her second stay at Calcott House?'

Her smile was undisguised now, deprecating, apologetic. 'I knew that was what you were going to ask! I'll be happy to answer you, to tell you the truth this time. I don't need to think about it any more, I've thought about it enough; it's been bothering me a lot.' She drank her coffee. 'Yes, I did have some contact with Julie after she left here in May. I went over to see her in the caravan she was renting.'

'When was this?'

'I don't need to think about the date, either,' she answered readily, smiling again. 'I'm quite certain of it. I guessed you'd find out sooner or later that I'd been over to see her; I've thought about it a lot since the day you called here, asking about her. I did think once or twice of ringing the Cannonbridge police station, asking to speak to you, so I could tell you about it.' She moved her shoulders. 'But that seemed to make it serious and important, as if I'd been trying to hide something – which I hadn't. And I kept thinking: Julie's bound to walk in here one of these days and none of that will matter any more.' She gave a sigh. 'The day I went over to the caravan was Thursday, May 18th. I was there a few hours. I went over in the morning and got back here around tea time.'

'Why did you go over?'

'It was Julie's idea,' she answered without hesitation. 'She phoned me a couple of days earlier. She said she was leaving Calcott House. It was very pleasant and she'd very much enjoyed staying there but she wasn't ready to come back here yet, she felt she needed more time. Calcott House was too expensive to stay there any longer. She'd found a cheap caravan on a farm. She suggested I might like to go over there for a day, the break would do me good.

'I said I'd like that very much – and, of course, I wanted to take a look at her, see if she was all right, in a good frame of mind. So we settled on the Thursday. We had a nice drive round the countryside; we stopped for lunch at a pub.' She smiled. 'My treat – I knew she was watching her money.'

'Did she say anything about her plans?'

She shook her head with decision. 'Not a word. And I didn't ask her. I knew she didn't want to be pressed. There was no kind of hassle between us, no awkward questions; in fact, really no questions at all. We just spent a quiet few hours together.'

'Did she mention meeting anyone in particular? At Calcott House? Or anywhere else?'

Again she shook her head. There was a brief silence and then Lambert said gently: 'Why didn't you mention any of this the last time I called?'

She gave him a contrite, rueful look. 'I know you're going to think me a very silly woman but I shall have to put up with that, it's no more than I deserve. It was on account of what I'd said to the Eardlows, Julie's relatives. At the time Mrs Eardlow rang, saying they'd been expecting to hear from Julie but there'd been no word from her, I had a lot on my mind. An old aunt of mine, over ninety – she'd been living on her own ever since she'd been widowed – had been found dead in bed; she'd gone in her sleep.

'She'd never made a will and the upshot was what you can imagine. The cottage and her bits and pieces of furniture, pictures and ornaments, things she'd always treasured but never thought were worth anything, well, of course, everything put together amounted to quite a sum.'

She made a face. 'That brought them all round like flies round a honey pot. It was astonishing how many relatives and in-laws started putting their oar in; they were sure she'd have wanted them to have something, saying how good they'd always been to her – half of them hadn't been near her for years, afraid they might be called on to do something for her – and there was I in the middle of it all, trying to sort it out.'

She expelled a long breath. 'Anyway, all that kerfuffle was going on at the time the Eardlows rang. I wasn't in the least worried about Julie. I just told Mrs Eardlow she was on indefinite leave from her job; I didn't know where she was but I was sure they had no reason to worry.'

She gave him a direct, open look. 'All that was absolutely true. Mrs Eardlow never said a word about going to the police. It wasn't till you called here that I had any idea it was all being taken so seriously. When you started asking me questions I suddenly remembered I hadn't said anything to Mrs Eardlow about going to see Julie in the caravan – it had simply never crossed my mind at the time. I did think of mentioning it to you then but I thought it might seem strange, not having said anything about it before.'

She gave a placatory little grin. 'I don't suppose you remember exactly what I said but I didn't actually tell you any lies. I never said I hadn't seen Julie or had any kind of contact with her after she went off.' She waved a hand. 'I'm afraid you jumped to that conclusion yourself and I let it stand; I couldn't see it would matter all that much. I knew Julie was perfectly all right when I left her that day and I was pretty sure other folk must have come across her afterwards.' She paused. 'Someone must have done, surely?'

Lambert gazed back at her. Mrs Norbury and Simon had seen Julie no fewer than three times after May 18th. Julie had called on Mrs Venables on May 22nd, on Eva Simcox as well as Mrs Norbury on May 23rd. He didn't spell out those facts to Audrey but he did agree, yes, she had been seen by other people.

'There you are, then,' Audrey exclaimed with manifest relief. 'I know it was wrong of me but I haven't actually hindered your investigation, have I? If I had told you earlier about the visit, it wouldn't have made any difference at all, would it? You

163

wouldn't be any the wiser now about where she is.' Lamber acknowledged by an inclination of his head that this was so.

'You don't need to tick me off about my misdeed,' she went on, almost gaily. 'I've learned my lesson. If ever I find myself in any sort of situation again where I have to tell the police anything' – she rolled her eyes – 'God forbid – nothing personal, but God forbid, all the same – you can be absolutely certain I'll tell them everything I know, probably a good deal more than they want to know, to be on the safe side.'

When Lambert left the cottage he drove on till he came to a lay-by. He sat in his car, digesting what Audrey had told him. It all seemed straightforward enough. Why then did he have the gut feeling that she still hadn't told him everything she knew or guessed?

Maybe Julie's disappearance had nothing whatever to do with her snooping round after Olive Hammond but was connected with some aspect of the life she had been leading before he encountered her at the side of the road, back in April – some aspect of her personal life at Honeysuckle Cottage or her working life at the *Millbourne Advertiser*. Why had she left her job? Why had she left the cottage? What was it that had bothered her so much that she needed such a prolonged time to think?

He sat frowning out through the windscreen. Another word with her boss, Donald Fielding, might not come amiss. Yes, that was what he would do. He switched on the engine, pulled out of the lay-by and drove on into Millbourne.

The streets were fairly crowded but he was lucky enough to snap up a parking space close to the town centre. He made his way along the main street to the offices of the *Advertiser*. In reception he asked the pretty blonde at the desk if he could speak to Mr Donald Fielding; he didn't tell the girl he was a police officer.

'I'm sorry,' she told him. 'Mr Fielding's not here just now. Thursday's one of his busiest days. He isn't even in Millbourne. He does the rounds of the other newspapers on a Thursday. It isn't at all a good day to try to see him without an appointment.' She did her best to be helpful. 'If it's really urgent, I could get a message through to him at one of the other offices.'

'No, it's not that urgent,' Lambert said. 'Thanks all the same.'

He asked what time Fielding might be expected back in Millbourne.

She couldn't tell him exactly. 'It varies quite a bit. It might be as early as a quarter to three, could be as late as a quarter to five.' The most usual time was around three.

'I'll come back later,' he decided.

'You'll probably be wasting your time,' she warned him. 'I can't imagine him seeing anyone without an appointment on a Thursday, whatever time he gets back.'

'I'll chance it. Thanks for your help.' He didn't leave his name. As he turned to go he saw nearby a table stacked with copies of the *Advertiser*. 'All right if I take one?' he asked the girl.

'Help yourself.' She waved a hand. 'That's what they're there for. The latest edition, hot off the presses.'

He left the building and stood outside on the pavement, glancing up and down the street. Not far away, on the other side of the road, he saw the offices of another newspaper, the *Millbourne Echo*. Presumably the conventional, paid-for, weekly paper, long established, traditionally run. He glanced in the other direction and spotted a pub. Close to the pub, a newsagent's.

He crossed the road and went into the newsagent's. He bought a copy of the *Echo*. It was, as he had guessed, a weekly paper, fresh out today. With both his papers tucked under his arm he went along to the pub.

It was by now turned 12.30; there was a fair sprinkling of customers in the public bar. He ordered a drink and stood with it in a corner of the bar where he could casually watch the door. He made a show of reading his newspapers.

The patrons were a run-of-the-mill bunch: businessmen grabbing a bite and a drink before the next appointment, shoppers giving their feet a rest, old ladies, old men, killing time, dodging loneliness.

As the hands of the wall clock drew nearer to one o'clock a different, more convivial type of customer began to appear. Habitués, known to each other, hail fellow well met, a free and easy give and take of noisy banter. They settled in groups near the bar. Their loud exchanges left no room for any mystery; they were clearly journalists and other employees from the *Echo* and the *Advertiser*.

Still Lambert watched and waited.

165

Shortly after one the door pushed open and a man came in, alone. Very thin, with gaunt features, hair streaked with grey. He stood by the door, glancing round. He held himself in a deliberately loose, relaxed posture, he kept a would-be carefree smile fixed to his face as he slid his eyes over individuals, groups, giving a nod here, a wave there. Once or twice he received in return a brief, muted greeting but no one hailed him with pleasure, no one gestured an invitation to come over, no one offered him a drink.

He's my man, Lambert told himself. He folded his newspapers and clutched them high against his chest. He made his way over to where the newcomer still surveyed the room with his unwearying smile. His gaze travelled over Lambert, came to rest on the newspapers bundled into Lambert's grasp. Their eyes met.

Lambert addressed him in a matey fashion. 'Bit of a scrum in here. Can I get you a drink? I'm over here on business; this isn't my usual pub. I'm not too fond of drinking alone.'

'I'll have a drink with you,' the gaunt man answered. 'An alcohol-free lager.' His voice disclosed a fair level of education, a slight local overlay.

'It's what I'm drinking myself,' Lambert said. 'I'm driving. Can I get you something to eat? I'm having a sandwich.'

'Yes, I'll have a sandwich. Whatever they've got.'

They edged their way with their booty over to a far corner where a couple of shopping women were gathering up their bags, about to leave.

CHAPTER 23

'They're a lively enough crowd in here,' Lambert commented as they settled themselves down at the table. 'They seem to be from the newspaper offices along the road.'

The gaunt man nodded. 'I used to work for the *Echo* myself.' Lambert allowed his face to express interest. 'Beasley,' the other enlarged. 'Frank Beasley. I did all the usual stuff, some features and personality interviews, but what I was best known for was a regular financial column. Aimed at the general reader, very popular. ''The Money Game'', it was called. I did it for years.' He scanned Lambert's countenance for any sign of recognition. 'Frank Beasley,' he said again.

'Yes, the name does ring a bell,' Lambert acknowledged with not even a passing bow at the truth. 'Very nice to meet you.'

Beasley's face lit up. He sat back in his chair and began to eat his sandwich with a good appetite. He didn't ask Lambert what work he did, where he lived; he didn't even appear to notice he hadn't been given Lambert's name in return for his own.

'I started work at the *Echo* the moment I left school.' Beasley's voice held the remnants of old pride. 'I never wanted to do anything else.' He hesitated and then plunged on. 'I'd have been there to this day if it hadn't been for a piece of utter folly on my part.'

He looked across at Lambert. 'My own fault entirely, couldn't blame anyone else.' He gave a mirthless grin. 'Doesn't make it any easier to bear. Driving under the influence. Lost my licence.'

He hesitated again, stared into his glass. 'That wasn't the whole of it. I'd been knocking it back all evening in a pub in the next town. I was driving home; I fell asleep at the wheel. I ran into a line of cars parked on a bit of an incline. They bunted each other down the slope, across a road, smack into the front of a shop.' He closed his eyes. 'An elderly couple, been visiting the married daughter in a nearby house, they'd just got into their car, near the bottom of the line.' He drew a shuddering breath. 'The old man had a heart attack, died next day in hospital. I got a suspended sentence, a heavy fine. Lucky not to go to gaol.'

He took a long drink. 'That was the end of everything. Broke the wife's heart. She'd been on at me for years about my drinking. I wouldn't listen, I knew it all. Used to kid myself I drove better after I'd had a skinful.'

He held up his glass. 'This stuff's all I touch these days; I had to learn my lesson the hard way. I do a bit of freelancing, magazines, mostly. I get the odd piece in a newspaper but never in the *Echo*, never once since the day they kicked me out. I don't try there any more.'

He swirled the lager in his glass. 'The missus died a couple of years ago. She never really got over it.' He stared at the eddying liquid. 'It's supposed to get easier as time goes by but that's not been my experience. I find it gets worse.' He glanced about. 'I come in here most days. Gives me some sort of feeling I'm still part of things.' He gave another cheerless grin. 'And I can keep my ears open for the gossip – can't do without that in my trade.'

Lambert gestured at his copy of the *Advertiser* lying on the table. 'What about the freesheets? Do they take anything from you?'

Beasley's sombre expression lightened fractionally. 'Yes, they do take my stuff. I often get a piece in the *Advertiser*. Donald Fielding's a very decent chap – he owns the *Advertiser*.' He smiled. 'I've known him since he was a baby in a pram, that never hurts.'

He jerked his head. 'Smart chap, Fielding. Smart businessman. Hard-nosed as they come, of course. You can't succeed in the newspaper game if you go pussyfooting about; it's dog eat dog all along the line. But Fielding isn't a one-hundred-per-cent dyed-in-the-wool son of a bitch, like a lot of these self-made men.'

'Self-made?' Lambert echoed.

'I'll say he is. He's about as self-made as any man could be.' Beasley's voice and manner were energetic now; he seemed to have been temporarily jacked up out of his brooding despondency. 'He could hardly have come from much lower down the social scale. Illegitimate, abandoned by his own family, raised by a woman no blood kin of his, a woman who took him in

168

out of the pure goodness of her heart. And now look at him today. All set for greater things. He hasn't got anywhere near as far as he's going to get, not in my opinion.' His voice held a strong note of admiration. Lambert could detect no trace of envy or sourness.

'Fielding's a widower, same as me,' Beasley went on. 'His wife died a few months ago. She'd been an invalid for years – multiple sclerosis. It came on a year or two after they married; there were never any children. In her best patches she did good work for MS, raised a lot of money. And Donald always did what he could in his papers: publicity, appeals, and so on. She was a courageous woman; they thought a great deal of her in Millbourne.

'Her parents were well known locally, well liked, well respected. Her father was a parson and her mother was one of those salt-of-the-earth women – WVS, Meals on Wheels, every kind of local charitable work. They're both dead now, her parents; she was their only child.'

He finished his sandwich. 'I wouldn't be at all surprised if Fielding doesn't marry again before long.' He gave Lambert a knowing look. 'And I wouldn't mind betting good money on the name of the lady: Miss Isobel Gresham.'

'Gresham?' Lambert repeated. The name seemed vaguely familiar.

'George Gresham's daughter,' Beasley enlarged. 'You must have heard of him – Gresham Enterprises. Very successful businessman. Tycoon, I suppose you could call him by this time. Made his money in industry, manufacturing, in the south of the county. Got out of that when he saw the signs. Went into printing and from that into publishing. Then he started buying up local newspapers, then an advertising agency, after that it was freesheets. From what I hear now he's into videos, local radio, satellite TV, every form of communication.'

'Does his daughter work in the business?'

'Isobel? No, she's not the type. She's not a university graduate or anything like that. She hasn't got her father's brains, though she's intelligent enough. She's not a young girl; she must be over thirty now. She keeps house for her father, has done since her mother died, some years ago. Very natural, sensible, domestic sort of woman, Isobel Gresham, quiet and unassuming,

169

gives her father a good, stable background. Very important, that, to a high-flier like Gresham.

'Not that Gresham's one of these jet-setting whiz kids, far from it. Austere, strait-laced sort of chap, not interested in frills, extravagant living. He's a lay preacher – not just for the look of it, either; he believes every last word of it.' He smiled. 'Doesn't stop him driving a hard bargain. But he's a very fair employer from anything I've ever heard, not the type to grind a man into the ground.'

He drained his glass. 'Next thing we'll hear, you mark my words, Gresham will have bought out Fielding's group of free-sheets and Fielding will be going to work for Gresham Enterprises – at the top level. Suit the pair of them very well, that will.

'Gresham's taken a real liking to Fielding. Both of them self-made men, on the same wavelength. Fielding's been over to Gresham's place quite a bit recently. The three of them were at a local charity do together a couple of weeks back. I was there myself. I saw the way Isobel looked at Fielding – and the way Gresham looked at the pair of them.

'Nothing Gresham would like better than to see Isobel settled, happily married, give him some grandchildren. And a son-in-law who can take over the empire one day. Gresham hasn't got a son, just Isobel. He's bound to start thinking about what'll happen to everything he's built up, after he's gone. And I'm sure Fielding would appreciate a normal family life now, no one more so. However devoted he was to his wife, it must always have been a difficult situation. I don't imagine he's any plaster saint; I dare say he's had his share of temptations over the last few years. There's never any shortage of good-looking young women in newspaper offices – and a good many of them more than ready to make a play for the boss.

'If he has been having a bit on the side, I imagine he'll have put paid to it pretty smartly by now; he'll be keeping his fingers crossed no word of it leaks out to George Gresham.' He grimaced. 'And that the girl can be trusted to keep her mouth shut. Not always the case nowadays; there isn't the same code about these things any more – kiss and tell seems to be the order of the day.'

He shook his head. 'A man in Fielding's position can easily get himself into a vulnerable situation. His wife being as highly thought of as she was, for her charity work and the way she coped with her illness – and with her being the daughter of her parents – local opinion could soon turn against Fielding if there was any whiff of carrying-on while his wife was alive.

'But I'm sure Fielding would always have been very discreet. The last thing he'd ever have wanted would be to upset his wife. In spite of all the difficulties over her illness, he had a lot to be grateful to her for.'

'In what way?' Lambert asked.

'When Fielding married her he had just the one freesheet, the *Advertiser*. Starting that took every penny he could lay his hands on. But his wife had quite a bit of capital – from her grandmother on her mother's side. She let Fielding have the lot. He was able to start up a second freesheet. When that prospered he started up another, and so on. They all did well. The money began to roll in. He was able to buy a very nice cottage for Audrey Tysoe, to pay her back some of what he owes her.'

Lambert just about managed not to jerk bolt upright in his seat. 'Audrey Tysoe?' he got out in as casual a tone as he could muster.

'That's right. Audrey used to work for Fielding till she retired. It was Audrey brought Fielding up; it was she gave him his start in business. I've known Audrey all my life. I lived a couple of streets away from her when we were kids. Little terrace houses, no gardens, opened straight onto the street, just a paved yard at the back.

'Audrey and I went to the same school. She was no dummy, I can tell you. Very hard worker, never anything showy, but plenty of good grey stuff up here.' He tapped his forehead. 'And plenty of good sound common sense. I don't suppose she's ever in her life done or said a foolish thing.'

Lambert asked if Beasley would like another drink, another sandwich.

'That's very civil of you.' Beasley was looking a good deal more lively and cheerful than when he had entered the pub. 'I'll have the same again.'

When Lambert came back from the bar Beasley was leafing through the *Advertiser*. 'Well set out paper,' he commented. He made a start on his sandwich. 'Audrey Tysoe ran the personnel side of things for Fielding. First class, she was, too.'

'How did she come to bring Fielding up?' Lambert asked. 'Was she ever married?'

Beasley shook his head with vigour. 'Not Audrey. Never even had a boyfriend. She was always a dumpy little thing, never anything to look at. She got polio when she was seven or eight; there were quite a few cases in the town. It left her with a limp.'

He took a drink of his lager. 'She had brothers and sisters, all older than her – her mother was middle-aged by the time Audrey was born. They all did quite well, decent jobs, got married, set up in homes of their own. Then the father died. Mrs Tysoe's health wasn't too good by then. Audrey was the only one left at home; she was still at school. When the time came for her to leave school the rest of them took it for granted she should stop at home to look after the mother, run the house. She'll never get married, they said. With her looks and that limp. They didn't bother to dress it up; they had no thought for her feelings.

'Audrey knew when the chips were stacked against her. She didn't make a fight of it; she accepted she was going to have to buckle down to things at home. None of the others was willing to chip in with any money. There was a pension from the firm the father had worked for – he was a clerk with a builders' supply merchant. The pension was just about enough to manage on.

'But Audrey did hold out for one thing, right at the start: the house, and any savings the mother had, would all have to go to her absolutely on the mother's death, the rest of them must give up any claim.' He grinned. 'There was one hell of an argument but in the end they had to agree, she had them over a barrel – there wasn't one of them wanted any part of the bother of looking after the mother.

'Audrey went straight off to a solicitor; she had the whole thing properly drawn up.' He gave an admiring nod. 'A young girl, straight from school, you've got to hand it to her. After a year or two Mrs Tysoe's health got worse, she started getting confused – Alzheimer's. In those days they called it getting senile.

'When Audrey was around eighteen, a girl she knew, a girl we'd both been at school with, got herself into trouble. Brenda Fielding, her name was; she was always feckless. She lived at home with her father, a real tyrant. Her mother had cleared off years ago with another man. Brenda had been knocking about with a local lad. His parents were very strict, very upright, some hellfire brand of religion. Of course Brenda got pregnant.

'When she told the lad he buckled at the knees. He didn't wait to find out what his parents would have to say, he scarpered with the speed of light, never seen round these parts again. Of course it wasn't long before Brenda's dad noticed his daughter's belly swelling. There was an almighty uproar. As soon as he knew there was no question of her getting married, he slung her out on the street.

'She went straight round to Audrey Tysoe's and threw herself on Audrey's mercy; she didn't know what else to do. Audrey didn't think twice about it; she took her in. She didn't bother to ask her mother's permission – her mother didn't know what day of the week it was by then.

'The rest of the family were horrified when they found out but Audrey told them to mind their own business and let her mind hers. She was never short of character and guts. If she made up her mind to do something, she'd go ahead, come hell or high water.

'Brenda stayed on with Audrey after the baby was born. She wasn't much of a mother and she was pretty hopeless round the house. She always seemed to resent the child. She was soon back at work again – she had a job in a factory – and Audrey was looking after the baby as well as everything else.

'Then Brenda found herself a man who wanted to marry her. He had no idea she had a son and she had no intention of telling him. She knew she wouldn't see him for dust if she opened her mouth.

'She asked Audrey if she'd be willing to keep the child, raise him. No need for any formal adoption. Brenda had no wish to keep in touch with her son and she didn't offer to send any money for his keep.

'Audrey didn't need to think it over. She loved the boy, she knew she'd never have a child herself. It was a relief to know Brenda would be out of the picture for good. To all intents and purposes Donald would be her own son.

'So that was that. Brenda got married and took herself off. Audrey's mother died a year or two afterwards. Audrey invested what money her mother left. She came round to see me about it, asked my advice; she made sound investments. She'd always been thrifty, always managed to save, however little she had.

'When Donald was old enough for school, she took a secretarial course at the local college, then she went to work for an agency, so she could always be free in the school holidays.

'Donald did well at school. He was a clever, hard-working lad. He was devoted to Audrey, never got into any sort of trouble. As he got older, fourteen or fifteen, he started asking me questions about newspaper work; he showed a strong interest in it.

'When the time came for him to leave school, Audrey talked it over with me. She asked if I'd put in a word for him at the *Echo*. He started there as soon as he left school. And a very good journalist he made too. He was ambitious from the word go. I always knew he was going places.

'It was Audrey who put up the money when he started his first freesheet. She sold the terrace house and handed him the proceeds. The pair of them moved into a cheap rented flat. She gave him all her savings and the investments she'd made. The whole lot put together was just about enough to give him a start.

'The *Advertiser* was a success from the beginning. It was tremendously hard work getting it off the ground. Sometimes Donald would be slogging away right round the clock. Audrey worked for him full time, and a good deal more than full time, many a week. He's never forgotten what she's done for him and he never will. I don't believe there's anything in heaven or earth she wouldn't do for him.

'When he got married, Audrey went on living in the flat on her own till Donald bought Honeysuckle Cottage for her. She'd always dreamed of living in the country, having a garden. When she got to fifty-five he talked her into retiring on a handsome pension; he told her it was about time she started taking it easy.' He drew a sighing breath. 'I've seen very little of Audrey since I was booted out of the *Echo*. Not that she ever turned her nose up at me over that, she's not the type, but it was a long time before I could look anyone properly in the face again.

'And of course Audrey doesn't come into town much these days, she spends a lot of time in her garden. It must be a couple of years or more since I last had a real chat with her. I see her once in a while, to give her a wave, maybe a word or two. I saw her one day this last week, getting on her bus. She looked very well.'

He laughed. 'A woman like that, all that character, all that energy, intelligent, capable, determined, dogged, you wouldn't think she'd still be going round by bus, you'd think she'd have learned to drive a car. But she never did.'

Lambert's eyes jerked wide open. 'She never learned to drive? Are you sure?'

Beasley looked surprised. 'Of course I'm sure. It's been a joke between us for years. I was forever teasing her about it. I used to tell her: "Every chit of a girl in your office can drive a car, but not you. You ought to be ashamed of yourself."

'She always said it comes naturally to young girls today, learning to drive, they've been brought up with cars, but she grew up in the age of buses. She would never have a lesson, never wanted to.'

'Maybe she learned to drive after she retired,' Lambert said casually.

Beasley shook his head. 'That she hasn't. When I saw her the other day I pulled her leg about it again. I said she had no excuse now for not buying a car and taking lessons, she had all the time in the world. She just laughed and said: "Not me – you'll never talk me into it. Buses suit me fine."'

A quarter to three at the earliest, the pretty blonde in reception had said Fielding would be back. But Lambert was taking no chances; he walked in again through the doors of the *Advertiser* shortly after two. The blonde was no longer in evidence; her place had been taken by an equally attractive redhead.

Lambert again went into his spiel, this time with slight variations and some additional queries. He learned that Fielding visited each of his freesheet offices at least twice every week, sometimes three or four times – plus the round of all the freesheets he made without fail on Thursdays.

Lambert told the girl he would wait, on the chance that Fielding might be willing to spare him a few minutes when he arrived.

Affixed to the wall in the waiting area were several boxes containing leaflets and brochures, advertising and publicity handouts. Lambert stood glancing through them.

In one of the leaflets he came upon a map showing the location of all the freesheets in the group. He sat down at a table and studied the map. According to the leaflet there were now seven freesheets in the group.

One location in particular caught his attention: a town only a couple of miles from the farm where Julie Dawson had rented the caravan.

Shortly after three Donald Fielding came striding into the building. His sharp gaze swept round the reception hall, coming to rest on Lambert who had risen to his feet the moment he caught sight of Fielding. The sergeant received the instant impression that his presence in reception had caused Fielding no surprise.

Fielding nodded over at him amiably enough, raising a hand as if to say: I'll be with you in a moment. He went up to the desk and spent a minute or two talking to the redhead before walking across to where Lambert stood waiting.

Fielding held out a hand. 'Sergeant Lambert!' His manner was briskly affable. 'I hear you've been waiting some time. I'm afraid you've picked one of my busiest days.'

Lambert asked if he could spare a few minutes and Fielding made no objection. He paused in his outer office to tell his secretary not to put any calls through for the present, he didn't want to be disturbed. In the inner office he waved the sergeant into a chair and took his own seat facing Lambert across the desk.

'Well now,' Fielding began pleasantly. 'How can I be of help?' He halted suddenly. 'I take it you've no news of Julie? That isn't why you're here?'

Lambert shook his head. 'No, no news.'

'Well now,' Fielding said again.

'I'm going to ask you a question,' Lambert informed him. 'I'd like you to think well before you answer.' Fielding made a slight inclination of his head. 'Did you have any contact of any kind with Julie after she left Honeysuckle Cottage in May to pay her second visit to Calcott House?'

A look of mild amusement flitted over Fielding's face. 'Be sure your sins will find you out,' he said lightly. 'Yes, I did see Julie once after she left Honeysuckle Cottage in May. It was on a Thursday, when I was doing my rounds. I can give you the date.' He consulted a desk diary. 'May 18th.'

He sat back in his chair. 'Julie rang Audrey Tysoe and invited her over to the caravan for the day. Audrey doesn't drive so she asked me if I could give her a lift; it wouldn't be much out of my way to drop her off and pick her up again in the afternoon. Of course I said I would.

'I didn't go into the caravan when I dropped her off but I did go in when I picked her up again. I didn't stop long. Julie looked very well but she told me she still wasn't ready to come back to work. I didn't press her. I told her to take all the time she needed. It was all perfectly friendly.'

'You said nothing about this visit the last time I was here,' Lambert pointed out.

Fielding raised his shoulders. 'I never actually said I hadn't seen Julie. You didn't ask me specifically.'

'It would have been the natural thing to mention it.'

Fielding grinned. 'In the ordinary way, of course, I would have mentioned it, but Audrey Tysoe had asked me not to. She phoned me one day in June; she sounded worried. She said she'd had some relatives of Julie's on the phone, asking if she knew where Julie was. After the call she realized she'd forgotten to say anything about going over to the caravan. If the Eardlows rang me, would I mind not saying anything about the visit either? It seemed a fuss about nothing to me, but I said OK, if that was what she wanted – Audrey can be a real worrier.'

He grinned again. 'Then you turned up. Audrey was in a bit of a state after you'd spoken to her at Honeysuckle Cottage. She rang me to say she'd still said nothing about going to the caravan; she'd been in two minds about it but she was afraid it would seem odd to mention it now when she'd said nothing before. If you called in here, asking questions, would I be sure to say nothing about the visit? I told her for heaven's sake to stop worrying, forget it, she was blowing it up out of all proportion, I certainly wouldn't drop her in it.'

'I spoke to Miss Tysoe again this morning,' Lambert said. 'As I dare say you're well aware.' Fielding made no response to that. 'Miss Tysoe admitted she did go over to the caravan to see Julie but she said nothing about getting a lift from you. She allowed me to understand she'd gone over there alone, that she'd driven over. She didn't tell me she's never driven in her life.'

Fielding smiled. 'I'm sure she didn't tell you any outright lie. I'm sure if you'd asked her how she got to the caravan she'd have told you I gave her a lift.'

'There's such a thing as lying by omission,' Lambert observed.

'Be fair,' Fielding said in protest. 'It's your job to ask the right questions. Does it really matter how Audrey arrived at the caravan? If she'd gone over there on a bicycle or a bus, what difference would that make to anything? You're not telling me Julie vanished into thin air the moment Audrey and I drove off from the caravan that Thursday? Other folk must have seen her.' Lambert gave a brief, acknowledging nod. 'And what about Julie's things in the caravan?' Fielding went on. 'She must have cleared them out before she left. And she must have returned the keys at the end of her booking.'

'Yes, all that was certainly done,' Lambert conceded. 'But

anyone could have done it. There's nothing to prove it was done by Julie.'

'And I take it there's nothing to prove it wasn't done by Julie, either,' Fielding countered sharply.

Lambert gave him a level look. 'Is there anything else you haven't bothered to mention because you were never directly asked? You didn't, for instance, make a second visit to the caravan? On the following Thursday? May 25th?'

Fielding's expression changed abruptly to one of piercing alertness, tinged with anger. 'Why should I want to go over there again?'

'Perhaps Miss Tysoe asked you to give her another lift to the caravan. Or maybe you decided to call in again yourself to have another word with Julie, as you'd be over that way.'

'I never went near the caravan again,' Fielding insisted with force. 'I had no reason to. Audrey never asked me for another lift over there'. He came to an abrupt halt, made a visible attempt to regain his composure.

Lambert felt like a man on the edge of a precipice. He could still step back. He could forget about Fielding, about Audrey Tysoe. Forget about Julie Dawson. He could drive back to Bowpatch, pack his things, set off tomorrow back to Cannonbridge and his everyday life.

For a moment he was powerfully tempted. He made ready to push back his chair, rise to his feet.

But he couldn't do it.

'I put it to you,' he said to Fielding in the tone of a man about to advance a philosophical proposition, 'that your relationship with Julie Dawson over the past two years was a good deal more than that of employer and employee, that you had her move discreetly into Honeysuckle Cottage because of that relationship.'

Fielding sat very still, his expression hardened into granite.

Lambert plunged on. 'One day back in the New Year your personal situation alters suddenly with the death of your wife. Soon afterwards it begins to look as if your business situation might also alter drastically. The arrangement with Julie doesn't fit the new situation on either front; in fact, if even a whisper of it gets about it might gum up the works, put paid to your chances of branching out, making a new start in both your business and your personal life.'

179

Fielding sat like stone.

Lambert swept on. 'You don't want to cast Julie off without a thought, you want to be fair to her. You offer to make some sort of provision, help her to find a new job somewhere else. References, training, contacts, anything she needs she can have. But she's got to go – and go permanently.

'She's knocked sideways. She'd imagined the situation could go on for years, she'd felt settled in it, content. She may even have fancied there might be a possibility of marriage one day. She doesn't want to leave, doesn't want to be paid off. But you're adamant.

'She needs time to think, to decide what to do. She cuts and runs for it – back to the village where she was born. And when she does think it over, maybe she's not in the least inclined to be cooperative, maybe she point-blank refuses to be cast aside so easily.' He leaned forward. 'I put it to you again: did you go back to the caravan on Thursday, May 25th?'

Fielding looked across at him. 'That's quite a scenario you've dreamed up there.' His tone held a note of detached, professional appraisal, like an editor considering the work of a cub reporter. 'You'll be able to take up crime-fiction writing when the day comes for you to leave the force.' He inclined his head with a half-smiling look. 'That day may come a good deal sooner than you bargain for if you make a habit of pitching into respectable citizens the way you've just set about me.'

He linked his hands behind his head and leaned back, tilting the front legs of his chair off the floor. His eyes never left Lambert. The quality of his gaze hardened, sharpened. He ran a penetrating newspaperman's eye over the sergeant, noting his casual clothes, the length of his hair. He swung further back in his seat; it looked for a moment as if he might topple over but he maintained a precarious balance at a point where he was able to glance through the central arch of the desk at Lambert's feet, shod in their holiday trainers.

Fielding dropped his hands from behind his head. He allowed the legs of his chair to bang down again on the floor. His look was edged with amusement, burgeoning triumph.

'Would it bother you at all,' he asked with an idle, matey air, spiced with derision, 'if I were to ring Cannonbridge and ask to speak to your superior officer? If I told him I wasn't altogether pleased with your way of going on? If I threw in a few words

180

like harassment and persecution? The police are a touch sensitive these days about complaints of that sort – particularly from someone with a bunch of newspapers at his back.'

There was a brief silence. 'You don't answer,' Fielding pursued with relentless mockery. 'You amused yourself just now with a little guesswork about me, it's only fair I should be allowed to return the compliment.' He put the tips of his fingers together. 'My guess is: you're not here on official duty at all. You're playing a lone hand.'

Lambert said nothing. His whole attention was riveted on keeping his face, his posture, calm and unmoving. But it was this very absence of any hint of response that told Fielding at once that he had struck home. He threw back his head and laughed in genuine amusement.

'By God!' he exclaimed when his laughter had moderated. 'That *is* what you're up to! You've been told to drop the case, there's nothing in it.' The last of his laughter vanished. 'But you can't let go, can you?' He leaned forward, his voice low, full of controlled menace. 'You met Julie, you took a shine to her. So you decide to play Sir Galahad. You get yourself some time off, you take a snoop round on your own.'

Lambert sat mute and rigid.

Fielding's voice was bitingly cold. 'And if you can't come across any crime, that's no problem, you can always invent one. I don't know if you make a habit of amusing yourself in this way but you've as sure as hell come to the wrong shop this time.'

He fell silent for a moment before erupting again with savage force. 'If you ever so much as show your face round here again I'll personally see you live to regret it. Get out!' he ordered with dismissive contempt. 'Clear off before I decide to make that phone call!'

Lambert got to his feet. 'Close the door behind you!' Fielding commanded. 'Some of us have honest work to do.'

By the time Lambert got back to his car he was overwhelmed by a wave of black depression. It was not the smallest consolation to realize that if the chances of his folly had taken his feet in through the portals of Calcott House instead of through the swing doors of the *Advertiser*, it could just as easily and predictably have been Evan Marchant who dispatched him with a flea in his ear.

It was as much as he could do to start up the engine, give his attention to the traffic, slide into the stream of vehicles, following them blindly, anywhere, away from Fielding, away from the *Advertiser*, from Millbourne.

Some fifteen minutes later, without any very clear recollection of having negotiated such things as traffic lights or roundabouts, he found himself on the edge of town, heading into open country.

The sky had darkened. A fierce squall of rain blew up suddenly. His windscreen ran with water.

He spotted a lay-by ahead. He pulled in and switched off his engine. He sat with his eyes closed and his head sunk on his chest, trying to still the voices in his brain.

At last, after a lapse of time he couldn't measure, he sat up and opened his eyes. He felt shaken and exhausted as if he had by a hair's-breadth just escaped total disaster.

Ah well, no use sitting here brooding. What was done was done and couldn't now be undone. Better turn round, head back for Bowpatch.

He switched on the engine. The rain had stopped, the sun had broken through again and was shining brilliantly. As he began to move the car out he saw, a little way ahead, a magnificent rainbow arching across the road.

He switched the engine off again and got out of the car. The air smelled fresh and sweet. He stood looking at the rainbow, at the beautiful, dazzling, translucent colours. He felt some measure of peace begin to return.

As he watched, the central span of the arc began slowly to fade and dissolve. He stood unmoving. The dissolution gathered speed. Still he watched. Now there were only the twin piers of the arch, melting even as he gazed at them.

He got back into the car and pulled out. He drove slowly, passing between the last remnants of the airy columns. Half a mile further on he halted and looked back.

Of the whole vast, brilliant arch, so substantial seeming, so apparently tangible such a brief time before, not the faintest vestige now remained.

Mrs Inskip was busy in her kitchen when Lambert got back to Bowpatch. She heard him open the front door and came out into the hall.

'I hope you're going to be pleased with what I've done,' she greeted him. Slight anxiety showed in her gentle brown eyes. 'If you'll come into the sitting room you'll see.' He followed her along the passage.

'I went over to my daughter's today,' she explained. 'In the next village. She's been having a good clear-out and I had a look through the stuff she was getting rid of, in case there was anything I could use. She'd put all this lot out.' She gestured at a couple of large, bulging bags of stout brown paper. 'Children's toys, rag books, puzzles, games, all things her two have finished with. She was going to give them to a jumble sale but I said no, I'll have those, I know just the right home for them.'

She peered earnestly up at Lambert. 'Don't you think Cicely Jerrom would like them? I thought you might take them along to Greenfield; I'm sure Hilda would accept them from you.'

'I'll take them with pleasure,' Lambert promised. 'I'll make sure Hilda understands how kindly you mean it. I'll be leaving after breakfast in the morning; I'll drop the bags in on my way.'

A thought struck Mrs Inskip. 'Tomorrow's Friday – the Jerroms might not be in; they might be doing their weekend shopping in Yelmerton.'

'Don't worry about that,' he reassured her. 'I can always take the bags round the back of the bungalow, leave them somewhere safe. I can write a note and slip it through the letter box.' He carried the bags up to his bedroom and set them down beside the chest of drawers.

By the time he had eaten his supper his gloom had lightened considerably. He said goodbye to Mr Inskip before he went to bed, knowing Inskip would be up and out at work before his own foot touched the bedroom floor in the morning. And he decided to give Mrs Inskip the present he had bought for her now. She received it with a lively show of pleasure.

'While I think of it,' she said on a sudden recollection, 'I'd better have your Cannonbridge address, in case anything comes for you after you've gone, or I find something you've left behind.'

In the kitchen he brewed himself the final dose of Hilda Jerrom's herbs. He carried the steaming beaker upstairs and set it down on his bedside table.

He paused in the act of removing his jacket, dipped into a pocket and drew out the envelope Simon Norbury had given him. He regarded it with a wry smile, turned it over and glanced again at the jottings.

There were still two abbreviations, Mgt and Frs, he hadn't been able to make anything of at all. Just as well. He gave a little snort of self-mockery. God alone knew what further idiocies he might have embarked on if he'd had two more folly-fallen paths to blunder along.

A thought struck him: maybe Julie had managed to work something out for those two abbreviations; maybe she had got onto one – or both – of the folk they stood for.

Then common sense reared its head again. No more of this nonsense, he commanded himself. Put it behind you.

He gave a final dismissive shrug of his shoulders at the entire lunatic episode. His brain, rational and positive, the authoritative, clear-headed overseer, directed his fingers to crumple up the envelope and its contents, and drop them in the waste bin.

But his fingers, perverse and wilful, refused to obey. Operating on some obscure, covert level, instinctive, intuitive, far removed from the sway of reason, his recalcitrant fingers obstinately returned the envelope to his pocket.

It was past eight when Lambert woke after a sound sleep that had restored his spirits to their usual state of cheerfulness. He got out of bed and went over to the window, drew back the

184

curtains. A light, wreathing mist enveloped the landscape but already the sun showed the first signs of its struggle to break through.

He turned from the window. After all, things weren't too bad. He had escaped – admittedly by the skin of his teeth – any real damage to his career. It had certainly taught him a lesson. Oh yes, he acknowledged fervently as he went along the corridor to the bathroom, the lesson had burned into his soul. Never again such wayward follies – never, never, never again.

But it hadn't all been a total waste of time and effort, he consoled himself as he ran the taps. He had had a holiday of sorts, he felt a lot fitter; he appeared, touch wood, to have shaken off the last remnants of his malaise, no coughing or sneezing this morning, not a solitary twinge or ache. He stared at his face in the mirror above the washbasin. His skin was definitely a fresher colour, his eyes brighter, less like those of a stricken toad.

Downstairs he ate with relish a last leisurely breakfast. His spirits continued to rise. There was still the weekend before him after he got back to Cannonbridge, no reason why he shouldn't enjoy it. One or two old friends lived not too far distant from Cannonbridge, friends he had rather lost touch with in recent times; he could ring round, see if he could meet up with any of them. Plenty of interesting things to do and see within striking distance of Cannonbridge, only a question of taking the trouble, making the effort.

He went upstairs to finish his packing. And while he was at it, while he resolutely pursued the last of his holiday mood, why not treat himself to another superb lunch at Calcott House? Take a pleasant stroll round the gardens, then a really slap-up meal, hang the expense.

He stowed his dressing gown and slippers in his bag, crammed in his washing things. And all the while, at some profound level of his brain, his subconscious beavered away at its task, dogged and persistent, occasionally shafting up a message, utterly indifferent to skittish shifts in direction on the part of management up top.

Lambert remembered he had left his toothbrush in the bathroom. He went along to get it. He came back and put it in with his toilet things. He began to close his bag.

At that moment a thought flashed up into his brain. He halted

185

in his task, his hands idle over the straps. Olive Hammond might be back at home in her cottage by now, returned from some brief holiday or errand of mercy. He could just pop over there, take a gander, then it could all be wrapped up and put away, laid to rest and forgotten, in company with all the other dead ducks and red herrings of his years in the force.

He jerked back into motion again, closed up his bag. Yes, that was what he'd do: drop the toys in at Greenfield, then call in on Olive, then on to Calcott House for lunch, then off to Cannonbridge. He whistled a tune as he went downstairs and took his things out to the car.

Mrs Inskip was in the garden, picking over the strawberry beds for jam-making. He went across to say goodbye. As he walked back to his car he heard the hollow, mocking notes of some laggard cuckoo echoing across the fields.

The air had brightened, the mist had almost gone. The day gave promise of heat. He reached the T-junction where the turning led off to Greenfield. He uttered a sound of irritation as he realized he had left behind the bags of toys Mrs Inskip had given him. He knew precisely where they were at this moment: on the other side of his bed, on the floor beside the chest of drawers – out of range of his final checking glance round the room.

He was strongly tempted to forget the toys, drive on towards Olive Hammond's cottage. But Mrs Inskip's kind, anxious face floated up before him. How disappointed she would be when she came across the toys. Cicely Jerrom would never now rejoice over them; they would go to the next church bazaar – Mrs Inskip would never be able to bring herself to walk up the front path of Greenfield, press the doorbell, attempt to hand them over herself.

He gave a long, noisy sigh. Nothing for it but to do the decent thing, turn round and go back.

The sun finally broke through as he pulled up outside the cottage. Mrs Inskip was in the kitchen, hulling her strawberries. She was delighted to see him. 'A letter's come for you,' she told him. 'In the ordinary way I'd have redirected it right away and given it back to the postman, but I'd been up to your room a minute or two before and I saw you'd left the toys behind. I took a chance you might come back for them.' She handed him the letter.

Lambert recognized the handwriting of his Cannonbridge landlady.

Across the top of the envelope another hand had penned in bold capitals: TRY YELMERTON, with the *M* heavily underlined. 'It's been to Yelverton, in Somerset, by mistake,' Mrs Inskip commented. 'You can see the second postmark – of course that's delayed you getting it. They read the *M* as a *V*. That does sometimes happen; it's an easy mistake to make.' She picked up the two brown-paper bags. 'While you're reading your letter I'll take these out to your car.' She smiled. 'I'm making sure you don't forget them this time.'

Lambert slit open the envelope. Inside was a second envelope directed in a schoolboy fist to Detective Sergeant Lambert at his Cannonbridge lodgings. He saw from the date stamp that it had been posted four days ago.

Inside was a neatly written letter from Simon Norbury. It began with laboured apologies. Simon had remembered something but he didn't know if it was important or not; he had been wondering whether to write and mention it. 'I'm off to Turkey tomorrow,' he went on, 'so in the end I decided I'd better tell you, just in case. It was the last time I saw Julie, on the Tuesday, May 23rd – I'm quite certain about the date. We were talking about books. She said she had some books back in Millbourne, in Honeysuckle Cottage, books she didn't read any more; she might let me have them for my collection. I said that would be marvellous, it was very generous of her. Then we started talking about other things and we played a game of chess.

'When she was going she said, "Don't get your hopes up, this isn't a definite promise, but you might have those books before you go back to school." She knew I would be going back on the Friday, June 2nd. She said she'd probably be going over to Honeysuckle Cottage; she had some unfinished business to sort out in Millbourne.

'I never heard any more from her. I wasn't really disappointed about not getting the books. I thought she'd changed her mind and decided to keep them herself. After I got back to school I forgot all about it.'

The air was warming up. The sun shone down with increasing brilliance as Lambert set off again towards Greenfield. I could nip over to Millbourne after lunch, he mused. Pay a call on Audrey Tysoe at Honeysuckle Cottage. One question he'd dearly like to put to her: had Julie called in after May 23rd to pick up the books for Simon?

He reached the T-junction and turned for Greenfield. As he straightened the car he caught sight of his hair in the mirror. It was actually starting to turn up in little curls. Must get it cut today or tomorrow without fail; the Chief would have a fit if he could see him now. He wondered how the Chief had enjoyed his cruise. And the widows. Maybe one of them had managed to get her hooks into him. He grinned at the notion. That would be the day.

He came into sight of Greenfield, serene and peaceful in the golden sunlight. Hilda Jerrom was stooping over a border in the front garden. She straightened at the sight of the car and stood watching as he got out. Her face wore its customary wary look. Her gaze came to rest on the brown-paper bags he carried. She didn't call out in greeting as he approached.

'I'm glad I caught you,' he said as he opened the gate. 'I wasn't sure if I would. I thought, being Friday, you might have gone into town for the weekend shopping.'

The wariness began to dissolve. 'We never go into town on Friday or Saturday, far too crowded for a wheelchair. We get the shopping done early in the week, then Cicely can enjoy it in comfort.' She smiled. 'She looks on it as a great treat.'

'It's because of Cicely I'm here.' He explained about the toys, scrupulously careful to avoid any hint of charity or patronizing attitudes, any suggestion that the Greenfield household had been a topic for discussion. He allowed himself to bend the truth a little, giving Hilda to understand that passing on the toys to Cicely had been his idea and not Mrs Inskip's.

The last of Hilda's wariness had melted away by the time he finished. She gave him a broad, open smile. 'It was very kind of you – and Mrs Inskip – to think of Cicely. I'm sure she'll be delighted.'

He made to hand her the bags. 'I'm just off,' he said. 'Back to work on Monday.'

She didn't take the bags. 'You've got a moment, surely, to give her the toys yourself.'

'Yes, of course.'

She turned towards the house and he fell in beside her. 'She's in the sitting room,' Hilda said. 'I was thinking of bringing her out onto the verandah, now the mist's cleared.' He had a sudden sharp sense of the loneliness and isolation of their existence, of what a major event a casual call must be in such restricted lives.

'You must have a cup of my coffee this time,' Hilda declared in a tone that brooked no refusal. 'You haven't tasted my coffee. Herbal, of course. I think you'll like it.'

'I'm sure I will,' he answered heartily. 'By the way, I really must thank you again for the remedy you gave me the other day. It's completely cleared my coughing and sneezing, and got rid of all my aches and pains. It gave me some good sound sleep into the bargain.' He grinned. 'You ought to market it, you'd make a fortune.'

She looked immensely gratified. 'I'm glad it helped.' She paused and then said in a rush as if offering an answer to some unspoken question: 'We've never been able to mix locally, things being as they are. You see how it is.'

He gave a nod. 'I understand,' he said with sympathy. 'It must be very difficult for you at times, but you seem to manage extremely well.' She looked pleased at that.

He followed her in through the front door. 'Cicely's busy doing your squirrel jigsaw puzzle,' Hilda said as she led the way into the sitting room. 'She's very fond of it. She does it once or twice every day.'

At the sound of voices Cicely looked up from the puzzle. Her face broke into a beaming smile as she caught sight of Lambert. She stretched out both hands towards him in joyful welcome. He went over to where she sat in her wheelchair before her table, the trolley at her side. Hilda remained by the door, half turned towards the kitchen, watching the scene with obvious pleasure.

'I've brought you some books and toys,' Lambert said. He set the bags down on the floor while he cleared a place on the trolley.

Cicely leaned across and opened the nearest bag. She began to take out the contents: gaily coloured picture books, wooden construction toys, small dolls and farmyard animals, games, puzzles. She drew trembling breaths of happiness, pressing her lips together or opening her eyes wide at some particularly enticing item, flicking a rapturous glance at Lambert every few seconds.

189

'I'll go and make the coffee,' Hilda said from the doorway. She went off to the kitchen.

Cicely came upon a tiny baby doll in a minute cradle. She ran a caressing finger over it, then stretched out a hand towards her Victorian jewel box which Lambert had moved to a lower shelf of the trolley. She couldn't quite reach it; she glanced up at Lambert with appeal. He picked up the box and held it out to her. She didn't clear a space for it on her table; she raised the lid and lifted out the top tray, handed it to Lambert. She laid the baby doll in its cradle carefully down in the main compartment, then returned her attention to the brown paper bags, delving in for further treasures.

She picked out two more diminutive pieces, stroked them lovingly, considered them, made to drop both into the jewel box but considered again, dropped one in and put the other aside. Lambert stood holding the box and tray, watching her absorbed endeavours with indulgent amusement.

She found two more midget pieces and began the same process of assessment. Lambert glanced down into the jewel box, handsomely lined with red silk. His gaze strayed idly over the contents. Everything on a miniature scale: trinkets from Christmas crackers, prettily coloured beads and marbles, mother-of-pearl buttons. He smiled as he spotted the bright new penny piece he had seen Cicely swipe so skilfully.

He froze suddenly, staring into a corner of the box. He slid a glance at Cicely; she was wholly engrossed in her ponderings. Quietly and gently he set down the tray on the top shelf of the trolley. He dipped his fingers into the corner of the box and drew out a small object. He stood looking down at it; he felt the hair rise along his scalp.

It was a good-luck charm, made of pine, a mellow, golden shade of wood, satin smooth, beautifully made, carefully fashioned into a four-leaved sprig of clover.

He stood transfixed, his brain swept by a rapid surge of thought. Simon made a special charm for Julie, Mrs Norbury had said. A four-leaved sprig of clover. Julie said she'd always carry it.

CHAPTER 26

He set the jewel box silently down on the trolley. Cicely was still lost in blissful contemplation. She didn't glance up as he went noiselessly from the room, out into the passage, easing the door shut behind him. He moved soundlessly towards the kitchen.

On his right, the larder door stood open. He could see Hilda, perched on a step-stool, reaching up for a cake tin. She turned her head at his approach and gave him a cheerful smile. 'Wondering where I've got to?' She held out the tin. 'You can take this in for me. Some of my cinnamon and raisin cake. I know you'll like it.'

The door had a lock with a big, old-fashioned key. In the instant before he slammed the door shut and turned the key he saw Hilda's smiling look alter abruptly to open-mouthed astonishment.

He dropped the key in his pocket and darted towards the back door. He had a sudden vision of the Chief's appalled, astounded face. Behind him Hilda's voice called out in tones of incredulous outrage: 'Let me out of here! Let me out!' She banged on the door panel, rattled the handle.

He snatched open the back door. Outside, on the left, a flight of steps led down to a cellar. He plunged down the steps, tried the cellar door. It refused to yield. He raced back up the steps, back into the house, into the kitchen. A door faced him in the opposite wall. He seized the knob and the door swung open, revealing another flight of steps, plainly leading down into the cellar.

He switched on the light and went down at a rush. From the larder the thumping and shouting grew ever louder.

The cellar was large, laid out as three separate rooms. He shot into each in turn, looked swiftly round. A boiler room for oil-fired heating, a workshop, well fitted out, a storage area.

Everything orderly, scrupulously clean. No sign of any damage or interference to the concrete flooring, the brick walls. He flung open cupboard doors, threw back the lid of an old leather cabin trunk, looked inside a chest freezer.

He leapt back up the steps, into the kitchen, out into the brilliant sunshine. The banging and calling had ceased. He knew what she was up to now – casting feverishly about for something to force the lock or smash down the door.

On his right, the carport, sheltering the station wagon. He glanced into the vehicle, looked behind it.

Beyond the carport a small tool shed, unlocked. Inside, a wheelbarrow, garden tools, an old macintosh, ancient hats.

Further on, two greenhouses, full of produce.

Over on the left, screened by rustic latticework smothered in rambler roses, an oil storage tank raised up on a brace of brick supporting walls four feet high. The space beneath the tank had been boarded, furnished with a door. He stooped and peered inside: a concrete foundation, undisturbed; garden oddments, watering cans, flowerpots.

He straightened up and sent a raking glance round the garden, tranquil in the sparkling sunlight. Before him lay a herb garden, vegetable beds, rows of soft fruits. The air was full of fresh, flowery, green-leaf scents.

He set off again, running past an orchard area, a shrubbery, into a magnificent stretch of wild garden. No path, no tracks visible through the lush meadow grass. Birds sang from blossom-laden shrubs. Clouds of butterflies rose up from a great drift of purple foxgloves as he plunged through a sea of flowers.

In front of him a belt of soaring trees ran right across the garden, up to the boundary on both sides. A tall wooden gate, robustly built, stood halfway along the belt of trees. He ran up to it. It was roped tightly shut, top and bottom, additionally secured with a padlock.

He contemplated for an instant running back to the tool shed for some implement to batter down the gate but thought better of it. He would force a passage through. He stepped back and surveyed the trees. They were at their least dense over on the right, against the boundary.

He ran along and managed to push his way through, emerging into undisturbed, knee-high grass. The boundary trees towered even higher, their unchecked branches thrusting freely out.

Ahead of him, on the right, he saw the gated entrance he had noticed that first evening, strolling round Greenfield in the twilight. It gave on to a weed-infested drive leading to a garage on his left, a solid, brick-built structure, forty or fifty years old. He ran over to the garage. On either side of the timber door was a small-paned, iron-framed window, whitewashed over on the inside.

His first lunge at the doors told him he was wasting his time. They were secured by a mortice lock as well as by bolts top and bottom. He glanced round for a stone to smash in a window-pane. As the glass shattered under his blow the words 'criminal damage' flared briefly in his brain.

He cupped his hands round his eyes and stared in. Closely draped in old curtains and bedspreads was the distinctive, rounded, beetle shape of a small car.

He ran round to the back of the garage to see if there was any way of getting in. Tight up against the rear wall of the garage, under the overhang of trees, stood another small car, covered with an old tarpaulin tied down, weighted with bricks and stones. He wrenched the cover away.

The car was a white Mini. The number plates had been removed. The rear bumper was new.

The Mini was empty. He tried the boot; it was locked. He'd have to smash down the garage door, get a look inside the other car. There'd been an axe in the tool shed by the house. As he turned from the car he saw another shed, brick built, substantial, over on his left, close to the boundary, under the canopy of trees. He plunged towards it through the tall grasses.

A makeshift curtain of thick sacking obscured the small, single-paned side window. The door was of heavy timber, with a strong padlock.

He took a good run up and launched himself at the door. The timber creaked and groaned. At his third kick the padlock burst free.

He pushed open the door. A powerful, sickening stench surged out at him. He had to fight down a terrible heave of nausea. He snatched a handkerchief from his pocket and clapped it to his nose.

The inside of the shed was in darkness except for the waver-ing, green-tinged half-light filtering in through the doorway.

On his left he could make out a number of old tea chests and packing cases stacked against the wall.

The sacking was tightly nailed to the window frame. He ripped it down and a fraction more light came in through the dusty glass. He sent a ranging glance round the gloomy interior.

Dangling from the rafters hung long strips of rag thickly encrusted with dead flies. Scattered about the floor and shelves stood bowls and basins choked with insects. His forehead broke into a damp sweat.

Two high-backed armchairs draped in old sheets and blankets stood with their backs to him, facing the wall opposite the door. Beneath the drapes he made out the outlines of two human forms, leaning back in a parody of ease. Waves of sickness swept over him. He shuddered, retched, regained control. He nerved himself to advance gingerly. He approached the first chair.

Protruding from the edge of a blanket he saw the crook of an elbow, a slender elbow in a sleeve of fine, smooth cloth of muted grey-green check.

His horrified gaze travelled on, to the adjoining chair. Sticking out from under the drapes was a short, broad foot, encased in a laced walking shoe of stout oxblood leather.

CHAPTER 27

On Thursday evening in the third week of September Lambert left work on time for once. He was off to Greece with friends early on Saturday morning, for a holiday booked months before. He was very much looking forward to the break after a furiously busy couple of months. Chief Inspector Kelsey had got back from his cruise to be faced with the shock of the Greenfield discoveries and the realization of how his sergeant had been spending the previous two weeks.

Lambert hoped to finish the bulk of his holiday preparations during Friday morning and intended driving over to Pennyhill after lunch to see Mrs Osgood – and Cicely Jerrom. He had contacted Mrs Osgood very soon after the horrific disclosures at Greenfield, to explain what had happened and the present plight of Cicely, alone for the first time in her life. The moment Mrs Osgood had been able to draw breath after this bombshell she had offered to take Cicely until some decision could be made about her future.

Cicely hadn't been told, and would never be told, anything of the appalling happenings; she had been given to understand that Hilda had had to go away for a time. She had taken her removal from Greenfield and the abrupt vanishing of Hilda from her life with more calm than might have been expected – but she was not, after all, unaccustomed to change; she had had a number of previous moves and had been looked after by various people. She had been overjoyed to see Mrs Osgood again and seemed to feel she was being given a treat in going to stay with her.

Mrs Osgood would dearly have loved to have Cicely to live with her permanently but it was scarcely a realistic notion. Cicely might be expected to live many more years and Mrs Osgood was turned seventy. The social services quickly came up with the name of a home not far from Pennyhill, a highly regarded private establishment, purpose-built, for residents with a range of handicaps and disabilities. It possessed first-class facilities, provision for physiotherapy, and a well-trained, caring staff; it offered a variety of activities, frequent outings, contact with the local community and neighbouring churches. Mrs Osgood agreed the home would be by far the best option for Cicely, providing her with much-needed stimulus and companionship. And it was near enough for Mrs Osgood to be able to look in regularly.

Lambert hadn't seen Cicely since she went into the home but he had heard early on from Mrs Osgood that she appeared to be settling in well and enjoying herself. He had rung Mrs Osgood a few days ago to tell her he would shortly be off on holiday and to inquire about Cicely. She hadn't directly answered his query but asked if he could possibly spare the time to come over before he left; she would like him to see for himself how Cicely was getting on.

The afternoon was fine and sunny as Lambert got into his car and set off for Pennyhill. The Greenfield bungalow and its contents were in the process of being sold. Faced with incontrovertible evidence, Hilda had made no attempt to deny any of what had happened but had cooperated fully with the police. She had made up her mind to plead guilty to every charge, rejecting with contempt any suggestion of entering a plea of diminished responsibility. The trial was still some distance away but she showed no sign of budging from her refusal to spend a single penny on any kind of defence. She was determined that the entire proceeds of the Greenfield sale should go to swell Cicely's trust fund which had been much depleted over the last ten years. She had made no attempt to persuade the authorities to allow Cicely to be taken to see her; she had no wish to distress and confuse her sister.

She had answered readily every question put to her. She told them in a calm, passionless manner about the death of Alfred Raybould. While staying in the house to help nurse him she had prepared and given him to drink a pleasant-tasting herbal and plant concoction made according to the recipe her mother had always used to put down old and ailing household pets. Raybould had drunk it without protest, scarcely aware that he was drinking it; he had died peacefully a little later. Cicely had known nothing of this.

But Nurse Olive Hammond had known or guessed sufficient to enable her for ever after to levy blackmail on Hilda. Hilda had struggled to pay up over the years until Olive's increased demands, after she bought her country cottage, pushed Hilda over the edge. She could make no further retrenchments. Life was difficult enough as it was; it would be impossible if she had to pay over more money. She decided to end matters once and for all.

But she made out she would go along with Olive's demands. She asked her to come over to discuss details in an amicable fashion. Would she call in the evening, after Cicely had gone to bed? Olive was happy to agree.

Hilda conducted the interview in an amiable atmosphere, chatting easily to Olive about the cottage, Olive's present way of life and future plans. Nothing she learned caused her to have second thoughts about the scheme she had devised; she was certain she could get away with it.

In the course of their chat she plied Olive with a glass of the same pleasant-tasting concoction. Ten years had gone by since the death of Alfred Raybould and in all that time Hilda had paid up without once challenging Olive; Olive had no idea that Hilda's attitude had in any way changed. She readily took the drink and drank it with enjoyment; she even asked for a refill. She soon passed painlessly into a deep, final sleep.

Hilda drove Olive's Volkswagen round the bend of the lane and in through the side entrance at the far end of the garden. She removed her own station wagon from the garage and locked the Volkswagen away inside. Olive's body she put in the shed. Before many days had passed she set about constructing a carport by the house for the station wagon.

Some time later Julie Dawson turned up on her doorstep, wanting to locate Olive Hammond, asking a number of questions. Hilda chatted to her, asking some questions herself. She discovered Julie was on holiday in a caravan; she learned all she needed to know.

It was a warm day and Hilda offered refreshment. Julie accepted gratefully and drank with pleasure a glass of the lethal concoction. At some point Julie must have dropped the cloverleaf charm and Cicely must have picked it up, without Hilda's knowledge. But Cicely had known nothing of Julie's end, any more than she had known of Olive's.

197

Hilda drove Julie's Mini down the lane and in through the side entrance, parking it tight up against the back of the garage, covering it with a tarpaulin. Julie she put in the shed, beside Olive. That night, during the hours of darkness, with Cicely sleeping soundly in her bed, Hilda drove over to the caravan and removed Julie's belongings. She put the key of the caravan into an envelope and slipped it into the agency letter box. When she got back to Greenfield she stowed Julie's possessions away in the shed.

Hilda declared that she had felt and still felt no compunction at the deaths of Alfred Raybould and Olive Hammond. But this was plainly not so in the case of Julie Dawson. 'I had no choice,' she told Kelsey, looking earnestly up at him. 'Julie was very sharp, very inquisitive. She'd have hung on like a terrier.' Her voice had faltered for a moment. 'She would never have let go.'

The postmortem examinations had confirmed the cause of death in the case of both Olive Hammond and Julie Dawson as the ingestion of powerful plant-derived alkaloid poisons, squaring precisely with the recipe Hilda had described.

But the body of Alfred Raybould had been cremated and it was now impossible to determine exactly what had caused his death. Hilda had clearly done her best to kill him and she certainly believed she had succeeded. But other folk in Pennyhill had died in the same outbreak of illness. The doctor who attended Raybould was retired now and living in Scotland. He had been contacted and proved well able to remember the case. He had had no shred of suspicion over Raybould's death, nor a moment's hesitation in writing out the death certificate. He was positive then and positive now that Raybould had died from the illness that had put him in bed.

It was perfectly possible, Kelsey had in the end concluded, that Raybould could have been very close to death when Hilda gave him the draught and may well have died before the draught had had time to take effect.

One thought still woke Lambert sometimes in the night. Hilda, it appeared, had never had the slightest inkling of his true identity but had fully believed him to be a holiday-maker. He shuddered at the recollection of the cheerful way he had swallowed the drinks she had offered. It made his hair stand on end even now to contemplate what might have happened if he had chanced – as he so easily might – to give himself away.

CHAPTER 28

The afternoon grew increasingly warm, the sun shone brilliantly from a cloudless sky. When Lambert stopped for petrol he bought a can of cola from a chill cabinet and pulled into the next lay-by. He took off his jacket, leaned back against the upholstery and took a long refreshing drink.

Donald Fielding and Audrey Tysoe had been appalled to learn what had befallen Julie Dawson. They both cooperated whole-heartedly with the police, explaining now what they had been reluctant to tell Lambert earlier, for fear of being thought to have been in some way involved in Julie's disappearance – and for fear of Fielding's relationship with Julie becoming public knowledge locally.

Fielding readily disclosed that he had been on intimate terms with Julie for some two years before the death of his invalid wife. He had always been aware that Julie was confident they would marry if he became a widower, although he had been careful never to encourage her in that belief.

His wife had died in the spring and not long afterwards he had been approached by the media magnate, George Gresham, with a view to a takeover of his freesheet enterprise and a prime position for himself in Gresham's empire. In the course of their dealings he met Gresham's daughter Isobel, his only child, and they became friendly. The friendship deepened. Gresham looked on with favour and the question of marriage began to arise – with all that might imply for a son-in-law capable of one day stepping into Gresham's shoes.

Gresham was an austere man of strict principles and inflexible moral views. Fielding knew that any knowledge of his relation-ship with Julie would imperil both the takeover and the mar-riage. He strove to put an end to the relationship with Julie, being careful to let her know nothing about the Gresham con-nection. He offered her generous inducements to move right away from the area, declared himself ready to make any reasonable provision she might ask for.

But she hadn't proved very amenable. She had been hurt and upset. She had gone away for a break, to think things over, decide what to do.

When Audrey Tysoe asked him if he would give her a lift to the caravan in the course of his rounds, he took the opportunity to ask Julie if she had made up her mind about what she intended doing – and what she wanted from him. She told him she hadn't yet reached a decision but expected to do so shortly and would be in touch.

Later, after the Eardlows began making inquiries, it started to look as if Julie had disappeared. Questions began to be asked; he was afraid to reveal his involvement with her. He had no idea where she was but as time went by he was forced to contemplate the possibility that something untoward might have happened to her. If that proved to be the case and it eventually came to light, the details of her private life would surely be explored in any police investigation – and could soon become a matter of public knowledge. He shrank from the thought of the local townspeople learning that he had been involved with a girl on his staff while his wife – so well regarded locally – was alive. And he shrank even more from the thought of those facts reaching the ears of the Greshams, father and daughter.

Lambert took another drink of his cola. In spite of all the media space devoted to the Greenfield murders, Julie's relationship with Fielding had not so far emerged and it seemed probable now that it would not emerge. As far as Lambert could ascertain, the takeover and the marriage were both still on the cards.

He finished his drink and deposited the can in a litter bin. He got back into his car and pulled out of the lay-by.

Evan Marchant and his wife had proved hard nuts to crack, in no way minded to cooperate with the police, stubbornly denying any hand in the death of Mrs Marchant's mother, any blackmailing of themselves by Nurse Hammond.

It was impossible now to discover precisely how the old lady had died as her body had also been cremated. And it was difficult to see any very strong motive for dispatching her. She was well advanced in years and couldn't have been expected to live a great deal longer. The hotel would in any event go to the daughter, her only child. All the crime – if crime there had been – would seem to have achieved was to remove the formidable, obstructive presence of the old lady from the lives of her daughter and son-in-law and give them the ownership of the hotel a little earlier.

True, the hotel books did indeed plainly show that Olive Hammond had never paid a penny for her room and board but the Marchants blandly explained that as an expression of their gratitude for Olive's care of the old lady. A very generous expression, maybe, but since when had generosity been a crime?

One point, however, still remained, not to be quite so easily explained away: the swift sacking of Eva Simcox, immediately after she had sought out Nurse Hammond to express her unease about the old lady's death. Eva's statement was forthright and could be considered damning but it was unsupported by any other evidence – and the word of a dismissed employee could never be relied on to carry much weight in court.

But the statement appeared to put fear into Marchant and his wife. Confronted with it, questioned about it, they fell at first into a mulish silence but then withdrew for some private discussion, returning before long to say they now realized they may have been overhasty in their dismissal of Eva – understandable enough in the light of their grief and upset at the old lady's death, but nevertheless somewhat unfair, as they now acknowledged. They would be prepared to offer Eva a sum by way of recompense, the amount to be determined by the solicitors of both parties, under the Chief's scrutiny.

As Kelsey couldn't see any realistic chance of a case against the Marchants ever reaching the courts, this proposal was agreed and was currently being put into effect.

And that, in all likelihood, would be the end of the matter.

Luke Marchant had proved a good deal more ready to talk than his brother. He knew nothing of the circumstances of the old lady's death; he had arrived at the hotel for the first time only after her funeral.

But he admitted he hadn't been entirely frank in what he had earlier told Lambert. He had in fact seen Olive Hammond on one occasion after she left the hotel to move into her cottage. She had returned to collect the plants and cuttings she had asked for. He had handed them over and she had paid him for them. She had left at once, intent on getting back to the cottage to set the cuttings in the ground and water them in.

When questions began to be asked about Olive's whereabouts, every instinct told Luke to deny having laid eyes on her after she moved out of the hotel. The last thing he needed was to be mixed up in another police inquiry about a female; he had had more than enough of that at the hospital where he had worked before coming to Calcott House. He had eventually been cleared in that investigation but the case had never been solved and the rumours and whispers had refused to die down; he had in the end felt driven to leave.

Luke added with a wry trace of a smile that he had had one further reason, a good deal more trivial but compelling nevertheless, for denying he had laid eyes on Olive: he hadn't wanted his brother or his redoubtable sister-in-law to know he had been selling plants.

CHAPTER 29

Lambert reached a junction and took the road for Pennyhill.

Mrs Wynn-Yeatman had returned to her nursing home improved in health and spirits after her stay by the sea. Once she had recovered from the shock of what the police had to tell her she felt able to talk to them and in fact welcomed the opportunity at long last to speak the truth. She accepted that she couldn't expect to live many more years and she wanted to make her peace with society before she died. Her step-grandson, Martin, was now of age, no longer a minor to be protected at all costs. At her request he flew over from Canada where he had now finished at college and was about to enter the family business. He was happy to make a full statement of the events of that Friday evening, greatly relieved to be rid of the weight that had lain so long on his conscience.

Abbott, the young man Martin had run down and left unconscious in the lane, had made a good recovery and had long ago put the episode behind him. He had a positive attitude to life, was doing well in his job and had a steady girlfriend.

Mrs Wynn-Yeatman was resolved, even at this late stage, to do all in her power to make amends. She offered to pay a substantial sum to Abbott by way of compensation, the amount to be determined under an official eye. She intended also to repay to the insurance company the money they had paid to the owner of the burned-out car. She felt a sense of natural justice in these offers as the whole of her estate – apart from minor legacies and charitable bequests – would go to her step-grandson, so that these two large payments in recompense would in effect be coming out of Martin's pocket.

Martin had been only fourteen years old on that Friday evening and a considerable share of the responsibility for the cover-up of his offence must be laid at Mrs Wynn-Yeatman's door. In the seven years since then Martin didn't seem to have put a foot wrong. There was every reason to suppose he would make a good citizen and little would appear to be gained by dealing harshly with him, blighting a promising and useful career before it had fairly begun. All this would be taken into account and it was highly unlikely that any steps would now be taken against Martin – or, in view of her age and health, her sincere wish to make amends, against his stepgrandmother. Abbott for his part was happy to go along with Mrs Wynn-Yeatman's proposals. He felt that justice would now at last be done and he had no desire for anything beyond that; there was nothing vindictive in his nature.

There was a lull now in the afternoon traffic. Another fifteen minutes or so would bring Lambert to Pennyhill. It occurred to him that he might take Cicely some little present. In the next village he spotted a gift shop; he stopped and went inside. After a few minutes' browsing he found a small china basket of flowers he felt sure would please her. He had it prettily wrapped and returned to his car.

Arthur Langstaff and his wife had got back from their tour of the United States in the middle of August, to find the police wanting to talk to Arthur about what dealings he had ever had with Olive Hammond and what he could tell them about a will purported to have been made by his uncle, Bert Langstaff, but never found.

Arthur's immediate reaction was to sit tight and deny everything but a moment's reflection told him that his bank account, with its record of payments to Olive Hammond going back to a time shortly after old Bert's death, would speak loudly and unequivocally to the police. So he squared his shoulders and opened his mouth.

Yes, there had been a will. He had come across it very soon after his uncle died. But it was scarcely a credible document. It hadn't been drawn up by a solicitor but was homemade, drawn up by old Bert himself; it had been neither dated nor witnessed. It had left the whole of Bert's estate to his sister-in-law and her husband but Arthur couldn't see that it could have any force in law. Nor, in his opinion, did the in-laws have any moral claim to Bert's money. Arthur believed there was a very big question mark over the tactics the in-laws might have employed to persuade the old man to make a will in their favour, when every natural law would indicate Arthur as the obvious beneficiary. To allow the will to come to light would only involve him in an expensive and time-wasting dispute; he was certain the estate must come to him in the end. With all this in mind he had no hesitation in destroying the will and had never suffered the smallest twinge of conscience about his action since.

But Olive Hammond, he very quickly discovered, had known of the existence of the will. She had always kept her ears pricked for gossip and had heard some time before of the in-laws' claim that Bert was leaving them the property. She had had occasion to call on Bert professionally from time to time in his final years. She had mentioned what she had heard and he had confirmed the in-laws' story. After Bert's death, when no will was found, she realized Arthur must have destroyed it. But she was, as ever, open to reason in such matters. She was willing to button up her mouth in return for a regular payment.

Both in-laws were now dead and there had been no children or any other close relatives. The husband had died first, of liver failure; his wife followed him a year or so later. She had spent the last months of her life in a nursing home, incapacitated by a stroke, unaware of anything going on around her, totally dependent on state benefits. Neither of them had made a will, neither had had anything to leave. 'If they'd got their hands on any part of old Bert's money,' Arthur declared with conviction, 'they'd have drunk every penny of it. It would just have sent them to their graves a few years earlier.'

There was no way now of knowing the truth about the will. Taking it all round, it would seem that no charge could now lie against Arthur Langstaff.

By way of drawing a line under the past he proposed making a sizable donation to a charity, suggesting one devoted to the treatment and rehabilitation of chronic alcoholics as being the most suitable.

At the next crossroads Lambert made the final turn for Penny-hill, driving now through remembered countryside, lush and mellow in the approach of autumn.

Hilda Jerrom had remained resolute in her decision not to see Cicely. She had gone even further and made it known she intended never to see her again. She believed her sister had little or no concept of time and wouldn't be upset or puzzled by the fact that Hilda was no longer part of her daily life. Hilda was positive this was by far the best thing for Cicely and was certain she would settle in good heart into her new and stimulating life among people who were kind to her.

Hilda maintained that Cicely must surely have a valid claim against Olive Hammond's assets as the money Hilda had paid out to Olive over the last ten years had rightfully belonged to Cicely and had been paid without her knowledge as hush money for something of which she had known nothing.

Olive had made a will leaving everything to her sole relative, her cousin in Hampshire. The will stated that if he were to die before she did, the money was to go to a named nurses' charity. The cousin was an old man and had no wish to drag matters out. He had been appalled at what the police had told him about Olive's death and what had led to it; he wanted to make what redress he could for Olive's misdeeds. He had declared his intention of repaying into Cicely's trust fund an amount – plus interest – equal to what Olive had extorted from Hilda, an amount easy to ascertain as Hilda had kept a careful note and could produce cheque stubs in proof.

Olive's other blackmail victims were making no claims on her estate. There were still, according to the list Olive had jotted down on the back of the envelope, two victims Lambert hadn't managed to track down and who were not now ever likely to be found. It seemed probable that the old Hampshire cousin would spend his remaining days in a good deal more comfort than he had expected. He had no surviving relatives and had made it known that whatever was left of his windfall should go on his own death to the nurses' charity Olive had named.

There could be no dispute over anything Julie Dawson had left. It amounted to very little, mainly personal possessions and books. In the absence of a will it would go to her elderly relatives, the Eardlows.

CHAPTER 30

Mrs Osgood was on the lookout for Lambert and opened the door of her cottage the moment his car halted by the gate. She looked much more her old serene self again than when he had last seen her, distressed and shocked, after the dreadful revelations at Greenfield.

'I'm so glad you could come,' she told Lambert. She gave him a quick cup of tea and a piece of cake before they set off for the home, on the outskirts of a neighbouring town. Lambert asked how Cicely had settled in but she would still give him no direct reply, merely repeating what she had said on the phone, that she would like him to see for himself.

She had been to the prison to visit Hilda. 'They were terrible things that she did,' she said with a sorrowful shake of her head, 'but I've known her since the day she was born. I can't turn my back on her now.' She added with a long sigh, 'She must have felt fearfully driven. Living that isolated life, things would have got out of all proportion.'

Hilda had inquired with keen concern about Cicely but remained adamant about not seeing Cicely again. 'She won't change her mind,' Mrs Osgood said with certainty. 'I'm sure she's right in that. Cicely lives in the moment, she always has done. If she's happy here and now, that's the sum total of it as far as she's concerned; she'd never give a thought to anything – or anyone – else.'

They reached the home, a large establishment standing in spacious grounds. Cicely wasn't expecting them; Mrs Osgood had been told she was welcome to call in at any time.

They made their presence known at the front door and were received by a member of staff, a middle-aged woman with a competent air and a friendly manner. 'Cicely's out in the garden,' she told them. She took them along a path, across a stretch of grass. 'I think you'll be pleased with her,' she added with a smile. Some distance away, in the sparkling sunshine, Lambert could see Cicely, sharing a garden seat with a younger woman. 'That's her special friend,' the staff member said. 'I'll leave you to it now.' She turned and went off.

Cicely and her friend were watching with lively interest a game of clock golf taking place nearby amid a good deal of laughter and banter. Cicely's wheelchair stood beside the seat. She looked happy and relaxed. She was neatly dressed, her hair clean and shining, becomingly arranged.

At the sound of their approach she sent a glance in their direction. Her gaze fell on Mrs Osgood; her face broke into a beaming smile. In another instant she caught sight of Lambert. She got to her feet, clapping her hands in delight. Her friend rose to help her but Cicely shook her head and the friend stood back.

Cicely uttered a half-whispered 'Hello!' and then an instant later, her smile even more radiant, a louder, stronger 'Hello!', confident and joyful.